I0618920

HEART OF THE SEASON

A HOLIDAY ANTHOLOGY

THE AUTHOR TRANSFORMATION ALLIANCE
COURTNEY KONSTANTIN   ALLISON K. GARCIA
KAREN LOPEZ   M.T. DECKER   LINDSAY DETWILER
R.K. FULTZ   TOM FOWLER   N. TERRY   K. MCCOY
MYRIA WILD   KATRINA ROSEMOND

"Apocalyptic Christmas" © 2020 by Courtney Konstantin
"Melt Into Me" © 2020 by Allison K. Garcia
"Paul Dupré: A Cajun Country Christmas" © 2020 by Karen Lopez
"Christmas Delivery" © 2020 by M. T. Decker
"The Christmas Guest" © 2020 by Lindsay Detwiler
"Last Wishes in Cowboy Country" © 2020 by R. K. Fultz
"The Pilfered Presents" © 2018 by Tom Fowler
"Christmas, Cocoa, and Keychains" © 2020 by N. Terry
"The Smallest of Gifts" © 2020 by K. McCoy
"Miracle Dawn" © 2020 by Myria Wild
"Kindness and Fresh Snow" © 2020 by Katrina Rosemond

Collection compiled by Audrey Ann Hughey
Formatting by Tom Fowler
Cover Design by Nydia Pastoriza

All rights reserved. This book or any portion thereof may not be reproduced nor used in any manner whatsoever without the express written permission of the publisher except for use of brief quotations in a book review.

The stories in this book are works of fiction. Names, characters, events, places, and incidents are products of the authors' imaginations or used fictitiously. Any resemblance to actual persons, living or dead, or events, is entirely coincidental.

CONTENTS

THE CHRISTMAS GUEST
by Lindsay Detwiler

LAST WISHES IN COWBOY COUNTRY
by R. K. Fultz

THE PILFERED PRESENTS: A C.T. FERGUSON SHORT STORY
by Tom Fowler

CHRISTMAS, COCOA, AND KEYCHAINS
by N. Terry

THE SMALLEST OF GIFTS
by K. McCoy

MIRACLE DAWN
by Myria Wild

KINDNESS AND FRESH SNOW
by Katrina Rosemond

APOCALYPTIC CHRISTMAS

BY COURTNEY KONSTANTIN

APOCALYPTIC CHRISTMAS

The wind howled outside the concrete walls of the indoor sports park. The low murmuring of other survivors tickled Crystal's ears until she fully woke. She laid staring at the ceiling of her tent for a few moments more. Each morning she found herself rehashing how she ended up here, living inside a tent city, hiding from zombies.

A waitress who just happened to be unlucky enough to have the late shift. Crystal had always hated the late shifts. Customers were always far and few between, tips lousy, making Crystal feel like she was wasting her time. However, when she looked at the day the apocalypse all started, maybe the late shift was what saved her life.

"Mommy?"

Crystal turned her head and looked over at the smaller cot next to her. Her 5-year-old daughter Lucy looked at her through one eye as she rubbed the other with her fist.

"Morning, baby girl," Crystal whispered.

Lucy smiled before stretching and sitting up in her bed. They had learned early on to keep their voices low and their conversations private while inside their tent. While her daughter puttered around getting dressed, Crystal remembered how they had come to live in the encampment.

In the beginning, Crystal avoided everything that moved. Early on, it was clear the zombies only reacted to you if they saw you. They had initially stuck with the cook from the restaurant Crystal worked at. When the first person with a zombie bite had collapsed into one of their booths that first night, Jorge had been the first to realize there was an issue.

Jorge was also the night manager of the restaurant and never batted an eye when Crystal asked if Lucy could sleep in a booth when she was working the night shift. That had saved her and Lucy that night. They were already together, and Crystal didn't have to risk either of them to get to her from the babysitter's.

Jorge was a bulk of a man, strong and dominating. However, he had a soft spot for Lucy. That was how they lost him after a week. A zombie had come out of a bathroom stall before they knew to check everywhere. Jorge had tossed Lucy back into Crystal and the zombie bit down on his arm before he could stop it. He killed it immediately, but Crystal and Jorge knew what a bite meant.

Lucy still asked about Jorge, sometimes forgetting that Crystal had explained he was gone. It always broke Crystal's heart to remind the little girl, but she also wasn't going to lie to her. The current situation didn't really leave room for fairytales. But did it leave space for any happiness? That was what had been missing for her daughter.

They found their current group after being on their own for two weeks. Those two weeks were dark for Crystal. She didn't know a thing about surviving beyond their basic needs. Jorge had taken the time to show her how to kill the zombies, but her skills were lacking. She also could barely handle the smell or the gore without losing her lunch.

For two weeks Crystal kept Lucy in an upstairs apartment they found open. When they started checking doors, Crystal was waiting for someone to shoot her. She didn't even know how to pick a lock, so finding something open and empty was a blessing. From that apartment, they listened to the apocalypse rage outside the walls.

On a supply run, Crystal and Lucy ran into a couple that was coming out of a storeroom in the store they were in. Crystal thought about running, but the woman immediately saw them for what they were: struggling to survive and not a threat. The couple invited Crystal and Lucy back to their group.

When they were brought into the indoor sports building, given their own six-person tent, cots, and food, Crystal could have cried with joy. It was the first time in weeks that she felt like her daughter was safe. The first night when she curled up to sleep, she was actually able to sleep and not sit up watching Lucy.

"Mommy, what day is it?" Lucky asked, bring Crystal back to the day.

She climbed from bed and joined her daughter at the small calendar they had hung in their tent. They checked off the day each morning together. Though it continued to depress Crystal as she watched the days tick off. They were two months in now and there was no sign of rescue or improvement. All forms of communication had been cut off early on. There was no government presence to be seen.

Crystal crossed off a day on the calendar and realized they were almost halfway into December. Sadness spread through her heart as she thought about the coming holiday. Thanksgiving had come and gone without a word in the group. Crystal was never huge on Thanksgiving, so it didn't bother her. But Christmas was a big deal, especially for a five-year-old.

Her mind was still on trees covered in twinkle lights and colorful wrapping paper when they joined the group for breakfast. Lucy was one of five kids in the group of thirty people. Two of the kids were older and couldn't be bothered with a 5-year-old. The other three were around Lucy's age, and the four were thick as thieves within a few days.

"Slow down, Lucy," Crystal said, as her daughter shoveled eggs into her mouth until her cheeks bulged.

Lucy's response was muffled, and she had to stop when she almost choked on the food.

"The kids will be there in a few minutes. They have to eat their breakfasts too. Once you're done, you can play. But lessons later," Crystal said.

Crystal decided to ignore the small eye roll that came from Lucy. So far, the other parents hadn't tried to teach their kids. On the other hand, Crystal had collected supplies on each run she went on to be able to teach Lucy the basics of reading, writing, and math. So far they were practicing the sounds of the ABCs and writing letters. Lucy wasn't a fan, as she didn't see anyone else doing what she had to. Crystal made sure to give her plenty of rewards, so her daughter did as she was told.

"Hey, Crystal," a man said as he joined them with his breakfast.

Antonio was a good-looking man with a bald head and sleeve tattoos. Crystal had labeled him the muscle in her mind. His look was slightly deceiving as well. He seemed to love the kids. He was always grabbing toys whenever he was on a run. He was teaching them how to kick a soccer ball and throw a baseball.

"Hey, Antonio. Gotta say, the chickens were brilliant," Crystal said, holding up a fork of scrambled eggs.

"They weren't easy to catch, little bastards. But having fresh eggs isn't something I'll get tired of."

The backdoor of the sports building led into a fenced-in area, which had been adjusted to create a chicken coop. Antonio and his group had brought back five chickens the first run and another six the next run. One older couple had owned chickens before the apocalypse and were grateful to have the task again. Now eggs were aplenty and they could all use the regular protein.

"Headed out today?" Crystal asked.

"Yeah, like always. Did you need anything?"

"Maybe I could come along. I know I'm not scheduled until next week, but there's something I want to check out," Crystal replied. She had an idea forming, but she needed supplies to see if it was possible.

"Sure, anything for you doll," Antonio gave her a dazzling smile before returning his plate to the kitchen area.

Once Lucy was settled with the parents of her friends, Crystal went to her tent to pack her bag. She sat on her cot with a small notepad and started making a list of supplies she could hope to have.

Knowing everything fell apart in late September, she realized a lot of what she added to the list wouldn't be in stores. She sighed, wondering how talented and creative she could get.

Antonio let her have the front seat, for which Crystal was thankful. It wasn't that she didn't trust the other men on the run, she just didn't really know them. Each of them had hit on Crystal at one time or another, something that annoyed her greatly. It's not that Crystal had lived her life as a nun, she'd had boyfriends. Lucy's father had been a long-term one, which left as soon as the idea of being a father entered the picture.

The apocalypse wasn't the time for her to even think about romance or basic carnal needs. And that's what these men had been after. From what Crystal had heard around the group, the two guys liked to hit on any woman that walked through the doors, so she knew to not feel special. Since she turned them down, they had left her alone and that's all Crystal could ask for.

Crystal watched as buildings passed outside her window. It was hard to believe, sometimes, that everything had crumbled around them. Dried blood was splashed across buildings, some neighborhoods were gutted by fire, while some looked completely normal. Except for the times that the mindless zombies wandered through.

As they rounded a corner, Crystal saw one of the stores she wanted to check.

"Can we pull in there?" She asked Antonio.

"It's a craft supply store," Antonio replied hesitantly.

Crystal wondered if she should explain her plan or just be vague. Celebrating the upcoming holiday might be the furthest thing from most minds. But for Crystal, giving Lucy a Christmas was moving up to her number one priority.

"I want to find some supplies. It's halfway through December, Antonio. Do you know what that means?"

"We're halfway through another month of survival?" He replied.

"For a child, it's almost Christmas," Crystal said. Sounds of disbelief came from the backseat and she shot them a look that spelled out what would happen if they didn't keep their opinions to themselves.

"Christmas? Crystal, that's not a priority. I'm sorry. We can't risk time and resources for a holiday."

"Ok, maybe it seems silly. But as a mother, I really want to give my child some happiness. Maybe it would do everyone a little good. Lucy needs this," she reasoned. Antonio still didn't look convinced.

"Look, if nothing else, we can get supplies for mending clothes and any of the canvas tents. I doubt anyone really looted this place already," Crystal said.

"We do need some fabric to patch up some things," one of the men spoke up from the backseat. His voice was unsure, clearly afraid Crystal would bite his head off if he disagreed with her.

With a sigh, Antonio finally agreed. The men all had guns to pull once they stepped out of the vehicle. Crystal only carried an expandable baton. It worked to knock down the zombies when needed and if she tried hard enough, she could eventually kill one. She didn't really trust herself with a firearm.

They approached the entrance to the store and found the glass to be intact. Antonio tried the swinging door, but it was locked. He looked around them first, before nodding to the men. One of them stepped up with the butt of a rifle, cracking it against the glass a few times until it shattered open. The noise was enough to make Crystal cover her ears and that meant it called anything in the area, living or dead.

They all stepped into the dark store. Crystal clicked on her flashlight and began to swing the beam from side to side. Their footsteps crunched through the broken glass and the sound seemed to vibrate in the store. They waited together, one keeping an eye outside and the others looking around the store for movement.

When nothing came, Crystal released a breath that was sitting deep in her chest. A shiver passed through her at the thought of fighting zombies in the dark, and she was certain that was one thing she could pass up. The men of the group were more used to supply runs, and she could only imagine the things they saw each time they were out. It wasn't unknown that Crystal was a little soft.

"Lead the way," Antonio whispered.

Crystal wasn't sure on the layout of the store, so she tried to use her flashlight to see the hanging aisle signs. She found fake flowers and grabbed a few poinsettias. She continued to move until she found fabric and sewing materials. As promised they loaded up a cart with sturdy fabrics and sewing supplies. On a whim, Crystal grabbed patterns for different types of clothing, thinking about what she could make for Lucy if she had the right tools.

Slowly, they wandered back toward the entrance. Crystal's hopes were about to be doused until she saw a sign that said Seasonal. She quickened her pace and went right for it. The first things she saw were Halloween items. But on the other side of the aisle, red and green things started to catch her eye.

She began to pick out anything she could use for a Christmas celebration. Wreaths, ribbon, plain stockings, garland, and a fake snow tree skirt made it into her basket. Crystal began to feel excited by the prospect of pulling off the holiday. Just picturing the childlike bliss in Lucy's eyes when she saw everything prepared for Christmas, was all Crystal needed to keep packing things into the cart.

A low whistle cut through the air of the store and Crystal froze. It was the signal of trouble from the man watching the front of the store. Anthonio pulled on Crystal's shirt to indicate they needed to move. She began to push the cart, but he tried to stop her.

"I'm not giving this up now! I'll get it to the car," Crystal said in an urgent whisper.

"This isn't a necessity," Antonio replied.

"Maybe not to you," Crystal said. She felt like she was just going to have to repeat herself over and over again until the stubborn man got it.

Antonio huffed before heading straight for the door. Crystal pushed the cart quickly, following closely, having no idea of what was coming. When they arrived in the shadow of the front of the store, Crystal could see what the problem was.

They had parked the car in the lot, instead of right in front of the door. The look on Antonio's face said he wasn't happy with that decision now. There was a man looking into the driver's window of the SUV and two others at the back of the vehicle, cupping their hands around their eyes to look in the back.

"Well, not zombies," Crystal said.

"Doesn't mean it's better," Antonio replied.

"What do you want to do?" One of the men asked.

"Wait a second. If they try to steal it, we go out. If they walk away, we get out of here," Antonio said.

"How do we know they aren't looking for help?" Crystal asked.

"With that much fire power?" Antonio said as he gestured outside.

Crystal felt foolish when she saw the guns each man was carrying. She hadn't even noticed weapons when she looked out at first. Just another reason she wasn't meant to survive the apocalypse. With that thought still in her mind, she followed as Antonio led her away from the open door. She had to leave her precious cart of Christmas goodies because it made too much noise.

Tucked against a wall just to the left of the door, Antonio protected her with his body. It also prevented her from seeing anything that could be happening. She tried to peek around him and his arm shot out to push her back, causing her to lose her footing. As Crystal crashed into a stand of key chains and stuffed animals, she knew things were about to get bad.

Antonio spun around at the sound of metal clanging against the ground. Crystal was sprawled on her back, her legs caught in the stand. Tears had sprung to her eyes as she realized she sprained her ankle. When Antonio approached her, she was taken aback by the anger in his face.

"Jesus, Crystal! They are going to come in here now!" He whispered harshly.

"Me? Maybe you shouldn't have shoved me and I wouldn't have fallen," she replied, trying to keep from sobbing. Not only was her ankle throbbing, but she was embarrassed by her clumsiness.

"Antonio, they're coming this way. Maybe we should find a back way out," one of the other men hissed.

Antonio nodded and reached down to help Crystal to her feet. Disengaging her from the metal stand made more noise, but at that point keeping quiet didn't make any sense. Their companions ran toward the back of the store, where a second exit was assumed to be.

However, when Antonio got Crystal to her feet, it was clear she couldn't run.

"Just go," Crystal said, suddenly feeling sacrificial.

"Right. And you're going to just talk them out of taking you? With what, your keen wit?"

Crystal shot him another dirty look. As they tried to head away from the door a shot rang out behind them. Antonio's hold on her waist tightened, halting her progress. She looked at him, wildly checking for a wound, but it was clear the shot was just a warning. Antonio began to spin around, positioning Crystal behind him. She gripped the back of his shirt, pressing against his back, trying to make herself as small as possible.

"Sorry friends, didn't know this store was taken," Antonio said in his easy-going way.

"We ain't friends, dude," one man shouted back. Crystal couldn't see what was happening, but it sounded like guns moving.

"Ok, sorry. Let's just relax. We were just looking for supplies. But we'll head on our way."

"We want the woman," the man said without hesitation.

"The woman?" Antonio replied, feigning misunderstanding. Crystal knew exactly what they were saying. She couldn't stop herself from trembling.

"The woman with you. We know she's behind you man, we ain't stupid. We haven't seen any women lately. Well, alive at least," the voice said.

"She's not available, gentlemen. Sorry for the misunderstanding. She's with me."

The sound of a click told Crystal that wasn't the answer these men wanted. They didn't care for Antonio's smooth way of speaking. She was positive they wouldn't care if she was claimed by another man. Her mind was filled with the images of Antonio dying trying to protect her.

"Just go, Antonio," she murmured.

"Crystal, if there's a time for you to shut up, now is that time," he whispered back.

"You have till the count of 5 to send the woman toward us," the man yelled.

"Listen, I'm not trying to hurt any of you. But there's no way she's leaving my side."

"One!" The stranger yelled. There was a chorus of laughter from the other men with him, as if they were sure they were going to get their hands on Crystal because the man was counting down. Crystal wondered how men governed by the rules of a toddler actually were surviving the apocalypse.

"Two!"

"This is your last warning, gentlemen," Antonio called back.

It was then Crystal caught movement out of the corner of her eye. Their scavenging companions hadn't run for it as she had assumed. They were both stalking back to the men that were challenging Antonio now. Crystal could feel the shift in Antonio as he knew he wasn't alone either. The arm that had been secured around Crystal moved slowly to the handgun secured at his lower back. Crystal untangled herself from him to ensure he could move quickly.

"Three!"

"Now!" Antonio yelled next.

With that yell, the store became a cacophony of blasts. Antonio shoved Crystal, this time ensuring she sprawled across the linoleum. She couldn't be mad at him, as she crawled to hide behind the nearest display. Cowering, she covered her ears, gritting her teeth against the panic that rose up in her chest.

She didn't know how long it had been, but the noise turned into an oppressive silence. Crystal didn't move her hands, hoping she could keep herself in the cocoon she had created. She jumped back and banged into the wall when hands fell on her knees. When she saw it was Antonio, she threw her arms around his neck with a sob.

He stood with her still clinging to him. Since he didn't seem to know what to do with his arms, he wrapped them around her, hugging her tight.

"Hey, it's all good. You ok, Crystal?" Antonio asked. She didn't trust her voice, so she just nodded her head.

"That was nuts!" One of their companions said as he joined them.

Crystal looked over to both of the men, looking all of them over to ensure they weren't injured.

"We're fine. Those guys didn't even know those two were coming up behind them. They didn't exactly have situational awareness," Antonio said, dryly.

Crystal looked at Antonio. She was sure it was the adrenaline from the situation and him suddenly saving her life, but she was seeing him differently now. He had been so together, even with guns pointed at him and threats to his life.

"What did you do before this, Antonio," Crystal asked.

"I was a SWAT officer, before everything went to hell," Antonio replied.

The answer made so much sense, Crystal actually burst out giggling. Antonio had no idea what was so funny, but he smiled down at her all the same. He put an arm around her, squeezing her again.

"There was no way I was leaving you there," he said softly. His eyes were serious now, and the laughter died in Crystal's throat immediately. "Lucy would never forgive me if I didn't come back with her momma."

His seriousness and his hold on her caused Crystal to look away. She wasn't sure she knew what was swirling behind his dark eyes. And at that moment, with her heart slamming in her chest, she wasn't sure what she wanted to do with the knowledge. The mention of Lucy had also reminded her what she was doing there.

"Can we load up my Christmas decorations now?" She asked quietly.

Antonio laughed, making his chest vibrate against Crystal. He nodded before releasing her and they made their way back to the door. He took her hand and led her down a different aisle so she wouldn't see the dead men. He directed the two companions to push the two carts out that they had filled, and he took Crystal straight to the SUV.

The growling noise caught Crystal off guard, but she should have known Antonio was always aware. He pulled his handgun and shot the nearest zombie in the face. The sudden noise caused Crystal to jump. He pushed her toward the SUV and unlocked the doors. When she opened the passenger side, she saw more zombies appearing from around the side of the building.

"Let's hurry this up! I don't want to lose what we came here for, but we are about to be the buffet of this party," Antonio yelled to the men now running with the shopping carts.

Crystal was just barely putting her seat belt on when the SUV's back door slammed down and all of their supplies were in. All three men jumped in, just as the first zombie hit the front of the vehicle. Its face was decaying and Crystal was fairly certain it was missing an eyeball. She gulped down the bile that wanted to come up. For some reason, she didn't want to look weak in front of Antonio just then.

The SUV lurched backward, away from the approaching horde. Antonio slammed on the brakes and Crystal threw out her hands to brace herself on the dashboard. When she looked in the side mirror, she could see more shambling corpses coming from behind them. They were about to be surrounded. All because Crystal wanted some Christmas decorations.

"Hold on, we're going to have to get creative here," Antonio said.

Crystal made sure she had her seatbelt on. She grabbed the handle above her head as Antonio spun the SUV around and headed for an alley that ran behind the craft store. As they turned toward the back of the building, Crystal held her breath, hoping it was clear to the street. Her hope was dashed when they reached the far corner and they were stopped by a chain-link fence.

"Well, we aren't going that way," Crystal said. She looked at Antonio and didn't feel comforted by seeing a slight worry line between his eyebrows.

Antonio threw the SUV into reverse and floored the gas, heading back the way they had come. By the time they slid into the main parking lot, it was filling with zombies rambling toward them. Crystal had never seen so many in one place. The shootout had called them from all the surrounding neighborhoods, where the dead were wandering aimlessly.

Crystal let out a small scream when something banged against her door. When she twisted to look, the decaying face of a zombie was pressed against the window. It banged its mouth against the window, snapping its broken teeth at Crystal. She pulled back as if there wasn't glass between them, her back leaning into Antonio.

"Dude, go!" One of the guys yelled from the backseat.

"I'm going to try to go through. This might get rough," Antonio replied.

Slowly, the SUV moved forward, trying to push through the zombies. At first it seemed some were rebounding off of the bumper. They would change direction for a moment, bumping into others, some of them falling and taking a few with them. However, it was never enough to give them a break forward.

Crystal watched as some fell in front of the SUV and she cringed as she felt and heard the snapping of bones and squishing of bodies under the wheels. Antonio revved the SUV engine more as he fought to drive over the zombies that were falling below the vehicle. Suddenly, the forward motion stopped and Antonio cursed.

"What? Why aren't we moving?" Crystal cried.

"Too many under the car," Antonio mumbled as he threw the SUV into reverse and spun the wheel.

He rocked the car back and forth until they started forward motion again. He repeated the same steps a few more times before they completely stopped. Crystal felt like they had been in the SUV for hours, but in reality it had only been minutes. Now the SUV shuddered and pitched as the zombies ran into the sides. Crystal could feel tears threaten as she looked around at all the windows. There wasn't a clear spot anywhere.

"Antonio..." one of the men trailed off. All the passengers were coming to the same understanding of the situation.

"We can't just stay here," Crystal said quietly.

Antonio didn't answer. He continued to change gears on the SUV and tried to push the vehicle off the bodies that were collecting. Sweat had started to bead on his forehead and he slammed his hand into the steering wheel every time he shoved the gears back and forth. His frustration did nothing to calm Crystal's anxiety.

She reached across and grabbed the wheel, stopping Antonio. His wild eyes fell to her, and he took a deep breath.

"Stop. This isn't helping. We need a different plan," Crystal said. Her voice was much more confident than she was really feeling.

"There isn't one, Crystal. I think we're trapped," Antonio finally admitted.

The smell of the zombies began to permeate the air inside the SUV. The gag-inducing decomposition caused Crystal to cover her mouth. Antonio turned off the air and tried to close the vents, but the smell was already inside. After a few breaths through her mouth, Crystal was able to control her stomach.

Every window was full of faces, pressing close, trying to obtain their meal. They could see the living flesh inside the SUV and nothing was distracting them. Crystal couldn't help but stare at each face. Some seemed to be melting, the skin falling from muscle and bone revealed below. Some still looked bloody, recently turned and not yet completely falling apart. Those were the hardest for her. As she stared into the eyes of a zombie woman, her blonde hair knotted and pink in places where it had soaked in blood, Crystal had an idea.

"Seeing us is what gets them worked up, right?"

"I guess so," Antonio replied.

"What if they can't see us?" Crystal asked.

Antonio looked at her for a moment and then to the back of the SUV. He seemed to remember the rolls of fabric they had just packed into the back. Meeting Crystal's eyes, he nodded.

"It's worth a try," he said, as he reached forward and turned off the engine. Crystal barely registered the engine quieting, as the zombies were so much louder.

Together, Crystal and the men unfolded the heavy canvas they had scavenged. They used duct tape from the scavenging bag that was always kept in the SUV. Window by window, they hung the fabric to hide themselves from the zombies. Crystal was also happy to no longer see the dead faces, even though she knew they were still out there.

It took some time, but eventually it seemed like the zombies were losing their awareness of the people inside the vehicle. The grunts, groans and hisses seemed to slow before completely stopping. The dead were still out there, which was evident by the rocking of the SUV whenever they surged one way or the other. However, it didn't seem like they were actively trying to get in anymore. They were just aimless now.

The four people inside the SUV tried hard to be completely silent. The men in the back had split up to lay down. One was in the bench seat, the other went to the trunk area to lay there. They had pulled magazines from their backpacks, which Crystal found odd. Antonio explained in a low whisper that sometimes scavenging was lots of driving. The guys would read as passengers.

Crystal and Antonio were designated the front of the SUV. That left them with the front bench to share. They started with their backs to the doors and their legs next to each other on the bench. It wasn't the most comfortable situation, but as the day turned to evening, they realized they would be sleeping where they sat.

"Can I ask you a question?" Antonio whispered. He continued at Crystal's nod. "Where's Lucy's father?"

Crystal stared at him for a moment, caught off guard about the question. She would have been less surprised by a question about the weather. Since coming to the small settlement, Crystal hadn't been close to many people. She hadn't felt the need to share her life story. She helped where she was needed and she took care of her daughter. It was all life was about now.

"I wouldn't know," she finally answered.

"Like you didn't before this? Or you don't know because the world fell to pieces?" Antonio pressed.

"Like I didn't before," Crystal said. She then sighed, knowing she was being intentionally vague. Antonio was a nice man and she didn't want to make him feel like she didn't want to talk to him. "He wasn't keen on the idea of being a father. When I found out I was pregnant he bolted. That was almost six years ago now. Lucy and I were always fine on our own."

"Oh, I believe that," Antonio said with a silent laugh. Crystal had the feeling he was flirting with her, however the timing seemed pretty bad.

"I'm not sure what you mean. Is it my fantastic sense of balance that convinced you?" Crystal asked as she motioned to her sprained ankle.

Antonio got serious for a moment before sitting up and digging in his bag. He pulled out a first aid kit and motioned to her foot. Crystal didn't know what he could do to fix her sprained ankle, but she wasn't going to stop him. She nodded and waited with bated breath to see what he would do next.

The man was smooth, Crystal had to admit that. He slowly untied her boot, loosening the laces further than she normally would. This made the boot slip off easily, without jostling her ankle too much. The pain began to intensify as she lost the support of her boot, but the warmth of Antonio's hand quickly distracted her.

He rolled up the bottom of her jeans to expose her ankle high socks. Carefully, he peeled the sock down, his fingers grazing her skin as he went. Crystal tried to not react. She repeated to herself over and over that he was just tending to her sprain, nothing more. But the looks he seemed to sneak at her told a different story.

If they weren't in the middle of the apocalypse, sitting in a SUV, stranded and surrounded by zombies, Crystal may have winced at the fact that she hadn't had a pedicure in months. She was glad her polish free toes were clean and she had access to regular showers at the settlement. All of these thoughts flashed through her mind as the sock joined her boot on the floor.

"How does it feel?" Antonio asked.

"It's sore. I'm sure I can walk on it in a day or two," Crystal replied.

"I'm going to wrap it. The compression can help with the swelling. Then we should probably elevate it."

Crystal nodded and Antonio went to work. He carefully began to wrap a bandage around the arch of her foot. After a few loops, he began to make a figure-eight pattern around the back of her leg, around her ankle and around her foot again. She could feel the support and knew it was going to be an immense help.

Her breathing stuttered as he ran a finger between the wrap and her skin, checking how tight it was. Crystal knew he noticed, but he didn't behave as if he did. He carefully sat her injured foot on the top of his leg. He settled back and looked at her thoughtfully.

"So if your keen sense of balance didn't keep him around, he never got to see how awesome Lucy is," Antonio said.

Crystal had no idea how to reply. Her heart beat a little harder hearing this man talk about how wonderful her daughter was. Lucy's face flashed in her mind and she felt sadness for a moment. Her eyes filled with tears as she wondered what Lucy would think when she didn't get home for bedtime.

"Hey, hey, I'm sorry. I didn't mean to make you cry," Antonio said, leaning forward to grab her hand. She shook her head, not trusting herself to speak.

With a move of strength, Antonio pulled Crystal forward. He motioned for her to bend her legs and in a moment he had her leaning against him while he wrapped his arms around her. He comforted her, running a hand down her arm. Crystal could feel his face resting on her head and she couldn't stop herself from feeling good.

"I'm ok. I just worry. What will she think when I don't come home tonight? God, what if we don't get home at all?" Crystal whispered.

"We won't let that happen. It might take a day or so, but something will draw them away. Then we can clear out under the SUV and get home," Antonio replied, doing his best reassuring voice in a whisper.

The inside of the SUV was getting darker as the sun fell below the horizon. The four pulled together the food each of them had in their packs and determined if they rationed they would have enough for at least two days. Crystal had no desire to stay inside the smelly SUV for two days. She had a feeling as their bodies became ripe, the space would be even harder to stomach.

After a small dinner of an apple and an energy bar, they decided it would be best if one person stayed awake while the others slept. Crystal, being useless against the zombies, wasn't given a watch. She was sure she wouldn't sleep anyway, but she was happy to not have the responsibility.

Antonio was given the first watch. He insisted that Crystal lay on the bench with her feet in his lap. She felt bad taking up so much room, but Antonio pointed out that he was sitting up anyway, so it didn't make sense for her to be uncomfortable. Crystal propped her head up on the fake snow tree skirt. Almost immediately her eyes started to feel heavy.

"I can't believe I'm even slightly sleepy," she whispered

"Eventually your adrenaline was going to crash," Antonio whispered back.

"You aren't tired?"

"A little. But I know how to stay awake if I need to."

Crystal yawned and her eyes fluttered closed. She could already hear the two guys in the back snoring, one softly and the other less so. The noise didn't bother Crystal though, since there was still the noise of the zombies outside the SUV. She fell asleep soundly despite her worry and the smell of death.

It wasn't until the middle of the night that Crystal was awakened. She realized it was Antonio trying to get comfortable that had woken her. He had let Crystal continue to sleep on the entire seat, while he tried to sleep against the driver's side door. When she lifted her head, she could see one of the guys in the back sitting up, reading a magazine by a small flashlight. Antonio instantly sat up when she moved.

"Sorry. You don't look comfortable," Crystal whispered.

"It's ok. I didn't mean to wake you. You looked really out."

"Was I drooling or something?" Crystal asked, wiping her hand across her face.

Antonio laughed silently and opened his mouth to say something, when a loud shot echoed from outside. Crystal and Antonio froze their conversation. Both guys in the back sat up straight and waited. Another shot followed and another. The zombies outside of the SUV were beginning to make the sounds of hunger again. The vehicle rocked more violently as they bumped them from all sides.

The next shot seemed to be further away, but still clear for the group to hear. Crystal so badly wanted to peek under the fabric, but she knew it was pitch black outside and she wouldn't be able to see what was happening. When a fifth shot sounded, Crystal reached over to grab Antonio's hand. He squeezed her fingers, reassuring her once again that everything would be fine.

The shots became more and more distant. As their distance grew, the sounds and movements from the zombies seemed to dissipate.

Eventually the SUV didn't move and they couldn't hear any of the normal groaning from outside. The silence was heavy as they all waited, being as quiet as possible. Crystal felt like if she even took a deep breath, the zombies would come back.

Lights lit up the front of the SUV and Antonio grabbed his gun.

"Stay here. Not sure who this is," Antonio instructed Crystal.

He motioned to the men to follow and the three of them slowly opened their doors to peek at the newcomer vehicle. Crystal could see Antonio and watched his body language for any signs of how she should be feeling at the moment. When he relaxed, Crystal peeled back a piece of fabric to see what was happening. She couldn't see faces, but the way Antonio approached and shook hands, Crystal knew they were saved.

An hour later they were rolling to a stop in the parking lot of their indoor settlement. Antonio came around to Crystal's door and helped her to her feet. Her sprained ankle hurt, but she could limp and declined his offer to carry her. She already felt like a problem, she didn't want to seem like an invalid on top of that.

When they entered the building, it was surprisingly bright with most people awake and awaiting their return. Lucy came bounding toward Crystal and she had to carefully stoop to hug her little girl.

"What are you doing up at this hour?" Crystal asked her daughter. An older woman named Joyce joined them. She was the one that watched Lucy when Crystal would go on runs. She seemed like she would have been a great grandmother if she had been given the chance.

"She's the reason the team came after you all tonight. She refused to stop asking where you were. She wouldn't let anyone sleep until they went and got you," Joyce said.

"I told them, Mommy. You always say you'll be back to read to me before bed. If you didn't come back, that meant you needed help," Lucy said, smartly. Crystal couldn't help but smile at her, so proud of her acting so grown up.

"Well, ya know what, princess? I'm pretty grateful you made sure someone came to get us. Thanks, kid," Antonio said, ruffling Lucy's hair. Lucy beamed under his attention.

"You did good, baby girl. But it is definitely time for bed. Probably no story tonight," Crystal said.

Antonio gave a quick rundown of the day's events to the adults that were awake. Crystal avoided talking to anyone, embarrassed that her Christmas plans were what caused the whole problem in the first place. She limped her way to her tent with Lucy in tow. Just as they were unzipping the door, Antonio caught up with them.

"Hey, Crystal. If you wanted to finish your project, we could try again tomorrow," he offered.

"No. I think I'm done with silly ideas for the time being," she said. Then she lowered her voice so Lucy wouldn't hear from inside the tent. "I almost got three people in addition to myself killed today. For what? A silly holiday? I'm really sorry, Antonio. I don't know anything about what's really important, I guess."

"Oh, come on Crystal. It wasn't that bad. Everyone has close calls," Antonio said. He reached for her hand and Crystal let him hold it for a moment before she pulled away.

"Thanks for saying that. I'm really tired. See you later," she said. She noted the sadness on his face as she turned away. But she just didn't have the energy to think about her failure any longer.

Lucy let Crystal sleep in the next day. The little girl puttered around the tent until breakfast. She quietly told Crystal she was going to eat and Crystal nodded before turning over to go back to sleep. It was partially from the previous day and its stress, but it was also her sadness and depression that kept her in bed most of the day. She surfaced long enough to eat lunch and then summoned the energy to take Lucy back into the tent to work on her lessons.

After lessons, Lucy ran around the settlement with her friends and Crystal tried to concentrate on a book she had borrowed. Her mind kept wandering to Antonio. She felt extremely stupid to have insisted on the Christmas decorations. She didn't know why he had flirted with her and been so kind after that. Crystal blamed herself, why wouldn't Antonio as well?

Just before dinner, a person making a knocking noise outside of her tent woke her from a nap. She unzipped the door to find Antonio.

Lucy was with him, bouncing on her toes, her face flush with excitement.

"Come on, Mommy, you won't believe it," Lucy said.

"Shhhh, Lucy. It's a surprise for Mommy, remember?" Antonio said, his voice playful as he winked at Lucy.

"A surprise?" Crystal asked.

"Come one. Trust me," Antonio said, holding out his hand.

Crystal looked at him with a raised brow, but took his offered hand anyway. His was warm and calloused and her smaller one seemed to fit him well. As they walked between tents, Crystal wondered where everyone was. When they came to the center open area, her questions were answered.

Where an open meeting space once was, now a large, beautiful tree stood. It was covered in ornaments and bows. Wrapped gifts were being added under the tree. All the kids were running around talking excitedly about Santa coming in less than two weeks. Crystal spotted some adults using glitter puff paints to write the kids' names on stockings.

"Here's mine, Mommy!" Lucy exclaimed when Crystal walked over.

She pointed to a red stocking with her name written in pink across the top. Her daughter bounced and smiled before running and hugging Antonio around the legs.

"I don't understand," Crystal started to say.

"You were right. But not just about Lucy. The entire group needed this. Needed this happiness. If we're going to survive this, we need joy too," Antonio said.

Crystal couldn't fight the tears that came. She swiped at her face as they fell down her cheeks. She watched Lucy run to join the kids as they looked at the gifts.

"I don't have anything to give her," Crystal said, suddenly nervous about her daughter being disappointed after everything.

"Don't worry. We hit a toy store too," Antonio said with a laugh.

Crystal really didn't know what else to say. It seemed that Antonio had thought of everything. Down to the fake snow tree skirt she had grabbed from the craft store. It was now laid out under the tree with the colorful gifts laying on top of it. Even though much of the paper was plain colors or birthday paper, it didn't matter. It was all so beautiful.

"I have one more thing," Antonio said, his voice taking on a gruff tone.

Crystal turned to look at him as he held something over her head. Where he had found mistletoe, she couldn't begin to guess. Her face must have shown shock because Antonio grinned in his charming way. His free hand came to her face, and he used a thumb to brush away her lingering tears. His lips were soft where they landed just next to her mouth.

When she opened her eyes, Antonio stared right back at her.

"We have time," he said.

Hand in hand they circled the tree and Antonio showed her some ornaments he chose. Lucy ran around them, determined to show her mother every ornament she helped with, which to Crystal seemed like most of them. The last thing missing was a star on the top of the tree. Lucy was hoisted to Antonio's shoulders and she carefully placed the plastic star on top of the tree.

There may have been no twinkling lights or fireplaces, no huge turkey feast or eggnog, but for an apocalyptic Christmas, the holiday held everything that was dear for Crystal. For the first time, she found hope again. And she was going to do whatever necessary to hold on to it.

ABOUT THE AUTHOR

Though born and raised in Northern California, I spent the majority of my adult life in Las Vegas, Nevada. Now living in Oregon, life is slower and much less bright than Las Vegas. When I'm not lost in a flurry of writing, I enjoy hiking, reading (of course), travel (cruise obsessed), and quality time with my family.

It's cliche to say that I've wanted to be a writer since I was a little girl, because don't most authors say that? What is new is my obsession with the apocalypse and anything that could possibly cause the fall of our society as we know it. When I first decided to try my hand at writing a full-length novel, I started with romance. I just couldn't get it done. That was where the Sundown Series came into my life. When the Duncan Family was born, it was suddenly characters and lives I could sink my teeth into. I find myself being very emotionally connected to my characters, making it difficult to allow anyone to die. But how do you have zombies without people dying?

facebook.com/AuthorCKonstantin
twitter.com/CKonstantini
instagram.com/courtney.konstantin_author

MELT INTO ME

BY ALLISON K. GARCIA

CHAPTER 1

DONE WITH MEN

Callie threw her phone across the living room. It made a thud as it bounced off the cozy, light blue armchair onto the faded rug in her loft. Another failed relationship ended through text. This time she broke it off. Derek had barely been worth her energy. He'd told her he was living with his parents during the pandemic to help take care of them, but it had definitely been the opposite. She had personally watched his mother bring trays of snacks down to the basement where he lived in squalor with enough gaming equipment to open up his own store.

She was done with men. Now 34, she would adopt another cat and accept the title of "crazy cat lady."

Her phone beeped, but she ignored it and got off the couch. She needed some comfort food. And to get out of the house for a bit. She'd been working from home during the pandemic and only ventured out for food or Derek.

"No more Derek," she whispered to herself. "And..." She opened the fridge, confirming the barren tundra needed to be stocked. "...no more food."

Callie grabbed her favorite mask with kittens in Santa hats off the counter. She stuffed her feet into her fuzzy black boots, tugged on her pink hat and puffy black jacket, and wrapped the matching pink scarf around her neck. She slung her dark blue messenger bag across her chest, tucked her phone in her back pocket, and snatched her reusable bags off the hook on the wall. Sometimes she felt like she was going off to war instead of traversing her neighborhood.

"I'll be back later, boys," she called out to her two cats, Purrdy and Cutie, who sat entertained at the window by a pigeon on the fire escape. Purrdy was a "purr box" as her best friend, Hannah, had nicknamed him. She could hear him purr his way into the room, his little white boots gently tapping against the gnarled wooden floors. He was almost all black, even his face, so the purring was helpful for both of them especially at night, for him not to get trampled on and her not to get the life scared out of her. Then there was Cutie, a sweet tabby with the cutest little face when he fell asleep. Maybe she would come back with a little brother or sister for them instead of groceries.

Her stomach rumbled. Maybe not.

She'd just grab some food at the small grocery store two blocks down and drop by the taco place that just so happened to be across the street from Feline Friends, a local non-profit animal shelter.

Callie unlocked the deadbolt and stepped into the hall, taking one sniff of her live wreath before covering her face with her mask. She nodded at her elderly neighbor, Barbara, at the end of the hall. "Looks like it's a cold one out there."

Barbara lifted a crumpled tissue from her cane up to her nose with a shaky hand. "It's the wind that gets you." Barbara went on short walks around the block every day. Before the pandemic, Callie rarely saw her neighbors. She'd go to the office and out with her friends and hibernate in front of the television. Since March, she'd been working from home and quarantining except for her weekly trip to the grocery store, dinner at Derek's (provided by his mother, of course), and the occasional socially distant outing with friends. At first, she loved rolling out of bed and answering troubleshooting calls in her pajamas, but even her introverted self needed live people every once in a while.

Derek was always there, which was part of the problem. His gaming would take up half of her signal, and she'd lost connectivity more than once and had to boot him out of her place. Sometimes she'd take a walk around the block just to cool down.

Callie shook her head. She should've dropped his lazy butt five months ago, but the pandemic had her mind all screwed up and lonely for people. Derek had gone with his family down to South Carolina for Thanksgiving, and the week and a half without him were the lightest she'd felt in months. It finally gave her the clarity to realize that she didn't actually like him. She'd just been lonely.

To fight the loneliness, she started calling and video-chatting her friends more and slowly meeting her neighbors. So far she'd met Barbara, who went on short walks every day and had been a real-life Hot Lips Houlihan during the Korean war; Charlie and his partner, Leon, who were knee-deep in their newborn daughter's diapers; and Madeline, who was an oddball writer who sometimes had full-out conversations with her characters in the hallway. There was also a man and wife she'd labeled "Mr. and Mrs. Grumpster," a cute, soft-spoken Vietnamese family, and a half dozen other apartments of people in their three-story apartment building on the east side of Wesley, a small city in Northern New Jersey.

"That's one good thing about these masks," Barbara joked as she opened up her door and stepped into her apartment. "Blocks the wind a bit."

Callie smiled. "True. Well, you have a good day." She waited until Barbara closed the door and walked down the hall to the open stair-case. She leaned over the banister, looking down the three sets of stairs. The railings were decorated with a long string of tiny white icicle lights that blinked in unpredictable patterns.

Noises carried up through the stairwell: television, children's laughter, an argument, rhythmic bass beats. Sounds of life. Her loft was so quiet. Derek and his games were annoying, no doubt, but they filled the void. At this point in life, her friends were all coupled up, most of them with kids, and here she was starting all over again from scratch.

She got out her key and checked her mail. Mostly junk and two bills. She shoved it in her messenger bag, next to the one from earlier in the week she'd forgotten to pay, and then made an alarm on her phone to pay bills online when she got back home. Nearly all her bills were automatically debited from her account, except the bill for her root canal and crown from last year that she'd been paying a little bit on every month, one magazine subscription she'd been considering renewing, and the first bill for the new internet provider she'd switched to and had forgotten to set up online banking for.

Callie stepped outside into the frosty winter weather, squinting her eyes as an icy wind threatened to freeze her contact lenses. She fast-walked down the sidewalk, barely taking in the winter decorations around the block. Green garlands and snowflakes and red bows. A masked Santa Claus hopped from one foot to the other on the corner with his charity bucket extended. She tossed in a quarter and then made a beeline for the warmth of the local grocery store. They had a person sitting outside with a parka and an abacus, counting her as she went in. She felt really positive about this store, because they required masks to get in, had free paper ones for people who didn't have one, and only admitted a limited number of people.

She got a handbasket, promising herself not to fill it with only ice cream and chips to drown her sorrows. She'd already put on the "Covid-19," which is what Hannah said were the nineteen pounds everyone seemed to be gaining from sitting on their butt's all day, and she could not afford new clothes right now.

She wanted something delicious but easy. She vaguely recalled a recipe for pumpkin alfredo sauce. On a whim, she'd picked up a pumpkin last month and baked it in the oven. Apparently, pumpkins had a lot of filling, because she'd already made two pies, pumpkin bread, and had three containers of puree leftover in her freezer. She pulled out her phone and found the recipe.

"Pasta, pumpkin puree, sage, rosemary, butter, garlic, heavy whipping cream, and Parmesan cheese," she mumbled out loud. She had everything except the cream and herbs.

Callie walked to the fresh produce section and scanned for the herbs, grabbing some small sweet peppers that she liked in her omelets and a bag of onions. No herbs to be found. She harrumphed and made her way to the dairy aisle, grabbing a container of agave-sweetened gummy bears from the bulk section. She checked the freezer section, also no herbs. A blond, spiky-haired man in an apron bent over in the pet aisle. She paused for just a moment to admire the way his jeans hugged his backside before approaching.

"Excuse me, sir, can you tell me where to find the herbs?"

He stood up and turned around, only not to be a "he" at all. The woman smiled at her through her mask, and Callie turned as red as the sweet peppers in her basket.

* * *

VIOLET WAS USED to being mistaken for a man. But it was still annoying. She enjoyed being a woman, but she felt more like herself in a masculine-style presentation. "Were you talking to me?"

"Yes." The woman cringed, her face so bright red Violet could almost see it through her kitten mask. "I'm so sorry."

"Happens all the time." Violet shrugged and then gestured to her chest. "Most people notice these though."

The woman laughed nervously, glancing but then trying not to.

Hmmm. Was she family? Violet tilted her head to the side and looked her up and down. In the 90s and early 2000s, it was easy to tell, but once "The L Word" had all those lipstick lesbians on display, femme culture had risen up in the lesbian world. These days she didn't rely much on her gaydar. Any woman could be gay.

And why wouldn't they be? Women were gorgeous, soft, and sensitive. Sure, there was drama and soooo many emotions, but it was worth it every time. Not that there were a lot of "times" for her. She was what her friends called a "serial monogamist" and had three life partners: Natalie, who was an eternal teenager and still hitchhiking across the world at 45; Jen, who it might have worked out with if she'd ever agreed to therapy; and Layla, who apparently had been cheating on her with Jen for some time.

She'd been on a few dates pre-COVID, but no one special had emerged, and she'd given up and been binge-watching shows and keeping up with social media drama.

Violet looked at the woman's cute matching hat and scarf, her untamed brown curls, and dark brown eyes. Worth a shot. "What was it you were looking for?"

"Herbs," the woman choked out. "Sage, rosemary."

"Very 'Scarborough Fair,'" Violet replied.

The woman chuckled. "I've got this yummy recipe for pumpkin alfredo sauce. I mean, I've never made it, but it sounds amazing."

"For something like that I'd go for a fresh herb over a dry one."

"My thoughts exactly, but I couldn't find any in the produce section." The woman's pallor had settled to pink.

"There are some plants over here." Violet waved her over to the section near the window with live plants. "See, only $5 and enough for at least one batch of alfredo."

"Oh, I don't know about this. I kill everything I touch."

"Scary prospect." Violet took a stab in the dark. "What about all the women you date?"

The woman's eyes widened and her face pinkened again. "I'm not." She shook her head. "I don't."

Shoot. A sinking feeling took over but she overcompensated with a smile. "Sorry. Just thought you were cute. Worth a shot."

"Thanks, but yeah, I've only dated men."

Hmmm. Have only dated men. Not only date. Past tense. Was there still a possibility? Could she be one of the women who figured it out later? Not every lesbian was a gold star like her. There were plenty who had been married with kids and then emerged from their cocoon of compulsory heterosexuality and/or internalized homophobia to become rainbow butterflies.

The woman stepped closer to the herb plants, touching one of the soft sage leaves. "Anyway, I worry about keeping plants because I have cats."

Now this was something she knew about. "Both sage and rosemary are non-toxic to cats, so if you don't mind them munching on it or knocking it over, it should be totally fine."

"Cool." She carefully added the two plants to her sparse basket. "I'm ready to check out now."

"Oh," Violet chuckled. "I don't actually work here."

The woman put one hand on her ample hip. "Are you kidding me?"

Violet gestured to her apron. "I work at Friendly Felines. I came in for some cat food, but I'm in here all the time and know where stuff is. Thought I'd be helpful."

The woman laughed. "This was worth leaving the house for. Thank you, generous stranger. You've definitely brightened my day."

"I'm glad. It's Violet, by the way." She pointed to her name tag.

"Callie. Nice to meet you."

"Ditto." Violet sighed. "Well, I better grab that cat food before my boss wonders if I've fallen into a sewer grate or something."

Callie chuckled. "Well, I might end up seeing you later, because I'm thinking about getting another cat."

"Oh yeah?" Violet stood up taller. "That's awesome. We have some cuties right now. It's by appointment though."

"Oh." Callie's face dropped. "I was hoping to get over there today. Sometimes I forget things have changed."

"Ain't that the truth." Violet tugged her wallet out of her back pocket and plucked out a business card. "Ask for me, I'll hook you up."

Callie swallowed. Hard. "Okay, thanks." She paused for a moment, her hand on the card, before taking it. "I don't want to keep you."

Violet adjusted her mask and smiled with her eyes. "Callie, I look forward to seeing you again."

Callie nodded and did an awkward wave before walking to the register.

Violet went to the pet aisle, heart pounding. What was she even thinking? It was silly to focus on someone who hadn't even thought of dating women yet. She didn't want to be someone's experiment.

She grabbed the bulky dry food and tossed it over one shoulder, then grabbed a half dozen cans of wet food with the other hand.

Callie was walking out the door as she stepped up to register. Lord, she was beautiful. Not like a skinny runway model or a cookie-cutter Hollywood star, but in a classical Renaissance beauty. Something drew Violet to her.

If Callie showed up and asked for her, she'd play it by ear. Half of lesbian dating was wondering if the other person liked you as a friend or as more than a friend anyway. Wouldn't be that much different.

* * *

CALLIE WALKED MUCH FASTER than she would have normally.

What just happened?

People had mistaken her for gay for years. It used to piss her off when she was younger. People making assumptions, because it took her so long to get her first boyfriend. Sorry that she was more into books and computers than boys! And later because she wasn't married with kids.

Truth be told, previous to today, all those people had been straight and generally the offensive attitude they'd had was closer to "What? Are you gay or something?" That pissed off Callie more. She had friends that were gay, all the way back to high school. There was nothing wrong with it. Her parents were never very on board with her gay friends, but she was more evolved.

But in all her years, never had she been hit on by a woman.

Nor had she ever checked out a woman's butt before and liked it. In fact, she usually avoided looking at them. Ever since she was a kid in the locker room during gym class, she was super uncomfortable around women's bodies.

But today, she'd found herself looking. And feeling attracted to Violet. And for a brief moment considered...

She shook her head. No. No. She was 34. And most definitely not gay. Never had a gay thought in her head.

Callie stopped at a light and groaned. Except for that dream. Oof! And was that a dream. But, when she'd told Hannah, she reminded her about the Jungian interpretation that we are all the people in our dreams, so she'd believed she needed to reconnect with her feminine side.

She crossed the street, leaving behind her notions of going to the taco stand, unlocked the door to the apartment building, and headed up the stairs at a rapid pace, stopping on the second-floor landing for a moment.

Nope, this was silly. This couldn't be a thing. She would cook her pumpkin alfredo and forget about tacos and cats for the day.

CHAPTER 2

TACOS AND CATS

*C*allie was in the middle of a personal whirlwind. It'd been three days since meeting Violet at the grocery store, and she felt as though her life had been turned upside-down.

While most people during the holiday season were buying gifts and making plans with loved ones, she had been obsessively journaling. After fighting unsuccessfully for several hours to get the questioning out of her mind, she decided to do something she rarely did: think about her feelings.

Turns out she had a lot of them, because she had typed up 10,000 words in three days. She'd barely done anything else.

She'd looked back through her childhood and growing up years through the present, shocked that she hadn't figured this out sooner. She remembered playing doctor with her best friend in early elementary school, her slight fixation with Buffy the Vampire Slayer, sneaking over to her friend's house to watch The L Word when her parents were out, that one experience with the girl at church camp. Then there was her most recent series of celebrity "girl crushes." Derek had joked that they had the same taste in women, most recently it'd been Ruby Rose.

That was just the tip of the iceberg. She had literally blocked all of this stuff out. Or somehow she'd brushed each instance off, like it was no big deal. All together on the page, all ten thousand words of it, it was pretty conclusive. Plus, she'd taken no less than twelve quizzes and the consensus was that she was at least bisexual.

A mixture of excitement, fear, stupidity, and shock overwhelmed her one moment to the next.

Now it was Monday morning. How was she supposed to work with all this going on? She only had to hold it together until Friday when she had ten days off for Christmas. She was going to her parents' house an hour south in the small town she grew up in. Maybe time away from city life would give her the space she needed to get her head back on straight.

Ha. Straight. Was that even a possibility anymore?

* * *

Violet cleaned out another litter box, making it fresh for the two new rescues that were coming in today. It'd been three days and the cute girl from the grocery store had never called in.

No, she'd have to go home for the holidays and get another lecture from her mother about her poor choices in women. Now 40, her mother had given up on setting her up with her friends' sons and had resigned that Violet was a "career lesbian" without hope for salvation.

Violet only went home for Christmas, mostly to see her brother and sister and their families who came in for the holidays. They were both in hetero marriages with an average of 2.5 children. Meanwhile, Violet would have to go solo again, explaining that Layla was no longer in her life.

The only bright spot was her recent connection to an LGBTQ+af-firming church called HOPE in the area and their upcoming outdoor Christmas party in an arboretum right outside the city. Layla had some friends that went there and kept going on and on about it, so a little over a year ago she'd checked it out and had been surprised at how awesome they were.

She didn't have to dress up and didn't need a working knowledge of the Bible to get in. She had left her parents' church, labeled as a "heathen," when she was 16 and had made out with the pastor's daughter, Kim, in the choir loft. Kim was sent to an "ex-gay" Christian camp where she met her best friend/future wife. At HOPE, no one judged Violet for being gay. In fact, more than half the congregation was queer.

Violet had never felt safe around Christians before, so it was weird. She'd never stopped believing there was a God out there, but she thought she had been kicked out of the club for being gay. It was sort of amazing and wild to know people could be gay and a Christian at the same time. They'd been mutually exclusive. She had queer friends who were spiritual but most had left traditional religions behind.

Last fall, she'd found out about Jen and Layla and soon after that had sought comfort and support in HOPE. She'd walked in one Sunday on a whim after looking it up online a half dozen times and had seen a familiar face. Her former coworker named Pat, who was another gold star like her, came up and greeted her with a huge smile and a hug. She recognized several other people, too, and that, along with the free coffee and snacks, the affirming message, and the casual atmosphere made her feel safe.

She kept coming back, one Sunday after another, and soon she had a little family there. So when they started the LGBTQ+ support group, she'd joined in. Even though she felt secure in her sexuality, the premise of the support group was healing wounds the church had left in the LGBTQ+ community and she definitely had fallen into that category.

She'd met some really cool peeps and the support group had even continued through COVID with a supportive chat room and weekly video chats. She'd been to a few outdoor services and hadn't missed hardly any of the streaming Sunday services. She always learned something and there was a comfort in finding this new, positive community.

Violet had lost half her friends over the whole Jen and Layla fiasco. She had to admit that she'd been pretty bitter in the end. Half of her friends had sided with Jen and Layla and the other half with her. It made for a lot of uncomfortable stares during parties and at the lesbian bar in the south end of town and the gay-friendly coffee shop where all her friends hung out. Even though the city was big, the lesbian community was small. The L Word was pretty realistic in that aspect.

HOPE had helped her get to a calmer place in her heart, and she felt maybe she was ready for someone new.

Of course, her support group friends had warned her about getting her hopes up with the straight girl. Her friend, Jo, had just sent a laughing emoji, and even her own brain told her it was dumb. But still every time the phone rang or the door dinged open, she got her hopes up.

Why did God have to send that voluptuous beauty into her path if He wasn't going to follow through?

* * *

CALLIE HAD NOW DOUBLED her wordcount in her journal and at least a thousand were about how she needed to call Friendly Felines and ask for Violet. The business card yelled at her from her desk. She picked it up and flipped it over in her hand. She'd already worn one of the edges from that very movement.

She could lie to herself and pretend that she was uncertain about getting another cat, but the real truth stared her down. She was attracted to Violet and was afraid of what that meant.

"Oh my God, Callie. Get a grip." She tossed the card down and stood up, pacing around her living room. Purrdy weaved between her legs and almost sent her tumbling to the floor. "Silly kitty. Do you want to get squished?"

Purrdy meowed and rubbed against her calf.

She reached down and scratched his ear, and he fell onto the ground, exposing his tummy. "Oh my goodness," she used her baby voice. "Does kitty wanna belly rub?" She stroked his stomach, black with splotches of white. Cutie made his way over and flopped on the floor next to Purrdy. "Oh, two kitties want belly rubs? Good thing I got two hands."

She smiled as both of her cats stretched back, eyes closed, content looks on their faces.

"Do you want a new brother or sister or am I being crazy?" Cutie went to nip at her finger. "Is that a 'no'?"

Violet's face flashed in her mind. What was she so scared of? Being gay? What was so scary about that? Sure, her entire life would be flipped on its head, but if she'd learned anything while surviving a pandemic, it was that there was a difference between living and existing, and she wanted to live.

Plus, she wanted another cat.

Callie stood up and stomped over to the desk, picked up the card, and got out her phone. Her hand shook as she dialed the number. She held her breath. It rang once. Then twice. Then a third time.

"Friendly Felines, how can I help you?"

Callie bit her lip. "Hello, I'd like to set up an appointment with Violet."

"This is Violet."

Callie's breath caught, and all the words tumbled out of her brain. Say something. Anything. Nothing came out of her mouth.

"Is this the girl from the grocery store?" Violet asked, a touch of excitement in her voice.

"Yes," Callie managed to squeak out.

"Well, you've just made my day."

Callie's eyes widened.

"That was cheesy. Sorry. Let me try that again." Violet cleared her throat. "Hi, Callie, right? Glad you called."

Callie snickered.

"So, you want to get a cat?"

"Cat? Yes. A cat. I want a cat." Callie did a facepalm. What the heck was wrong with her?

"I mean…you don't have to get a cat." Violet lowered her voice. "We could just hang out."

"I definitely want a cat," Callie said a little too fast. "Or at least an appointment to meet the ones you have."

"We have three ready to go here, two new ones coming in, and a dozen that are being fostered right now."

THE AUTHOR TRANSFORMATION ALLIANCE

"Fostered?"

"Yeah, we don't have the manpower to keep them all here. Plus, the cats are happier in homes. You can foster to buy, as well, to see if the one you choose gets along well with your cats. We have two that wouldn't be a good fit, because they are not good with other cats. And, do you have kids?"

"Nope."

"Husband? Boyfriend?"

Callie smirked. "Just the two cats."

"Some cats don't like men. Have to ask."

"Mm hmm." Callie bit back a smile.

"My last appointment today is still available. 5:15?"

"I'll take it. I get off work at five, but I live pretty close, so I think I can make it."

"Don't worry. I'll wait."

Callie's stomach did a flip. "Okay, see you then." She hung up before she could say anything else stupid and then flopped face down on the couch with a moan.

"Purrdy, Cutie, it's official. Your mother is a total dork."

Cutie nudged her hand, and Purrdy purred loudly in her ear and kneaded her shoulder.

It was the closest thing to a pep talk she was gonna get.

* * *

VIOLET HUNG up the phone and grinned big. "You'll never guess," she called out to her manager/friend, Jessie.

"For real?!" Jessie called from the back room. "Grocery Girl?"

"Yes. And she's coming in at 5:15 for an appointment."

Jessie walked out. Her red stilettos clicking against the hardwood floors. She was the epitome of cool chic with her dark wash skinny jeans hugging her perfect curves, her black V-neck sweater doing the same, and dangly matching gold earrings and bracelet. Her bright red lipstick matched her heels and brought out her chestnut skin. She pulled her mask up, took one look at Violet, and shook her head. "Mm-mm, you can't meet her in that."

42

Violet looked down. Her raggedy old sweatshirt was covered in fur and smelled like old kitty litter, but her jeans were cute and she had her favorite pair of rainbow Chucks on. "I don't even remember what I have underneath this." She pulled off her sweatshirt and tossed it on the hook where she always left it for kitty litter duty and gave her simple t-shirt a sniff, wrinkling her nose. "Nope. I stink. What time is it?"

"Time for your break. Jaqueline's shift starts in twenty minutes, and I'm almost done with the grant proposal. What needs to be done still?"

Violet studied the area. The last five minutes had wiped her memory. "Let me think…oh, I need to put her name in the system. Oh gees. I didn't even get her last name."

Jessie rolled her eyes. "You've got it bad."

"Shut up, you." Violet inputted Callie's name and sparse information she'd failed to collect into the computer. She pulled up the schedule. "We have Ms. Hardy coming in a few minutes, then Mr. Sanchez at 3:30, and Callie at 5:15. Plus, that investor is supposed to drop by any minute now, and Wendy hasn't dropped off the two new cats yet."

"Oof, what an afternoon." Jessie leaned on the doorframe. "I did not wear the right shoes for this."

"Who do you think you're kidding? You're never wearing the right shoes."

Jessie coughed out a laugh. "Ain't that the truth. Did you put out food and water and give Jasmine her afternoon kitty treat?"

"Yes. And the litter boxes are all clean. I didn't vacuum or dust yet."

Jessie waved her off. "Jaqueline can do that. Go home. Take a shower. Get changed. Be back in an hour."

"Thanks, boss lady!" She blew her a kiss, grabbed her winter jacket and hat, and flew out the door.

Thirty minutes later, Violet was standing in front of her foggy mirror in her small bathroom, drying off. She tamed her hair with a bit of product and brushed her teeth. She walked down the hall to her bedroom and spent an extra few seconds picking out a cute long-sleeved tee in her favorite shade of cobalt blue that Layla told her brought out her eyes. She put on a fresh pair of jeans and stuck her feet back in her favorite Chucks. "What do you think, Gravy?" she asked her thick brown cat.

Gravy looked up for a moment and then went back to grooming himself on the bed.

Violet groaned. "You're right. I need to chill." She shook out her arms and stretched.

She stepped into her tiny kitchen, finishing the last bite of her turkey sandwich while she ran the dishwasher. When Violet bought the small, two-bedroom house with Jen ten years ago, it seemed perfect. Now, even with Gravy, it seemed empty and big. Truthfully, it wasn't bigger than a typical apartment in Wesley, but it was hers. She even had a tiny vegetable and herb garden in the back and a garage to park the car she didn't own. Instead, she used it as her workshop, where she tinkered with woodworking. Her front yard consisted of her small concrete porch and two snowy patches of dead grass hugging the stone path down to the main sidewalk.

Before heading out the door, Violet tossed her clothes in the dryer, threw on her winter garb, and grabbed her wallet, keys, and mask. She normally rode her bike to work, but she had another half hour to kill and she wanted to stretch her legs. It was only five blocks. She walked at a moderate clip so as not to get sweaty, enjoyed the scenery she usually missed flying by on her bike, and attempted to take Gravy's more relaxed view on life and chill.

* * *

CALLIE TRIED on her fourth outfit and was finally satisfied. Had to look good for those rescue cats, right?

Thankfully, her last call had been an easy fix, merely uninstalling and reinstalling a program and running a virus sweep, so she'd had time to get ready. Ready for what? She wasn't sure, but she headed out the door anyway.

As she turned the corner onto the road where Friendly Felines was housed, the aroma of fresh corn tortillas and seared chorizo, asada, adobada, and carnitas surrounded her. Her mouth started to water. The grilled cheese with tomato soup for lunch was already out of her system. There was no way she could resist eating dinner there tonight.

She walked by the stand, where a frozen family shivered on the metal stools and scarfed down their delicious tacos. She resisted the urge to stop and continued on to Friendly Felines, taking a deep breath before opening the door with a ding.

"Welcome to Friendly Felines. Are you Callie?" A woman in stilettos approached.

"Yes. I have an appointment with Violet," Callie stated, her voice shakier than she would have liked.

"She's finishing up with a phone call." The woman held out a clipboard with a QR code. "Can you fill this out while you're waiting?"

"Sure thing." Callie pulled out her phone, snapped a pic, and began to input her information into their online form. She stood near the wall of the small entrance room that housed a coatrack, a screen scrolling pictures of cats and their happy new owners, and a few plants. There also seemed to be an office in the back and a windowed room with free-roaming cats.

The woman cleared her throat. "Violet mentioned you already have a couple of cats."

"I do. A 3-yr old tabby named Cutie and a 2-yr old tuxedo named Purrdy, both males. Very friendly."

"That's great. Violet is wonderful with cats. She pretty much helped me open this place. It'd fall apart without her."

"I keep telling her to make me a full partner, yet she resists." Violet walked out of the office, somehow looking better than the other day at the store.

Callie felt tingles all through her body. She was definitely at least a little gay.

The woman put a hand on her hip and cocked her head. "And I keep telling her that's not how non-profits work." She shoved the clipboard back in a holder on the wall. "Well, ladies, I've got a date with my hubs. Momma's got the kids for a few days and I'm feeling feisty."

Callie felt heat rise to her face.

Violet snickered. "Jessie, you know you're just gonna catch up on Lovecraft Country."

She let out a roaring laugh. "You know me too well." She grabbed a peacoat and pulled a red hat over her natural curls, grabbing a black strappy purse from the office. "I sent Jaqueline home early. Don't forget to lock up."

Callie suddenly realized she was alone with Violet. Her stomach swirled and her heart picked up its pace. She redirected her energy to finishing the form on her phone and submitted it. She stuck it into her back pocket.

The boss whispered something to Violet as she passed her and headed out the door.

Violet clicked her tongue at her. She turned to Callie, her eyes smiling. "Ready to see some cats?"

Callie perked up.

Violet stopped in her tracks. "Sorry. Where are my manners? Do you want to take off your jacket?"

"That'd be great." Callie was starting to perspire under the extra layer. She passed it to Violet who put it on the coatrack where her boss' peacoat had just been hanging.

"Do you want any coffee or anything?"

Callie shook her head. Caffeine combined with her current anxious state would likely throw her into a panic attack. "I'm good, thanks."

Violet ushered her through the glass door into the windowed cat room. "As you can see, we've got five in here now. Buster and Isabelle have already been welcomed into the fold." She gestured to two striped kittens that looked like brother and sister, huddled up in a cat bed together. "We'd love to adopt them out as a pair."

Callie nodded. "They look pretty cozy." A gray cat rubbed up against her leg. "Well, hello there. Who are you?"

"That's Smoky. He's a cuddlebug." Violet scooped him up and held him like a baby, scratching under his chin.

Callie held out her hand and let Smoky smell it before petting him. "He likes you."

Callie smiled, suddenly aware that she was so close to Violet she could smell the sweet spice of her perfume. Before she could think, the words spilled out of her mouth. "You smell nice."

Violet glanced into Callie's eyes for just a moment before returning her gaze to Smoky. "Thanks. Probably my hair product."

Callie swallowed. Smoky jumped down out of Violet's arms. They stood in the same space for a moment, not speaking, until an orange tabby caught her eye.

Violet turned to stand beside her, reducing the space between them. "That's Naranjo. He's persnickety." At that, he hissed at one of the two newcomer kittens. "Great solo cat, but probably not what you're looking for. And Jasmine's hiding around here somewhere." She clicked her tongue. "Jasmine, where are you, baby?"

A sleek striped cat popped her head up from the top of the cat castle in the corner.

"There you are. Come meet Callie."

Jasmine studied Callie for a moment and then began to groom herself.

Callie smiled.

"She's a bit of a princess. Hence the name." Violet pulled a tablet from a holder on the wall. "Let me show you the others we have offsite in foster homes."

Callie could hear her heart beating in her ears. Violet shuffled through a dozen pictures, none of which Callie could pay attention to. All she could think about was how blue Violet's eyes were and how good she smelled and how soft her skin looked.

She shook her head. What was happening to her? Somehow admitting to herself that she was attracted to women had opened the floodgates.

Smoky rubbed up against her leg again. She pulled herself out of her trance and bent down to pet him. Smoky flopped onto his back. "Aww, this is exactly what my kitties do."

Violet squatted down next to her and rubbed his belly. "He is a pretty great cat."

They both pet him in silence for a moment, until Jasmine and the kittens made their way over.

"Look what you started, Smoky," Violet scratched behind his ear, and he curled up his front paws and purred.

"While I love all this attention," Callie said as the kittens nibbled on her shoelaces and Jasmine circled near her. "I think Smoky is the one for me."

"Yeah, he seems to really like you." Violet stood up. "We have to run a background check with your information."

"Make sure I don't have any cat felonies?" Callie joked.

Violet chuckled. "You'd be surprised. That usually takes a day or two, plus we need to get his papers ready."

"Oh, so I can't take him home today?" Callie frowned.

Violet cringed. "No, sorry. I should have explained that on the phone. I was a bit distracted when you called."

"Oh yeah?" Callie stood up and gestured out the window to the sidewalk. "Cute girl walk by or something?"

"No. I was distracted by the cute girl on the phone," Violet said, her voice smooth and slightly lower.

Callie lost the ability to speak once again.

A tiny, high-pitched cry broke the silence. One of the kittens had pissed off Jasmine, who was holding it down with one paw.

"Now, now, Jasmine, is that any way to treat your new friends?" Violet scooped up the kitten and its sibling. "I better put you two in your bed before you get yourselves in any more trouble." She carried the fuzzy, wriggling kitten over to the back corner, where there was a cage with bedding, a litter box, water, and food. She placed them inside and closed the cage door.

"What about the rest of them?" Callie asked, recuperating her voice.

"We don't like to take chances with the new cats. These guys have been here a while, so they're used to each other. They each have their own litter box and food bowls, and they share the cat fountain." She pointed to the babbling water dispenser in the corner. "Speaking of food, it looks like someone was hungry. Better restock before I close up shop."

Violet popped open a large food container and bent over to fill up the food bowls. Callie felt the heat rise to her face again, as she tried really hard not to appreciate Violet's jeans and what they hugged.

"What are you up to this evening?" Violet asked as she tossed the scoop back in the container and locked the lid.

Callie's brain buzzed with a thousand thoughts racing around her head at once. "Tacos," she blurted out loudly.

Violet snorted. "What's that now?"

"Tacos," Callie stuttered. "I'm going to eat tacos for dinner." She gestured wildly outside in the direction of the stand.

"Yeah, that place is so good. I should have stock in it." Violet patted her flat stomach.

"Wanna join me?" Callie asked before she had time to think.

Violet's eyes lit up. "Yes. I would love that. Just give me a minute to shut everything down for the night."

Violet made her way around the room, turning off electronics and lights, while Callie nursed the sinking feeling in her stomach. What did she just do? Did she just ask a woman out on a date? Or was it just friends hanging out and eating dinner?

She followed Violet into the main office and pulled on her coat and hat while Violet put the finishing touches on closing Friendly Felines. Violet locked the office door with a key from her carabiner and tugged the last coat off the rack. "Ready!"

Callie gave her an awkward thumbs up. Violet held open the door for her. "Thank you." Derek barely had the common decency to put the seat down for her. She smiled to herself. Guess she didn't need to worry about that if she was considering dating a woman.

She squinted her eyes against the cold as she walked into the dark night. Is that what she was doing? Considering dating a woman? Had she stepped into another dimension? Was she asleep and would awaken from an odd dream? Or was this actually happening?

Violet brushed up against her as she locked the outer door. "Excuse me, hun."

A heatwave rushed through Callie's body, taking the edge off the frozen tundra that was New Jersey in mid-December.

Date or not, Callie was definitely not dreaming.

CHAPTER 3

HOPE AND NEW BEGINNINGS

*V*iolet grinned big as she squinted through the predawn darkness at the new text that appeared on her phone. Every time a notification came in, she hoped it would be Callie. It was a very "Pavlov's dog" situation. Her phone had barely left her hand in three days.

Violet rolled over in bed, careful not to squish Gravy, who was curled up beside her. The other night's dinner was freezing, but the food was good. Once Callie had calmed down enough to speak full sentences after a while, they'd had a good conversation. She'd given Callie her number and was surprised to get a text from her before she'd even arrived back at her house. A simple statement about enjoying the evening and looking forward to hanging out again.

Since then, they'd texted every day. Only a few messages at first, but yesterday, they'd texted throughout the day and well into the night, having full-blown text conversations, mostly about their favorite fantasy shows. Callie's was Buffy, which Violet had never seen, and hers was Lost Girl, which Callie had never even heard of.

Violet turned her attention back to the text that had awoken her.

Good morning. Watched an ep of Lost Girl. So good.

Violet bit her lip and replied. You're up early.

Couldn't sleep.

Too excited about getting Smoky today? Violet wasn't supposed to work today, but she'd called in a favor from Jessie to do Callie's adoption.

That and it's my last day before my vacay.

Sweet! Doing anything special?

Not really. Going to my parents' for Christmas. They live in Kingsley. You?

I have a thing tonight for church—

Suddenly, an incoming call from Callie interrupted her text. She sat up quickly, hesitated for only a moment to answer, and it stopped ringing. She stared at the screen for a second and hit the call button.

"Hey, what's up?" Violet asked in her groggy morning voice.

"Sorry, my thumb slipped," Callie sounded vaguely panicked. "I didn't mean to call. It's so early. I probably woke you up."

"Hey, you're good. I've been enjoying our texts, but it's nice to hear your voice."

"Same. So, you have a church thing tonight?"

"Yeah." Violet relaxed back into her pillow. "Last year, my ex's friend told me about this LGBTQ-affirming church downtown. I had no idea how awesome it would be."

"Hmm...I don't think I've ever heard of an affirming church before. My church growing up definitely wasn't."

"Neither was mine. I was kicked out at 16 for being gay and never went to church again until last year."

"I'm so sorry. It's been a while for me too, but I thought the whole idea of being a Christian was supposed to be about loving God and your neighbors."

"Exactly." Violet sighed. "But that's why I love HOPE."

"I feel like I've seen that. Is that on 27th?"

"That's the place, but they're not having services in person right now because of the virus. There are a lot of people on hormones or with compromised immune systems, so it's pretty much all virtual, except for a few outdoor services. This one's a candlelight service. I'm excited. I've been streaming the virtual services and chatting with friends online and going to the video chats for my support group, but I miss being in that safe space and feeling all their love."

The line was silent for a moment. "That sounds really nice."

Violet noted a sadness in her voice. "It's being held at the arboretum. You ever been?"

"On a field trip once, I think. In the 90s."

"I didn't even know it was around back then." Violet did the math. "How old were you in the 90s?" Callie looked younger than her but not by a huge amount.

"I'm 34. You?"

Violet winced. Was six years difference too much? Screw it. "Forty."

"Wow," Callie said. "You look reeeally good for forty."

Violet chuckled. "Not just really good? Reeeally good?"

"I said what I said," Callie replied.

Now it was Violet's turn to blush. "Well, thanks." She took a breath and gathered some courage. "You could come with me tonight if you'd like...to the arboretum."

Callie's voice was slightly breathless. "I'd like that."

Violet felt a warmth cross over her chest. "It starts at 8. That'll give you enough time to bring Smoky back and introduce him to the boys."

"I hope they get along."

"It'll be fine." Violet added, "And if it's not, we'll find one that'll fit."

"Violet?" Callie asked, hesitancy in her voice.

The sound of her name on Callie's lips sent a wave of joy throughout her body. "Yes?"

"You wouldn't want to--? I mean, like not to do—Just for like..." Callie trailed off and then started back quickly. "Do you want to bring Smoky over here and have dinner before we go?"

Hope rose in Violet's heart. "That'd be great. I can do the last of the paperwork virtually. You wouldn't even need to come down to the office."

"I work from home, and I'm done at four."

"I can be there whenever. I have a confession to make." Violet sunk into her pillow.

"Oh yeah?"

"It's my day off. I asked Jessie to do your adoption just so I could see you."

Callie let out a bright peal of laughter. "I hope she's paying you overtime."

"She is, but I was willing to come in for free."

"You must really like your job."

"I do." Violet lowered her voice. "I also really like you."

The line was quiet for a moment. "I like you too. A lot."

Violet smiled. "That's good since you're going to hang out with me for what...six, seven hours tonight."

"Oof, that's a long first date."

Violet's mouth dropped open. She had labeled it. She wasn't just imagining things.

Callie started to backpedal. "Oh no. Did I get it wrong? Is it not a date? I'm just going to crawl into a hole now and die."

Violet stopped her rambling. "Wait, wait, wait. Yes. I very much want it to be a date. Second date, though. We had tacos."

"Does that count? How do you even know when dates are dates when it's two women?"

"Ah, the eternal question," Violet mused. "Sometimes it can go on for months and months with no one wanting to make the first move."

"Oh."

"You were bold, though."

Callie chuckled. "Apparently realizing I might be gay has made my filter fall out."

"Well, it's working for you. And for me."

The phone line crinkled in her ear. "Gees, I just saw the time. I gotta get ready for work. My first call's at eight."

"I've got your address from your paperwork. I'll come by a little after four. Can I bring anything?"

"French bread?"

"Perfect. See you soon." Violet hung up and released a long, excited squeal, causing Gravy's hackles to stand up.

She leaned forward and gave her grumpy feline a hug. "Gravy, you old curmudgeon. I've got a date tonight with a beautiful woman. And she likes me back."

He gave her a disapproving look and fell back asleep.

* * *

CALLIE JUMPED as the doorbell rang. This was it. Her first…wait, second…date with a woman. And she'd invited her into her home. Her home which she'd rapidly tidied up between customer calls.

She glanced in the mirror and ran her hand over her wild curls in an attempt to tame them. She looked out the peephole, and her cheeks stretched into a grin. She clicked the deadbolt and pulled open the door. "Hey."

Violet leaned on the doorframe, looking as tasty as the French bread in her hand. "Somebody order a cat?" She nodded down to the carrier at her feet with a sadly meowing Smoky.

Callie rolled her eyes. "Cute. Come on in."

Violet walked by her, her sweet spicy scent wafting past and causing the hair to stand up on the back of Callie's neck.

Callie closed the door behind them and took the French bread, bringing it up to her nose. "This smells so good." She looked at Violet's mask and realized she'd left hers on the counter. "Shoot. Mask."

Violet lifted her hand to her face. "I'm really careful. I wear my mask everywhere, I wash my hands all the time, I socially distance, and as far as I know, I haven't been around anyone exposed."

"Me too. I'm always masked except at home."

"So…we're good?"

"I think so. I'm happy to have you in my inner circle."

Violet raised an eyebrow.

"Of friends," Callie added quickly.

Violet pulled down her mask and laughed. "I'm just messing with you. I knew what you meant."

Callie looked at her fully in the face for the first time. "You're really pretty."

Violet blushed. "Thanks." She hung her jacket on the kitchen chair. "Oh, here they come."

They watched Purrdy and Cutie approach the cat carrier. The cats sniffed the carrier, circled it a few times, meowed, then rubbed up against Violet.

Violet knelt down. "I bet I know which one is Purrdy." She scratched her happy feline friend behind the ear. "And you must be Cutie." He put his front paws up on Violet's thigh, demanding attention.

"I put a special bed, litter box, food, and water for him in the walk-in closet so he could have some space for himself and get adjusted."

"Yeah, it's a little tricky with a one-bedroom. But if they are getting along okay with minimal hissing, you can let him out tomorrow sometime. He's pretty young still, and he's handled all the other cats well."

Callie picked up the carrier and brought it to the spacious walk-in closet in her bedroom. They stepped inside with Smoky and let him loose.

"Dang, this is a big closet."

"Some of the other residents with the same closets use them as a second bedroom."

"It's almost as big as my first apartment out of college."

Callie chuckled and watched Smoky sniff around and explore.

"He's feeling pretty comfortable here," Violet stated.

"How can you tell?"

She leaned in closer to Callie. "See how his ears have perked up and his tail's straight up? That means he's happy. If he was scared, he would've stayed in the crate or his ears would be back or he'd be hiding somewhere in here."

Callie nodded, hearing only half of what she'd said. Her heart was beating so fast. She'd never ever felt this way around a woman before. Suddenly, the space felt really small and she could barely breathe. "I guess we should get out of the closet now."

Violet smiled and followed her out. "There's a joke there somewhere."

Purrdy and Cutie hesitantly approached the slotted doors of the closet.

"Let's give them some space." Violet waved her back into the living room, sat down on the couch, and patted the cushion next to her.

Callie's legs quaked a little as she walked over and joined her on the couch.

"So, how are you feeling?" Violet asked, turning to face her.

"I think it went pretty well. No hissing's a good sign."

Violet looked into Callie's eyes. "That's not what I meant."

"Oh." Callie picked at a loose thread on the couch. "I'm a little nervous."

Violet nodded. "And that's okay. That's normal. This is new."

Callie felt tears threatening to rise and pushed them down.

"I'm not in any rush. I just think you seem like a pretty great person, and I want to get to know you better."

Callie let out a shaky breath. "Well, you have plenty of time."

A dimple appeared on Violet's right cheek. "Oh, by the way, six hours is pretty standard for a first or second date in the lesbian world."

"God, I could never stand that long on a first date with a man." Callie paused. "Come to think of it, that should've been a sign."

"Don't beat yourself up. A lot of women take longer to figure things out. It's pretty common."

"It is?" Callie sighed. "I mean, I did read a few articles and watch some movies."

"Oh, did you now?"

"Research." Callie cocked her head to the side. "Apparently I'm a 'baby gay.'" She used finger quotes.

Violet coughed out a laugh. "I don't think I've heard that before. That's perfect." She rubbed her thumb on Callie's shoulder. "Well, you're not alone. Half of my support group came out after thirty. There are so many things that lead women to figure things out later: expectations, culture, religion, the media, social pressures."

"That's actually really comforting." Callie felt a sort of peace overwhelm her and tears began to fall. "I'm sorry. I don't know why I'm crying."

"Hey, I remember when I realized I liked women. All the girls in eighth grade were going on and on about Jason Priestley after we'd watched 90210 at a sleepover, and all I could think about was Shannon Doherty's red lipstick." Violet sighed. "I felt so alone and scared that everyone would hate me or judge me. So I get it. It's scary."

Callie had no idea how the people in her life were going to react. She was barely understanding how to react herself.

Violet took her hand. "It's okay to cry. It's an emotional time."

"Yeah, but on a date?"

"Hun, if I had a dollar for every time me or the woman I'd been seeing cried on a date, I'd be a rich woman."

Callie laughed and wiped her eyes with the back of her free hand. "Thanks." She leaned her head on Violet's shoulder.

Violet squeezed Callie's hand and wrapped her other arm around Callie's shoulder, settling her in closer.

Callie stiffened for a moment and then let go of all the expectations of what needed to happen and what was happening and what was going to happen, and she relaxed her body against Violet's. For the first time in a long time, she felt somebody actually gave a damn. And not only that, but she felt safe.

She let out another breath and melted into Violet's embrace.

* * *

VIOLET STOOD next to Callie in the middle of a wide, open field at the HOPE candlelight service, bright stars shining up above them. She didn't want to get ahead of herself, but she'd never allowed herself to be vulnerable tonight like she'd been with Callie. They shared raw, open stories of their lives, watched one episode each of Buffy the Vampire Slayer and Lost Girl, ate way too much pumpkin alfredo, and laughed more than she had all year.

How strange it was to meet someone new in the midst of the most chaotic year in recent history, when she'd almost given up hope again of finding anyone on this lonely planet. But here she was, beginning something new, jumping in headfirst, no holds barred, ready for whatever came next.

Pastor Rachel, bundled up in her parka, spoke loudly into the clear night. "Over two thousand years ago, a little baby was born, on a night...probably a bit warmer than tonight." The group laughed. "And we always talk about the gifts they brought him: gold, frankincense, myrrh. Sometimes there's a drummer boy, maybe some livestock."

Callie chuckled next to her, cheeks rosy in the candlelight.

"But there was a bigger gift that He brought. Hope. And hope is a wonderful thing. And right now, in this crazy world, in the middle of all this chaos and loneliness and sadness and loss and grieving for normalcy, we could all use a little hope. Hope that things will get better. Hope that people will learn to love more than they hate. Hope that we will be truly and fully loved, exactly as we are."

Violet felt peace wash over her. It was something she had struggled with for a long time, truly loving herself. And she was still a work in progress. It took having people look at her with unconditional love for her to be able to look at her own self that way. She'd melted the wall of ice around her heart that she'd built after Layla and Jen, and she'd allowed herself to heal, enough to let in someone who needed her words of comfort.

"I want you to look at the person next to you and say one thing you're grateful for this holiday season."

Violet reached over and found Callie's gloved hand and intertwined her fingers with Callie's, giving them a squeeze.

"Hope," she whispered in Callie's ear.

Callie smiled and turned to face her. With her other hand, she reached up to stroke Violet's cheek. "New beginnings."

Violet lowered her forehead to Callie's, and they melted into each other in the cold winter air.

ABOUT THE AUTHOR

Allison K. Garcia is a Licensed Professional Counselor, but she has wanted to be a writer ever since she could hold a pencil. She is a member of Shenandoah Valley Writers, Virginia Writers Club, the Author Transformation Alliance, and is a Municipal Liaison for Shenandoah Valley NaNoWriMo.

Allison began her journey as a published author in 2013 with short stories, flash fiction, and even a comic. During the years, Allison and her works have won several awards, including 1st place in the 2018 Royal Dragonfly Awards Ebook Cultural Fiction. Allison's stories have been featured in two boxed sets, and she has three published novels: Vivir el Dream, Finding Amor, and Finding Seguridad. Allison also has approximately ten more novels waiting in the wings.

Latina at heart, Allison has been featured in local newspapers, radio stations, universities, and national podcasts for her writing and for her connections in the Latino community in Harrisonburg, Virginia. A founding member of her agency's cultural competency committee and a participant in several pro-immigrant rallies and other events in her region, Allison also sings on the worship team at church and enjoys spending time with her girlfriend, Melissa, and her son, Miguel.

View her Amazon page at Bit.ly/allisonkgarciaauthor

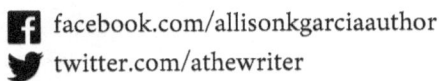

facebook.com/allisonkgarciaauthor
twitter.com/athewriter

PAUL DUPRÉ: A CAJUN COUNTRY CHRISTMAS

BY KAREN LOPEZ

PAUL DUPRÉ: A CAJUN COUNTRY CHRISTMAS

*I*t is the week of Christmas here at Green Valley. Green Valley always sounded more like a fancy grave place, rather than a home for men and women like me, those that seem to keep on living when most others have traded this life for a heavenly one. My wife journeyed over to the other side a good ten years ago. My second daughter followed her the next year. Sad. That was a sad, sad time.

Today, though, there are volunteers and visitors coming and going. They wish us happy holidays. A high school choir is singing over in the dining hall and one of the volunteers has taken hold of my wheelchair to push me through the hall toward it. That is when I pull my harmonica out of the pocket of my robe. Pressing it close to my lips, I play a few bars of the carol I can hear.

Surprised, the young man stops pushing me forward. He moves around so we can see each other and smiles as I play. Well, I can't play so long now. Not enough air in the lungs. One verse or a chorus is about all. When I stop, he asks me what is my favorite memory of Christmas? I point out the small alcove to the side of us that has a couple of chairs arranged around a low table. He easily steers my chair over and parks it next to one of them. Once we settle in, I answer his question.

When I was a boy most Christmas mornings were just as they were meant to be. It was difficult for us kids to sleep and before first light, my younger sister and I would scramble down the ladder from the attic into the large front room of the cabin. In this room, MaMa and Mamere prepared meals, weekly baths, and shooed the family cat off the long cypress table that commanded center stage. In the evenings, PaPa would light his pipe and take down his squeezebox from the shelf and play tunes until it was time to retire to our beds.

My name is Paul. Paul Dupre'. Growing up near Bayou Teche in a small community of Cajun folks, we celebrated most everything together. There were eight to ten families, more or less, depending on how many weddings and funerals happened in a year. Our lives were shaded by bald cypress trees springing up from the swamp and dripping with moss. We went to sleep with the music of frogs croaking and awoke to birdsong.

And for Christmas, we had the expectation of Pere Noel bringing our gifts through the winding bayous, small water trails, and shallow swamps. Seeing the bulge in our stockings hanging from the nail in those old cypress plank walls never failed to make our young eyes dance with joy. Or for muffled squeals to escape our mouth despite clapping a hand over it as quick as a wink. Of course, our weary MaMa and PaPa were forced to leave their warm bed and start the day. Missing out on seeing us pull our treats and toys from those hand-knitted sacks was unthinkable.

I know now we were poor. The poorest of poor if you count it up by paper money in a big bank somewhere. We were also rich. Rich in helping hands, loving hearts, and nature. Nature was our bank in those days. As long as a man could fish, trap, or hunt, there was no limit to the withdrawals his family could make. Counting all the stories told, music played, songs sung, and dances danced, our investments were solid and strong.

Now, no one ever saw Pere Noel. At least not until that Christmas eve of my seventh year. On that eve of Christmas, the sky was filled with dark, heavy clouds. At midday, it seemed quite dark outside, but PaPa insisted he had to make an errand over the bayou in his pirogue. He stood dressed in his hip boots which rose up his pant legs that were held up by suspenders riding over his shoulders. Atop his head was his wide-brimmed straw hat. It could shelter a man from the glaring southern sun or a light rain.

Our roads were the creeks, inlets, swamps, rivers, and bayous. You could navigate most any waters, excepting the gulf, if you had one of these flat, narrow, and pointy-ended boats. Swamps are boggy, so often PaPa would stand and pole by pushing the blunt-end paddle into the mud, moving him forward. Of course, Pere Noel made his visit to the girls and boys living in these watery habitats in his own pirogue. I do not know if he had a paddle like PaPa, but there were eight alligators that would pull him through the waters or walk his boat through the muddy marshes. Alligators move faster than most people think, with their strength and speed Pere Noel could get to everyone in one night.

Built on stilts, all the cabins stood off the ground. The way they perched up on long, lanky legs made you think of a lady holding her skirt up so as to not get it muddy as she walked along the small bayou's edge. Our home had three rooms and a sleeping porch that was used eight or nine months a year. The cypress floorboards were greyed by the weather but smooth from the years of boots and bare feet trampling over them. My PaPa stood there on the porch that Christmas eve squinting at the heavy sky with his arm around MaMa. She did not want him to go. Rains were sure to come in a torrent soon.

As he got his long paddle down from the porch rafter, he said, "My boat could make the trip to Chitamacha Bend without me. I'll be back in time to do the bonfires this evening. If the rains don't soak the wood too much. May have to let Paul and Colette put the hurricane lamp out here to guide Pere Noel to the house." He winked at his worried wife.

"Le Bon Dieu, there is no arguing with your stubborn self, so the saints and angels watch over you."

"Ma Cherie," he stooped to kiss her, "I'll be home in time for a big bowl of gumbo. You don't worry."

I watched from the window as he launched into the shallows and steered around the tree trunks that soon blocked him from my view.

MaMa called my sister, Colette, and me to finish up our chores. Overcast skies had not dampened our enthusiasm for decorating and preparing a tasty feast. With the dulled tin cookie cutters, we carefully carved out stars, trees, and bells from the flat dough Mamere rolled out on the well-floured tabletop. Sneaking a stray bit of the dough every chance I got, I could hardly wait for them to be baked. The whole room filled with competing smells to make a young boy's stomach growl in anticipation.

Just as we heard the first drops of rain fall onto the tin roof, I was seated next to my sister with a big bowl of popcorn. My job was to carefully push a needle into the heart of the open kernel while threading it into a long strand to wrap on the tree. Colette was too young to handle this job. Instead, MaMa was helping her color paper strips we would glue into a chain. The sound of rain beat like a big drum harder and harder. The room grew so dark, we had to light the kerosene lamps.

Even at seven years of age, I knew about fast-rising waters along the swamps. Water was our transportation. Water was where we found our meals. Water provided all manner of resources that made life possible. But fast-rising water was dangerous. It pushed against the banks. It beat against houses and gardens. The wildlife that lived within it were dislocated. Most dangerous of all it disrupted the current and sent pirogues down the wrong creek or out into the basin. If PaPa got caught in those bad currents, well a boy doesn't like to think on those things.

The storm raged. MaMa sang. I don't think our tree was ever so heavy with decorations another year. We couldn't get out and meet the neighbors to light the bonfires, the bonfires that lead Pere Noel in his pirogue to our houses during the night. Colette and I whispered our concerns to each other.

"MaMa," I asked, "how will Pere Noel find us with no fires to guide him? You can't even see the moon shining in the sky."

"Hmm, maybe we can leave a light for him on the porch. It is too early now, but before bed we can leave one of the lamps outside. What do you think?"

"But that is so small. The bonfire is big and bright," I answered unconvinced.

MaMa just smiled at me. And then, I saw her look up at the clock and she frowned. She got up from her rocker and opened the door. I followed her. Leaning to one side, I did my best to see what she was seeing. The winds blew the rain across our porch sideways. The heavy darkness of the storm obscured most everything from sight but our own porch.

MaMa began to pull the door closed again when a sudden streak of lightning blazed in the sky and illuminated the rolling dark waters outside. It was the first time I had ever seen the stillness of the green swamp water disturbed by anything more than a gentle ripple when PaPa pushed his pirogue into it. If the boat had been in its usual place, it would be afloat now. The muddy bog under the walkway was now a rushing stream. I saw it all in a flash. And then the thunder boomed so loudly that MaMa and I both jumped back, and she slammed the door on the storm.

While Colette and I argued over which end of the tree to start her paper chain, MaMa was bent over inside a cupboard. When she stood up, she had a hammer and a long piece of wire. I was curious about what she planned to use those for, then she handed them to me and picked up one of the lit gas lamps.

"Paul, come with me to the porch."

I followed her. It was less dark with the lamp in her hand but not much less. The wind was still howling at us. If MaMa had not been beside me, I tell you true, I would have run right back inside. I did not like it out there. No, not one bit, did I like it. Confused, I stood there obediently holding the hammer and wire.

"Take the wire and wind it on this nail here," Mama said as she held the light so I could see the nail. "Now, take the other end and wrap it on this one," she moved the light, so it illuminated another nail a few inches away.

Holding the light in one hand, she took the hammer and pounded the first nail in to make it tight around the wire. Once that one was secure, she wedged the brass end of the lamp between the wall and wire and told me to hold it from the bottom. Finally, she hammered on the second nail and wiggled on the lamp base to test it was steady.

"For Pere Noel," she whispered to me as she hustled us inside again.

We were both wet, but it was time to dress for bed. Colette was already in her nightdress. MaMa went to her bedroom. Mamere helped me out of my wet clothes, drying me good. Then I dressed myself for bed. It is funny the things a boy does not realize at the time. Now I know that light was for PaPa.

Colette and I said our goodnights to MaMere and climbed up to our beds. Just before I drifted off, MaMa came up and kissed us goodnight.

"Sweet dreams and bon noel."

That was the last thing I remembered before awakening. I thought it was morning, but it was still dark out. No light shone in from the one window in our makeshift attic sleeping quarters. On the roof, all I heard was a drizzle of rain. It was the creak of the floor from MaMa's rocking chair moving back and forth that woke me. That and the smell of dark coffee laced with chicory. She never said, but I believe my mother sat up all night watching and listening.

Pausing my story, I took a deep breath and then one more. Breathing, I've learned, is more important to life than even those waters I grew up on. Sometimes I think it's all this conditioned air I've been breathing the last 30 years that has made my lungs feeble.

"Mr. Paul? Are you feeling alright? Would you like something to drink?" my young companion asks.

I tell him that would be nice if he didn't mind. He flashes that bright young smile at me again and is back in two minutes. Carefully handing me a half-filled plastic cup of lemonade, he settles into his chair again. Thankfully he has the good sense to choose lemonade over that syrupy red punch. I drink half the contents before continuing the story.

Now, what was I telling ya? Oh, yes, Christmas morning.

Well, I sat there in my bed a little while wondering if it was too early to get up. I did not want to startle Pere Noel or prevent his visit.

At last, I decided if MaMa was up, it must be okay. So, I dressed quietly and went below.

"Merry Christmas, MaMa." Everything was so quiet, since the storm had stopped, so I kept my voice quiet too.

She quickly wiped her eyes with the corner of the apron she was wearing. "Merry Christmas, Paul," she smiled but her smile seemed sad.

I looked up at the wall and my sack stood limp and empty. Oh, no, was she crying because Pere Noel skipped us? No presents? Not even a handful of hard sugar candy? I didn't want her to feel bad even though I wanted to cry now too.

Standing in my bare feet on the handmade rag rug, I snuggled close to the arm of her chair. Big boys do not climb up into their mother's lap. And I was a big boy now.

Much to my surprise she put her arm around me and pulled me over, lifting me right up where I wished to be, all snuggled up like when I was a small boy. She held me close and hummed a tune. I don't remember now what it was, but I do remember feeling very special. Wrapped up in her sweet embrace, feeling the protection of her love on Christmas morning with no presents, I was comforted.

It seemed a long while we sat there together waiting for nothing in particular except the first streak of morning light through our east window. The first interruption was a morning bird call and then the creak of Mamere's door opening. Already dressed for the day she walked carefully to not wake anyone before noticing the coffee was made and keeping hot in the pan of water at the back of the old stove. Then she looked behind her and saw me curled up against MaMa's shoulder being rocked.

"Bon Dieu, is the child sick?" She was clutching an empty coffee cup in one hand and her rosary in the other.

"No, MaMere, we were just waiting together. Pere Noel has not come." There was a catch in my mother's voice, but she coughed to cover it up. "Time to get up, Paul." The words were spoken as I was deposited onto my own two legs again. "I'll let the lamp burn until full sunrise."

Mamere only nodded and turned to fill her cup. I knew something was very wrong, but my boy mind had not figured it out yet.

"Can I take PaPa his coffee? Is he sleeping late on Christmas?"

Minutes ticked by and neither woman answered me. I could carry a cup of coffee, so why were they both just looking at me as if I'd asked to wrestle a 'gator? I tell you it hurt my boy pride to think they saw me as inadequate to manage that small task.

Finally, my mother bent down and looked me in the eyes, "Paul, we must all say our prayers for PaPa to return to us safely. He is not home with us, yet."

"Oh," was all I could say. PaPa was not home. What did it mean? I kept looking at my mother waiting for my unspoken question to be answered. I forgot all about Pere Noel. All I wanted now was my own PaPa sitting down to breakfast with us.

We did the familiar. It is what people do while they wait and hope. MaMa cleaned and MaMere put on the corn grits and sausage gravy to cook. Colette came down the ladder all excited and then began to cry.

I put my arm around her. "Don't cry, little Colette. We love you. You are a good girl."

She rubbed at her eyes, but it took a minute for her tiny sobs to stop. The worst thing about no gift from Pere Noel is believing you are a naughty boy or girl. I went upstairs and brought down my sock monkey and gave it to her. It was one of my treasures and I had never let her hold it. Old as my eyes are today, I can still see the surprise on my little sister's face. We do not take notice of how growing up sneaks up on us in our childhood. That morning, my actions toward a younger sister were very big for a small boy.

Before we sat down to breakfast, I followed my mother out to the porch. She was untwisting the wire from the lamp we had put out the night before. The bog beneath our porch was a shallow pool. The end of our pier was covered with water that lapped up, making a stream beneath the boardwalk that led from porch to pier. A disoriented snowy egret stood on one leg on the submerged pier post looking around for breakfast.

A damp, chill wind pushed at my hair as I looked out. It was light out. A grey silver light that barely broke the cover of clouds. I stood looking as far as I could see into the swamp. If only my father's pirogue would come from behind one of those old cypress trees. If only. I felt a nudge on my shoulder. It was time to go inside.

As soon as the door was open, I smelled the gravy. Mmmhmm, just thinking of it makes my mouth water now. Four bowls were set around the table with steam rising from the hot grits inside them. Four bowls when there should have been five. I sat down next to my sister on the bench PaPa had made for us. One end of the table was empty, and I started to cry. I cannot tell you what it was I was thinking. It was more what I was feeling. It was a terrible fear. A fear of something gone and being lost forever.

Mamere started to ladle the gravy over one bowl of grits, but she sat that heavy iron skillet down again and turned around. I heard her sniffing like she had a cold and she kept wiping her face with her apron. Colette started to cry too. I think it was because I was crying. No one had told her anything about PaPa.

MaMa cleared her throat twice and tried to speak. It was no use, there was nothing doing but we all sat crying over our breakfast.

Sitting there with our hands in our laps and heads all bowed, I guess it looked like we were praying when the front door flew open and a big voice shouted, "Merry Christmas!"

I nearly fell off the bench I was so startled, but MaMa was half out of her chair yelling, "Mon Cheri! Mon Cheri!"

It was my PaPa! He was home. Somehow my mother recognized him, but it took me some time. He was covered in mud from his hair to his knees as he stood there in his sock feet grasping a damp burlap bag.

"What happened? Where have you been? Are you hurt? Le Bon Dieu, look at you?" That was my mother firing off questions as she hugged him despite his filthy clothes.

"I am not hurt. And I will tell all for a hot cup of coffee and a warm bath. Is that a bargain?" He spoke to her as he gave her hair a kiss, but he looked at the rest of us as he finished.

Mamere poured coffee into a cup and brought it over to him before herding us children into her room and closing the door. PaPa had asked for bath time which meant the rest of us needed to go away.

Sitting together on that patchwork quilt that covered her bed, MaMere told us the story of baby Jesus.

"A very long time ago, Joseph and Mary traveled to Bethlehem to pay their taxes. Lots of other people had to go to the same place. So, when they arrived, there was no place for them to stay. A kind man let Mary and Joseph stay in his barn. It was dry. There was clean hay they could sleep on, too. Because it was such a long trip, they didn't have time to go home again for Mary to have her baby. So, baby Jesus was born right there in that barn. The sheep and cows were the first to see him after his MaMa and PaPa. Outside, the world was so happy that the stars shone brighter than bright. It made some shepherds curious and as they were pointing at the sky, an angel appeared and talked to them. 'I bring you tidings of great joy. A king is born over there in that barn. Go see!"

"How did his MaMa Mary have any clothes or blankets for him?" Colette asked.

"Oh, I'm sure she had some extra wraps or clothing packed, cher. Now listen to what happened next. This is one of the reasons we give gifts to each other at Christmas time. There were also some very wise men who had big houses and lots of fancy things. They heard about the baby and brought him gifts. Gold. Frankincense. And myrrh."

"What? What is mur and the other stuff, Mamere?"

"You are full of questions little girl," Mamere smiled. "Gold is like money. The others are like herbs I think, but important in that time. The thing to remember is Jesus is a gift to all people from God. To honor baby Jesus, we give gifts. Mostly we love each other. Remember that most, my children. The best gift we ever get or give away is to love each other."

We both hugged Mamere and told her we loved her. I felt very happy. The story of baby Jesus made joy in my heart. Still, it seemed a long while before MaMa knocked on the door, signaling we could come out again. PaPa was all clean and Colette and I both ran over and hugged him. Hard.

Breakfast was eaten with everyone in their place. I know it wasn't as good heated again as it would have been before, but it was the best Christmas breakfast. We were together. All together.

At last, we settled around the table with the dishes cleared and PaPa told of his travels that Christmas eve.

"Well, now, I got over to Chitamacha Bend just fine and was paddling home again when the rain started to fall. Now, it didn't just fall a little. It didn't even fall a medium amount; this rain was like buckets pouring over your head. My good hat was no match for that much rain a falling."

"Oh PaPa, did your pirogue fill up?"

"No, Colette it didn't, but probably because it rocked so much in the current the water was sloshing out the sides. I paddled and paddled but seemed to get nowhere near home. All I could see was waters. I knew if I could just find the trees it would help me find home. I think I must have grown so tired from paddling; I fell asleep in my boat."

"You could have drowned!" My mother clasped her hand to her throat and tears gathered in her eyes.

"Now, now, I'm here. And I've got a tale to tell. Yes, I do."

"What is it, PaPa?" My curiosity was undeniable.

"I'm a tell you, Paul. I think I fell asleep. All I know is, I was in deep waters and it was dark as the iron skillet on that stove. No moon. No stars. Even if I had took up my paddle, there was no way to tell if I was going home or out to the Gulf of Mexico."

We all sat still with mouths agape. As a boy, I knew to respect the waters around us, but I had never felt afraid of them until that morning, listening to my father's story. Those rising waters could have taken him and his little boat out into the wide gulf. No man can paddle home from there.

"And that's when I heard 'em."

"What? PaPa, what'd you hear?"

"Them jingling bells. They was far away and soft at first. I kept listening and they got louder. Closer. I asked myself, could it be? Could it really be?" He looked at us, but no one tried to guess. Then he slapped his leg loudly and laughed, "And then I heard his 'gators a snapping!"

"PaPa!"

"Mais oui, I did! Coming right for me. And there was Pere Noel, himself, in his pirogue. I could see the faint light of his lantern a swinging from its post right behind me. His white beard reflected in the dim light. Sure enough, he had on those bright red suspenders and shiny black hip boots told in the stories. With eight alligators a towing him, he was upon me in short time. I hardly knew what to do but before I could say anything, I heard him call out 'PaPa Dupre, is that you?'"

"He knew you?" we all asked in unison.

PaPa slapped his knee and laughed again, "He did! Pere Noel, he know us all. He had no time to stop for long. Ya know. He's got a lot of houses to visit on the bayou. He tossed me a line and told me to hold tight. What do you know but I'm riding right behind ol' Pere Noel and his team, guiding me back to our own backwaters. Before we parted ways, he tossed me this sack. He laughed a jolly laugh and asked, 'You can bring those for me to your Paul and Colette, oui?'"

He stopped talking and reached over to pick up the rough brown sack laying on the floor next to him. Taking it up on his lap, he reached inside and pulled out a brown paper wrapping and then another and another.

"Well look at that," PaPa said when he pulled out his own gift, "this one is for me!"

There was a gift in that bag for everyone! Even for PaPa. A pair of bright red suspenders just like the ones Pere Noel wears himself. And that was how I knew it was true. It had to have been Pere Noel. No one else would have had a present for PaPa, too.

Well, that was the year I got this old harmonica you heard me playing a carol on before you asked me about my happiest Christmas. Since that Christmas, I have had the good blessings of nearly eighty more, and so many happy times. Gifts received and given, especially those years with my own children and then their children. But when I think about it, that was my happiest.

That Christmas when it rained so hard we could light no bonfires. It rained so hard Pere Noel skipped our house. It rained so hard no one went to ring the church bells for Christmas morning mass.

And that Christmas morning I sat in my mother's lap for the last time. I remember feeling like I was the most loved and special boy in the world as I sat there. Never guessing how frightened she was that her husband might never come home. And how happy we were when he did. They had many more happy years together and PaPa told his story again and again.

It has been longer than I can remember since I told PaPa's story. Today may be my last telling of it thanks to you asking. Ya know, if you visit me again, I may remember a few more old stories.

ABOUT THE AUTHOR

Karen Lopez resides in Louisiana. She loves to travel but the Bayou State has always been "home." She finds great contentment cooking in her kitchen and enjoys creating recipes.

Reading and writing are both lifelong passions. The author of *Shaw Point*, a historical fiction novel and a fantasy short story, "The Tide is Against You," she has also enjoyed blogging and writing articles and a few stories for local periodicals.

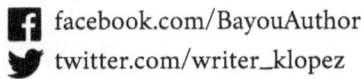

facebook.com/BayouAuthor
twitter.com/writer_klopez

CHRISTMAS DELIVERY

BY M.T. DECKER

CHRISTMAS DELIVERY

To say it had been a difficult year would have been an understatement, but if I'm being truthful, most years had been hard after Momma passed. After that, it was the old man and me against the world. Life wasn't all that bad and Dad always seemed to know when I needed a reminder that I wasn't alone.

During my first year in college, I was failing everything. I'd wake up in the middle of the night, my pulse racing like a kite on a frayed string as it slipped through my hands. That weekend, the old man showed up with an extra-large from Danny's and a 2-liter bottle of Cheerwine. We ended up talking the night away, nursing that pizza along until there was nothing but crumbs. He couldn't stay long. He had just been appointed Chief Deputy and his inbox was always full.

But he always managed to find his way to my dorm when things were getting tough. My first holiday back, that's when our tradition began. For Thanksgiving, we ordered a big spread from Gina at the diner and spent the night before Thanksgiving patrolling the interstate, doing our best to make sure everyone made it home.

I was a 'ride-along', a civilian watching my dad do his job. He said the people of Pruitt County had come to expect certain things, and holiday patrols were part of that expectation. After patrol, we'd roll into the diner and share our feast with anyone interested. On Christmas and New Year's Eves, we'd repeat the process, only we'd order ham or black bean soup for dinner

Every ride-along during winter break was time we spent together reminding us of how much we had. After graduation, I went to the academy and was hired by the sheriff's department. Sheriff Thomas had three years left to his term and the only time Dad and I were allowed to patrol as a team were the holiday patrols.

Each year the patrols got a little longer and the celebrations got a little larger. Gina was always there for us, giving us each a thermos of hot coffee as we began patrol. Time passed and Dad ran for Sheriff and won. His second term, he ran with me as his Chief Deputy. We officially met in the office once a week to go over what we needed and we'd meet unofficially every night for dinner. Once a month we'd go to Danny's Pizza for an extra-large pizza and all the Cheerwine we wanted.

Dad was grooming me to take over as Sheriff, but I wasn't ready. I definitely wasn't expecting him to be taken from me three months before the November election. I don't know if I was too young or if my heart wasn't in it, but Gina's brother Brett was elected.

Thanksgiving came and went, and I did the patrol alone. If Dad hadn't already placed the order, I would have gone home and crashed. That Thanksgiving we ended up celebrating my Dad's life. The dinner was the perfect send-off, but it made that empty seat next to me in the Durango that much harder to face on Christmas Eve.

I nearly lost it when Gina handed me two thermoses of coffee. She just kissed my cheek and told me I might need it. I accepted them with a slight salute, all the while praying I made it back to the car without losing it.

I miss my dad so much.

The patrol was quiet. There were a few calls that the State Troopers handled, a car ran out of gas with two men trying to get back home before the kids woke up, and truckers with their rigs decked out in colored lights, and 'I'll be home for Christmas' playing on the radio.

I tried singing along, but my voice cracked and there was a lot of dust in the car. I was about to head home and call it a night when I noticed someone walking along Denning Creek Way.

Denning Creek's in the middle of nowhere, and the only thing for miles was cold and wind. Sure, there were few houses along the way, but no businesses and definitely nothing that would have been open after 10 PM, especially on Christmas Eve.

I slowed down, noticing the duffel bag the man was carrying and the fact that he was wearing desert camos. He was a good ten miles from the interstate and I hadn't seen anyone driving down this road since about 20:00. I slowed and pulled in ahead of him waiting for him to make it to my door.

Rolling down the window I felt the cold chill in my lungs. I hadn't thought about how cold it had gotten, and he wasn't dressed for this weather. As he approached, I realized he was a Marine about my age, maybe a year or two younger. He didn't speed up or slow down, just kept moving at the same steady pace.

"Break down?" I asked as he set his duffel down and studied me.

"No, sir," he answered. "I was hoping to surprise my folks for the holiday. Just didn't think out the last twenty miles of the trip."

"So, you're local?" I asked.

"More or less. My folks are in Virginia. They have a cabin about three miles past the state line."

I nodded. "Climb in. I got a thermos of coffee to spare, and the heater is cranked up as high as she'll go."

He smiled and headed towards the passenger door. I waited for him to stow his gear and warm up as I offered him the second thermos Gina had given me earlier that night.

"Thanks. I was sure nobody was going to come along," he said as he rubbed his hands together and held them up to the vents to warm them. "You are a lifesaver."

I laughed. He'd been doing fine and would have made his folks place in a few hours, but he would not have been comfortable.

He sipped his coffee and smiled. "That is a damn sight better than the swill I've been drinking in Iraq," he commented.

"Tad far to travel on Christmas Eve," I replied.

He laughed and shook his head. "Nah, I left Baghdad two or three days ago. Went from there to Ramstein then I ended up at Dulles, my ride fell through, so I hitched from there, but my luck ran out when I got to the truck stop at the county line."

"Lucky you got this far," I commented, noting the tinge of blue in his fingers and lips.

"Yeah," he admitted. "I wasn't thinking about how cold it can get out here at night."

We sat in silence for a while until he sighed contentedly.

"This is the elixir of the gods," he said. "Been away long enough I forgot what real coffee tastes like."

I smiled. "Gina makes the best brew in the area, " I agreed. "By the way, I'm Che... "

I stopped and corrected myself. For the next 6 days, I was still Sheriff.

"I'm Sheriff Dustin Jamison," I said, offering him my hand.

"Sheriff," he said, obviously impressed. "Didn't think the folks in these parts would vote someone our age, Sheriff."

"They didn't," I admitted. "M'Daddy was Sheriff. He passed a few months ago. I was his Chief Deputy."

"Lance Corporal Terrence Tidings," the marine said offering me his hand.

I smiled as we shook hands and a slow winter's rain started up.

"Damn, I better get going," he said as he reached for the door.

"We better be going," I corrected as I radioed my status to dispatch. "Pruitt 101 to central, roadside assist on Denning Creek. I'll be heading to..."

I paused looking at Lance Corporal Tidings. "310 West Lafayette."

"310 West Lafayette..."

"Uh, Boss, there is no Lafayette west or otherwise in the county."

"Copy that. Got a Lance Corporal to deliver for Christmas."

"10-4. 101, should I start next in line?"

"Negative, Central. No vehicle involved."

The radio was silent for a minute and I could imagine Kathleen putting it all together. "County Council's not going to like it," she warned.

I laughed. It wasn't like they could fire me. "10-4," I answered and left it at that.

As we drove I had to ask, "What do you miss the most?"

The Lance Corporal smiled, a dreamy expression on his face. "Midnight mass. The whole extended family going to church, singing in the choir, and then coming home to a feast my Momma had worked on all day."

He'd missed midnight mass, but the feast was still an option. I handed him my phone.

He looked at it and then at me.

"Call your mom," I said, cause I knew if mine were alive, she'd be thinking of me out here alone.

"But she'll see me in a few minutes," he objected, and I could feel the excitement in his voice. The excitement you can only experience when you had given up on everything you wanted, only to have it granted.

"Call her," I urged again, because I knew I couldn't call mine.

He studied me for a minute and I saw the moment of recognition in his eyes as he teared up. Like I said, too much dust in that old SUV.

He dialed the number and put it on speakerphone.

On the third ring someone picked up and I heard a hesitant voice answering, "Hello?"

The smile on my passenger's face was brighter than the sun. "Momma?" he said. I could hear the joy in the woman's voice as we pulled into the driveway.

"Terry!? What number is this? Where are you calling from?"

I smiled at him and nodded as I turned on every light installed on the Durango.

"Look out the window..."

As I watched, the curtain near the front door moved. Three seconds later, the door flew open and the porch was teaming with people. Three generations of Tidingses and their extended family making more noise than I could have with an amplifier, and the joy was palpable.

I smiled and laughed as he waded through the assembled crowd to hug his momma, and then I found myself being pulled out of the SUV as well. I felt people patting my back, gently pushing me forward until I was at the front of the line, witnessing the Lance Corporal's reunion with his parents. And then his mother was hugging me as she cried. Her grip was strong, and her tears soft on my cheek.

"Thank you," she said. "Thank you for bringing my baby home."

It was an hour later when I clocked back on the radio. "101: back in county. Lance Corporal Terrance Tidings, home safe and sound."

"Copy, 101," Kathleen answered, then added, "well done."

I smiled. As I backed down the driveway, I swear I saw my dad sitting in the truck next to me, and he was smiling too. I'm pretty sure I delivered two sons home that night.

ABOUT THE AUTHOR

Software Developer, Musician, Composer, Lyricist, Journalist, Tech Writer, Sheriff's Reserve and Author are just a few titles M.T. Decker has held over the years. Growing up, her parents got her hooked on the works of authors such as Philip K. Dick, Harlan Ellison, Fredric Brown, J.R.R Tolkien and C.S. Lewis.

She loves developing software because you have to understand the businesses you are supporting and that means learning. Oddly, she's found that the same holds true for writing.

Prior to her foray into Flash Fiction, M.T. Decker never believed she could write a short story, but with inspiration from the authors she grew up reading, she learned that sometimes a short story can carry a greater impact than an epic saga.

Mary combines the talents of software design, critical thinking, and humor to bring her fiction works to life. Most recently, she has focused on expanding her title list to include editor and non-fiction author with her current project, "One Size Fits All, and other lies."

Mary believes that any situation you can laugh at is one that can't get the better of you, so she tries to make others laugh as well. Visit her at www.MTDecker.com.

facebook.com/DeckerMT
twitter.com/mishmhem
instagram.com/m.t.decker

THE CHRISTMAS GUEST

BY LINDSAY DETWILER

CHAPTER 1

The fire crackled and spit as she rocked in her chair, the subtle warmth a stark contrast to her bitingly bitter heart. It was Christmas Eve, a night when many filled holiday masses, family homes, and their hearts with the joy of the season. Once upon a time, she was one of them. She would slither into her shimmering red dress, gather with her parents at a family member's house. She would pass the gifts, laugh, and behold the wonder of the season.

There were the holidays, too, when she was his. She would walk into the room on his arm, the red lipstick he loved painted on her plump lips. They had enjoyed so many decades together, and her mind was filled with album after album of memories. The snapshots were vivid. The Christmas he'd bought her that scruffy dog from the pound. The lavish holiday party they'd thrown the year he got his promotion. The Christmas he'd bought her the vanity set that still sat in their bedroom upstairs. The year they'd had Molly, and the first year without her when she'd gotten married. Memory after memory floated through her as it did every year since he'd died five years ago.

Five years without him. Five years all alone, even in the middle of celebrations. Even that first year, when the family had rallied around her, she was empty inside. How could you feel the joy of the season in your heart when your true love was dead? She was bitterly cold, like the blizzard of '93. Every year since his death, she morosely found herself wishing that the perilous icicles hanging above the garage would pierce straight through her heart. She couldn't be that lucky, though.

This year was a new level of depression. Molly and Edward, her two kids, had each had two kids of their own who were grown. Long ago, the family holidays were magical and filled with joy. The laughter of small children filled their home, and they basked in the knowledge that their love story had built such a beautiful unit. As the years went on, though, times changed. People changed. They'd grown apart, the grandkids and great-grandkids too busy, too wrapped up in city life and traveling and all sorts of things. The holidays just weren't the same anymore. Charles, though, had helped her navigate the simpler, quieter holidays. She'd still felt that Christmas spirit in her heart as they sat by the hearth of their home, basking in the glow of the flames and their enduring love for each other, even when they had no true holiday celebration to attend.

But since he had died, that flame dulled. Christmas would never be the same again.

Her hands warming on her cup of tea, she stared into the fire and willed herself not to cry. It was fine. She was an old woman, safe and warm in her house. What more could she hope for at this point? She'd lived her life. She'd had her memories. Christmas didn't mean the same thing anymore to her, but nothing really did.

She would just have to numb herself to it all, like she was used to doing. She would sip her tea and go to bed. She would fall asleep thinking about her beloved Charles, patting the empty side of the bed as was her morose custom. She would drift off, wake up, and pretend it was just another December day. She would ignore the calendar. What did it matter, anyway? She never had anywhere to be these days.

She would answer the phone when Molly and Edward called on Christmas morning. She would listen to their excuses about how busy the kids were and how they just couldn't make it out. She would tell them it was fine. Because it was. After all, she didn't expect Cassie and Emily to return home from Paris to see an old bag like her. Mark was in the army, and Hank had a girlfriend in Colorado he was visiting. Everyone was scattered, she understood. And she certainly didn't expect Molly or Edward to travel back to see her with the weather being so bad where they lived. It would be fine, she would assure them. Because it would.

The neighbor had offered for her to come to their dinner, the sweet middle-aged mom with too high of a voice and too cheerful of a temperament. Margaret had turned her down. The only thing worse than being alone on Christmas was being alone in a stranger's house, the pitied old woman in the corner by the cheese table.

No, it was better this way. She would sit, lost in her memories, thinking about all those special years they'd had together. Still, as her mind drifted over it all, tears dampened her cheek. She could almost feel him next to her, laughing about her terrible eggnog. Holding out a specially wrapped present just for her. Sitting beside her at church, or just holding her hand by the fire as they talked about Christmases past.

It was never enough time. Never. Yet, she'd lived like so many do—thinking it would last forever. Thinking they were immortal, that death's icy fingers would never snatch them away.

When they had their eyes set on forever, though, death had stalked them and picked its first victim. Margaret was left thawing by an unmanned fireplace wallowing in pity, regret, and the knowledge that life would never have the same meaning again without Charles. She looked up at the ceiling, as if she could see straight to heaven, and shook her head.

Why did you leave me, Charles? Why?

And, as if the heavens had opened up and Charles was answering her, there was a clattering at the front door.

Her heart chilled as she wiped her eyes, wondering if that blue-eyed devil of a man had managed to deliver a miracle to her after all. It wouldn't surprise her. He'd always been a hopeless romantic. Feeling more alive than ever despite warning herself she was treading onto the unstable grounds of insanity, she rose from her chair. Her bones cried out slightly as she got to her feet. Ignoring the numbness tingling in her toes, she ambled to the door to see what sort of visitor had turned up after all.

But when she creaked open the door and the icy air bit into her flesh, she gasped at the sight before her and clutched at her chest. Life never lacks the element of surprise, after all.

CHAPTER 2

*T*he meow that the cat emitted was a soft whimper edging toward pathetic. The wind whipped around them, and Margaret pulled the collar of her shirt tightly closed to fight out the frosty air. The creature sat staring up at her, the porch light illuminating its white fur. It blended in with the coating of snow on the ground.

She shook her head. Poor thing, out on Christmas Eve, alone and cold. It was probably starving. She reached down gingerly to see if it would come near. It rubbed her hand immediately, its soft fur caressing her wrinkled hands. Her heart swelled.

"Come on, darling. Let's get you inside," she said, propping the door open a little wider. It needed no encouraging, for the cat scampered inside toward the warmth of the fire. Margaret smiled up at the sky, shaking her head.

The old coot knew she wasn't a cat person. He'd always wanted one, but in their fifty-three years of marriage, she'd never given in. She could picture him smiling that coy grin, shoulders shrugging in that way he'd done so many times over the years. In spite of herself, she laughed softly.

With the door locked, she immediately scurried inside to figure out what to do next. The cat shook itself off, headed straight toward the fireplace, and curled up beside it. Clearly, it was exhausted from its Christmas Eve adventure.

She didn't know how long it had been out. Was it someone's cat? She shook off the questions. First thing was first. She got down on the carpet beside the sweet creature. She stroked its head, examining it closely. It seemed to be in one piece. No obvious injuries.

"Okay, then. I guess we should find you something to eat," she responded. She stroked its fur once more, her heart swelling when the cat looked up into her eyes with its vivid glassy blues. It slowly blinked, as if in appreciation. Margaret smiled back at the cat as she stood, heading to the kitchen with a mission in mind.

It was late on Christmas Eve. All the stores in town would be closed. They would be closed tomorrow as well. What would she do? She didn't have any cat supplies, and there was no one to call.

She pulled open the fridge door. She would have to make do, she supposed. She scrounged around in the fridge, realizing for the first time the sad state of her meal preparations. Cooking for one just didn't seem worth the trouble. There were few things, in truth, that would be of interest to a feline, even one that was starving. She rustled in the freezer, then, wondering if there was some sort of meat she could thaw. Her eyes fell on the microwave dinner that would be her Christmas meal tomorrow. She sighed. That would be tomorrow's worry. She needed to get the cat some nourishment. Who knew how long since it had eaten?

She popped the unappetizing dinner into the microwave, watching it on the turntable. She felt something rub her leg and jumped. She was so used to being alone, she'd almost forgotten. She looked down to see the white cat rubbing her and purring. She smiled again.

After the five minutes passed by, Margaret put the meat on a plate —her wedding China. She didn't think Charles would mind. She placed it on the floor and watched the cat wolf down the meat. She pet it some more, sitting at the kitchen table while it finished its Christmas Eve meal.

The evening passed with Margaret finding blankets, making an impromptu litter box configuration out of an old container and some shredded newspaper. She talked to the cat, made sure it was comfortable. She made a list of all the items she would need to get as soon as she could get to the store. She considered a list of names for the unexpected guest who had shown up on a night that was no longer so bleak.

And just like that, Margaret realized she became a cat person quickly. It didn't take long. Within a few hours, she was attached to the creature who had seemingly picked her out of all the houses. She was obsessed, imagining afternoons they would spend together on the sofa watching soap operas. Picturing spring afternoons on the front porch. Why hadn't she thought of this earlier? A cat was just what she needed, a companion to pass the hours with. As she carried the newfound friend up to her bed, ignoring the potential that the creature had vermin, she tucked the sweet feline onto Charles' side of the bed. She smiled as it rubbed her face, purring as it curled beside her.

She drifted off to sleep thinking about how for the first time in a long time, she wasn't falling asleep completely alone. And for the first time in a long time, she wasn't dreading the next day or thinking of how to pass it quickly. She was thinking that she had a reason to get out of bed, a reason to get up, and some excitement in her life.

She didn't know how, but Charles had managed to send her the perfect Christmas gift after all. She fell asleep thinking of him, as she always did, but with contentment instead of emptiness.

But the next morning, she would remember why she'd given up on Christmas altogether, and why she was perhaps right to do just that.

CHAPTER 3

The knocking startled her awake, and it took her longer than normal to get her wits about her. She'd been up later than usual, she realized, as everything settled in her mind and the fog lifted. She glanced over to see the cat stretching languidly in Charles' spot. The knocking persisted, and she forced herself out of the warm refuge of the blankets. She tossed on a robe and moved as quickly as she could down the stairs. Meowing, the cat followed her.

The knocking continued, and fear settled in. Who could be knocking so violently on Christmas morning and why? Her heart fluttered as she feared the worst. An accident with one of the kids or grandkids. Some kind of disaster. She steadied herself for what was to come, braced herself for the Christmas morning sorrow that was certainly ready to be dropped on her. Inhaling, she opened the door cautiously.

But where she expected to see police or a familiar, tear-stained face, she saw instead an elderly man with blue eyes staring at her. He wore a winter hat and a scarf wrapped tightly around his neck. Snowflakes were gently falling in the morning sunshine. Bags under his eyes told her he was disheveled and distressed, but that was all she knew.

"Hello?" she offered weakly, her voice cracking from the lack of use.

"I'm so sorry to bother you, Miss," he murmured. He leaned on his cane, and she studied him, wondering why he was hobbling about the town's snow-covered sidewalks on Christmas morning. "I'm Fred Albertson from 207 Walnut Street, a few blocks over. It's just, well, have you seen this cat?" he asked, holding up a photograph of a gorgeous, pristine white cat cuddled up on a red blanket.

Her heart dropped and tears threatened to well. Margaret scolded herself for being so ridiculous. Still, sadness gutted her. She'd thought the cat was some omnipresent sign from the other side, some gift to get her through Christmas. She'd thought the universe had conspired to bring her a sense of joy, to assuage her loneliness. And now, on Christmas morning, sadness crawled back into the familiar spot. Loneliness drowned her. The cat had never been hers, after all.

She considered for a mischievous moment saying no. She considered shutting the door and pretending she hadn't found his cat. She thought that maybe she could convince herself she needed the cat, deserved the cat, more than him. The careless man had, after all, lost her. Finders keepers.

But the sorrow in his eyes met the sadness in her heart. She recognized that look of loss, of isolation, of bereavement. And perhaps it was that familiarity, that comradery in sadness, that softened her heart. Perhaps the cat hadn't been her Christmas miracle—perhaps it was the chance to give someone else a true gift that was her saving Christmas grace.

She swung the door open wider and invited the man in from the frigid temperatures, just as she had his cat the night before. The lone wanderer hobbled in on his cane, another refugee in the warmth of her home. She was prepared to explain, gathering her words as she led him into her house. She didn't need to bother, though.

For as soon as he stepped in, the cat left out a meow.

"Susie, oh sweetheart, thank God!" he proclaimed, and she saw the man cross her floor in what was probably record time. She saw the cat light up, and its excited meows resonated through the house. Her house was filled with a joy it hadn't seen in years. She stood back, a bystander in her own home as she witnessed the reunion. Her heart still sank as she realized her Christmas wouldn't be anything truly special once more. But witnessing their joy, she at least felt something. She felt alive. She remembered what it was like to have someone whose happiness mattered to you. She felt something. Period, end of story, there was victory in that simple point.

When the reunion had ended and Fred thanked her again and again and again, explaining the tale of the open door last night and the missing cat, she simply nodded in approval.

"I'm sure you have Christmas guests coming or places to be. We won't keep you," he offered.

She should have just nodded in agreement and let them leave. She should have just wished them happy holidays and returned to her dull morning of pretending it wasn't the 25th. But something had sparked in her. Maybe it was seeing the kindness in his heart. Perhaps it was the loyalty he showed for the sweet cat he called his own. Or, in hindsight, maybe after five years, it felt good to be in the presence of a man again.

Whatever it was, Margaret smiled back and replied, "I'm in no hurry. Can I make you a cup of tea? I'm sure you must be cold after knocking on all those doors."

He grinned back, his blue eyes sparkling under the brim of his hat. "I'd love that," he replied.

And so Margaret led him further inside, took his coat, and had tea with the stranger from a few streets over who very quickly didn't feel like a stranger anymore. They talked and drank. She passed him a pre-packaged muffin and he mentioned he liked the same kind. For an hour, she pretended that life wasn't so lonely and that her Christmas wasn't so sad. For a while, she forgot that it was Christmas at all. She basked in the company of him, of his dark, warm voice. He told her about Susie, about his deceased wife who had passed ten years before. He told her about his job in the mines he had when he was younger and his recent bowling score. He talked and talked. Mostly she listened. But she didn't mind.

After some time, though, it was clear that the cat was restless. "I didn't have any cat food. I did the best I could with a microwave dinner," Margaret confessed.

"Well, I'm sure she could use some food then. We've taken up so much of your time already. I can't thank you enough for taking her in, though. Who knows what could have happened," he said, standing from his chair.

Margaret's heart sank once more as he put on his coat and prepared to go home.

"You mentioned you and your late husband have kids," Fred said as he scooped up Susie. "Are they on their way?"

She smiled, her cheeks glowing. She'd told him too much. She hadn't wanted him to ask this, hadn't wanted a pity party. It had just come up in conversation. "No, they're quite busy this year. It's just me. But it's no big deal. Just another day, you know?"

She didn't ask about his plans. Didn't want him to think she was hoping for an invitation. She wasn't, of course. She'd had more than she could've hoped for, a nice morning tea with a kind soul. And a cat to keep her company the night before. Who knew, maybe she would just make her way to the pound the next day and find a cat of her own. No need to steal a neighbor's cat to find companionship. See, it is all fine, she told herself half-heartedly.

"Well, Merry Christmas, Margaret. We can't thank you enough, truly. It's a Christmas miracle," he said, his kind eyes sparkling as he looked at her once more.

"Merry Christmas," she offered weakly as she waved to him from the door. But it didn't feel like a Christmas miracle as she watched him hobble off with the cat in his arms. It felt like another goodbye, another reminder that the house was empty, that the only voice that ever filled it was her own.

She ambled back to her rocking chair, lost in memories and forgotten moments and the sorrow that Christmas had come to represent.

CHAPTER 4

*T*he afternoon passed in an unmarked, solemn fashion. Margaret busied her hands to distract her mind from the emptiness of the house. The short period of joy at finding the cat, at the tea with Fred, had underscored the dark, dismal silence of her life once they were gone. She'd told herself she could make it through another holiday season alone. Now, she wasn't so sure.

She dusted the ledges of the living room, ransacked the pantry for ingredients to make a sad excuse for cookies. She fiddled with her linen closet and organized the towels. She did plenty of pointless, cheerless tasks.

None of it worked.

Her mind was filled to the brim with images of presents and gold, glitzy bows. Of glazed honey hams and the laughter of children. Of twinkling lights and gingerbread in the oven. All of the things she would never have again.

She was settling in on the sofa, the fire failing to warm her deadened spirit. Even the Grinch from that story had a dog, after all. Margaret had, decidedly, no one. Nothing.

A honk sounded out front and interrupted her sad montage of

memories. Probably the neighbor's guests announcing their giddy arrival.

Another honk. Then another. Over and over the honking continued, until finally she arose from her chair like the proverbial Santa Claus to see what was, in fact, the matter.

Glancing out the window, her gaze landed on the dented, derelict station wagon sitting in her driveway. She squinted through the haze of the dirty window to see him waving at her.

Fred.

If he had lost that darn cat again, there was no hope for him. She was not, certainly not, getting involved. But he honked again, and she finally gave in. She pulled her shawl around her shoulders a little tighter, tucked her feet into slippers near her door, and carefully made her way out on the porch.

He rolled down his window.

"Hey, get your things and get in. Susie and I have a surprise for you."

"What are you talking about? I'm in no state to go out anywhere," she replied, imagining the wisps of her frizzy hair billowing even now. She self-consciously reached up to smooth them.

"You look wonderful. Besides, we aren't going far. I'm sorry for the honking. I know it wasn't the gentleman thing to do, but I didn't want to leave Susie alone out here. She's been known to get into mischief on her own."

Margaret stepped close to the car. Sure enough, the white cat was sitting in the passenger seat, meowing away at its adventure.

"Do you take her with you often?"

"Everywhere I go," he said, shrugging. "Now come on, lovely. It's cold, I'm hungry, and we've got a Christmas celebration to get to."

She opened her mouth to protest, excuses at the ready. She wasn't up for celebrating. She didn't like strangers. Her hair was a mess and needed to be washed. But before she could ruin it, she closed her mouth. Prompted by the sparkle in his eyes and the smile on his weathered face, she said the only thing she could.

"Be right back." And with a newfound sense of cheer, she went inside to find her perfect shade of red lipstick, a better sweater, and her bag.

It had been, after all, a long time since she'd celebrated, and she couldn't bear to miss it. Even if it did involve a man of somewhat questionable sanity and a cat riding shotgun.

CHAPTER 5

Wy hen he ushered her inside as he carried Susie in his arms, her eyes could hardly believe what they were seeing. His living room was a holiday spectacle. A beautiful white artificial tree sat in front of the window, lights and ornaments dancing on its branches. Soft holiday music played, and she recognized the singer as her favorite, Bing Crosby. It was simple but stunning when compared to her utilitarian house.

"Your tree is beautiful. You really go all out for the holidays then?" she asked with a smile as he put Susie down and reached for her coat.

"In truth, not usually," he admitted with a shrug. "It's just, well, after talking with you this morning and getting the sense you weren't really celebrating either, I thought maybe we could change that."

She paused, perusing his face. "So you did all this…"

"Today." He carefully hung her coat in the corner closet. She didn't move an inch, afraid if she dared to breathe, it would all evaporate.

The cat meowed as Margaret finally gained the courage to take a step toward the tree, her fingers carefully feeling the branches as her eyes danced over the lights. It was a simple tree at closer inspection. It offered the decorating skills of the typical man who had lived with a woman for years and wasn't used to taking charge of things like decorating. It lacked finesse and careful planning.

But it was the most gorgeous tree she'd seen in her eighty-two years of life.

"It's beautiful," she whispered, and she felt him come up behind her.

"I'm glad you like it. Susie and I just wanted to say thank you. Honestly, that cat is my whole world these days. And if you hadn't found her. . ."

Margaret turned to face him. Her heart leaped at the fact he was so close, she could feel his breath on her face. She reached out and patted his arm.

"I'm glad it all worked out. You really didn't have to go through all of this trouble for me, though. It's the nicest thing anyone has ever done."

"Well, there's more. I'm starving. Could you eat?" he asked.

"Always," she admitted, her stomach rumbling at the mere mention of food.

"I hope you like Chinese," he said as he offered her his arm and led her into his cozy kitchen. "It was the only restaurant open in town today, and I'm not much of a cook, in truth."

"I love it," she said. She inhaled the scents of a buffet of food. Fried rice, egg rolls, all sorts of meats covered paper plates in the center of his table. There were plastic utensils and paper napkins, but she wouldn't envy the Queen's Christmas dinner.

He pulled out her chair and she settled in. There was no shyness as they dug in, tossing Susie a bite or two here and there. They chatted about the weather at first, simple niceties to get warmed up. Quickly, though, they found themselves at ease in their conversation, as if they'd spent a lifetime across from each other at that dinner table. They talked about their mutual love for the theatre and how they hadn't gone forever. They talked about wishing they could be on a beach again, feeling the wind in their hair. They laughed about the thought of their wrinkled skin in swimsuits, prompting Margaret to spit out her fried rice and Fred to laugh until he cried.

"This is wonderful," he said as he refilled her glass of mulled wine. She'd never had the drink, but it was becoming her favorite.

"It is. Thank you."

"I must admit," he began after taking a sip. He looked at her, but his eyes were far away. "I haven't been one for celebrating these past ten years or so. Ever since Evelyn died, I don't know. It hasn't been the same. I've been empty. And we have a daughter, but she's so busy with her own life and kids and so far away. I hate to impose on her. So usually, it's just me and Susie and some Chinese food on Christmas."

She nodded, feeling the pain filling the air between them. "It doesn't get easy, does it? It's been five years since Charles died, and it never seems to get easier."

There was a pregnant pause between them as they both got lost in their memories.

But then, he pulled them back with a slap of his palm on the table.

"Maybe, Margaret, this is our year. What do you think? Let's stop feeling sorry for ourselves and living in the past. Maybe Susie knew what she was doing when she showed up at your door."

Margaret smiled, the mulled wine warming her body. His words warmed her spirit, though.

"I think she did. Maybe that unexpected guest was just what I needed, what we needed," she ventured. Her heart fluttered at the admission, but she felt soothed as she looked into his welcoming eyes.

"So let's make a toast. To this next year, and to next Christmas. May we find our friendship blossoming by next year at this time. May we find happiness in the year that comes. May we go on new adventures and make new memories so that next Christmas, we aren't just sitting around like two bags of bones feeling sad. Let's make this next year a year to remember."

"I'll drink to that," Margaret replied, smiling at the excitement of the possibility she could see in not just the next year, but in the man who made her come alive again. Who made her want to feel again. Whose sparkling blue eyes lit something in her she thought had burned to ash.

"Merry Christmas," she said, and for the first time in a long, long time, she meant it.

CHAPTER 6

ONE YEAR LATER

*T*he fire crackled and spit as she rocked in her chair, the subtle warmth from its glow matching the warm cat filling her lap. She rocked slowly back and forth, using the time alone to think about it all.

She thought about Charles, naturally, as she always did on Christmas Eve. She let her mind dance languidly over the moments and memories that had defined them as a couple. She glanced over to the Christmas tree in the corner of the room, the star on the top the one she'd found in the attic. The star he'd bought their first married Christmas. Fred had smiled and understood. After all, the skirt under the tree had been his wife's favorite.

That's how they were together. Love in your eighties, after all, was markedly different than the passion of the younger days. Gone was the conviction of a one and only. They both had loved before. They had both lost before. Both of their hearts still belonged, in part, to someone else. Still, in the loneliness of loss, they'd found a connection between them. And it was more than just a longing for someone to share their empty days with. In Fred's eyes, she saw the desire to feel again, to love again, to live again. She'd thought it had died with Charles.

He came back into the room now, two mugs of mulled wine filling the room with a hearty scent.

"My dear," he said, sitting down in the rocking chair beside her that he'd bought over the summer. She took the cup from him and Susie stirred but didn't get down.

"I swear she likes you more," he said, grinning. It was a running joke between them that ever since he'd moved in, the cat had abandoned his lap for hers.

"She knows who the better cook is," she teased back. Because in the past few months, she'd tried her hand at cooking again. She found that she really did like it when there was someone to enjoy it.

She'd, in truth, learned a lot about herself since Fred had come into her life one year ago. She'd learned that she wasn't ready to hole up in her house and spend her days among dusty relics of the past. She'd realized that she didn't have to sit around and wait for her children or grandchildren to want to visit. She'd found, most of all, that life with Fred was still filled with excitement.

From trips to the theatre to a trip to the beach over the summer, she'd found a new excitement for life with him. He'd wakened her up and made her realize that every day was a gift and that the best thing she could do was to continue to fill her memory book with new experiences. She wasn't ready to give up just yet.

"It's hard to believe that a year ago, Susie was just wandering into your house and bringing me with her," he said smiling as he looked into the fireplace. She turned to him.

"It really was a Christmas miracle, wasn't it? You finding her. You finding me."

He reached over and touched her hand, squeezing it. "It really was. Before that night, I just thought I'd live my days out alone. I thought the magic of Christmas was dead for me, buried in a bag of wontons and fried rice. But you made me remember, Margaret, how beautiful it all can be. I love you."

She was just ready to reply that she loved him, too, as she had so many times this past year. Because she did. The heart can bend and stretch to accommodate more than one love, she realized. There was no need for guilt. The heart could love again.

But before she could get out the words, there was a knock at the door. She looked at him, wondering if he was expecting someone. His grandchildren were married with families of their own all across the country. They weren't coming in. And her kids and grandkids were, yet again, too busy with their own plans. They were planning on a quiet night of Chinese food and Christmas movies, which was just what she wanted.

"Who could it be?" she asked, but he didn't look alarmed. He didn't even move. He kept rocking, staring into the fire as he sipped his drink.

"Go see," he said, and she eyed him with suspicion. Clearly, he was up to something.

She sauntered to the door, nervous excitement fluttering in her chest. She peeled the door open so slowly, peeking to see who would be there.

But she saw no one. She opened the door wider.

And then, looking down on the porch, the light illuminated two bright blue eyes. The cat sat in a wicker basket. Its red collar popped against its white fur. It left out a soft mewl. It seemed too young to even meow. A large red and green bow graced the top of the basket. Her heart spilled over with joy.

She picked up the basket and went inside, careful not to drop the bundle of sweet joy.

"Fred? What did you do?" she asked, but she couldn't keep the happiness from her voice.

He crossed the room, Susie beside him.

"Well, I heard a little rumor that last year, you tried to steal a poor guy's cat in the neighborhood. I thought I better get you a cat of your very own this year so you don't go stealing another one. After all, I don't need some other widower stealing your heart," he teased.

She reached down to scoop up the fluffy white cat, Susie meowing at the ball of fur in her arms. Her heart swelled as she crossed the room to plant a kiss on Fred's cheek.

"I love her," she said. "But I don't think you have to worry about me going to find another cat or widower. I think the two of you—

well, three, now—will do just fine," she teased. He wrapped an arm around her. "But I do love her. Oh, she's precious," she said. "And you're not half bad either."

They stood for a moment, the four of them taking in the beauty of the night and the fact that none of them were alone.

"Shall we start the movie?" he asked, and she nodded, putting the kitten down to get acquainted with its new home.

He went to the kitchen to make the extra butter popcorn, and she settled on the sofa. All around, holiday decorations covered every inch of the house. They'd spent the season making cookies and decorating. They'd bought gifts for the nursing home and the hospital, delivering beautifully wrapped presents last week. They'd spent the season together, finding ways to celebrate the small joys. The house was full and warm and Christmasy like it hadn't been for so long.

As she waited for him to return, a tear came to Margaret's eye.

She'd learned the hard way that nothing was forever. All of this beauty and fullness in her heart could be snatched away without a moment's notice. She knew that some year, she could find her house empty again and the second rocking chair reminding her that he was gone. She could find herself alone on Christmas, staring into the fire with a wistful heart and nostalgia plaguing her.

Still, she wiped away the tear. It wasn't this year. This year, the season was full of a joy she'd thought was gone. And even if in the future, she found herself alone, she knew it would be different.

Fred had reminded her that the season wasn't about feeling sorry for yourself. It was about finding ways to make your own joy. It was about finding ways to celebrate and to spread happiness and to give.

Most of all, he'd shown her that Christmas and life in general were about living in the moment and basking in the feeling of connection if you were lucky to find it with someone.

When he came back, the two cats trailing him, he settled in beside her.

She cuddled into him, knowing Christmas would never be the same again. For with that unexpected Christmas guest last year, Margaret had remembered that the real beauty of the season was that you never knew when the magic of Christmas would reveal itself. And she remembered that there was, even in the darkest moments, still Christmas magic to be found.

ABOUT THE AUTHOR

Lindsay Detwiler is a sweet romance author from Hollidaysburg, Pennsylvania, and a high school English teacher. She is also a USA Today Bestselling thriller and horror author under the name L.A. Detwiler. Her debut thriller, The Widow Next Door, is a USA Today Bestseller, and her novel The Diary of a Serial Killer's Daughter won the Readers' Favorite Bronze Medal.

Lindsay is married to her junior high sweetheart, Chad. They live in their hometown with their six rescued cats and their mastiff named Henry.

You can visit her website at www.LindsayDetwiler.com.

LAST WISHES IN COWBOY COUNTRY

BY R. K. FULTZ

CHAPTER 1

*J*couldn't believe she was really gone. My mother, Helen, died due to complications from dementia only two weeks earlier. She had fought like a warrior for the past three years. We would go out on weekend adventures, shopping and taking walks in the park before it got too bad. Dementia took its toll on her, stealing treasured memories. In the end, Mom didn't even recognize her own family.

Although I had siblings, everyone was scattered across the country. I was the only one that still lived in town near Mom. Although it had been two weeks, I hadn't had a whole lot of time to mourn. Mom had requested to be cremated and didn't want a service, so I had focused on planning and following through on her wishes.

I ran over everything in my mind while on the way to my mother's attorney for the reading of her will. My brothers and sisters would be attending virtually for this meeting. They all lived such busy lives and had children, so I seemed like the logical choice to take care of Mom. Divorced with my only child off at college, I didn't argue with any of them about the responsibility. She was my mom, and I would do it over a thousand times if I could.

I finally found the attorney's office in downtown Harrisonburg,

Virginia, and parked my car. Pulling down the visor, I took one more look at myself in the mirror.

"Keep it together, Riley," I muttered, staring into my tired eyes. The meeting was necessary, but it sure felt final. It would be Mom's last words in her life, the directions for her ashes and estate.

I took a deep breath and opened my car door. The bitter wind reminded me that Christmas was just around the corner. It was one month away. Of course, I didn't have any holiday cheer. It was hard to, with Mom gone.

I made my way to the front door and walked inside. It was a small office, and the receptionist was situated front and center.

"Good morning, may I help you?" she asked. The woman was prim and proper. She didn't have a single silver hair out of place in her shoulder-length locks. Her glasses were perched perfectly on her nose as she looked up over her computer.

"I have an appointment with Mr. William Carter," I responded. She nodded with an indication that she knew why I was there.

"He will be with you in a few minutes. Please have a seat," she offered.

I turned and walked over to a leather sofa against the wall. The reception area was quaint, and the walls were decorated with several photographs of local spots. I zoned in right away to a picture of a covered bridge surrounded by fall foliage. It was a place about thirty minutes north of here. I would take my mom and my son out there to visit and walk around. It had always been a peaceful place.

"Ms. James, you can follow me to the conference room." When I looked up, the lady from behind the desk was standing in front of me.

"Okay, great," I replied. She led me to a room filled with packed bookshelves at the end of the hall. As we approached, I saw a long wooden table with chunky legs and lots of chairs around it. The receptionist stopped at the doorway and swept her hand out to direct me inside.

"Please have a seat at the table. Mr. Carter will be over in a couple of minutes," she explained.

I stepped inside the room and made my way to the first chair at the table. My coat felt like it weighed twenty pounds. I unbuttoned and slipped it off my arms, then laid it on a chair nearby. My nerves took hold and made me fiddle with my hair as I pulled the chair out and sat down.

What has mom laid out? I wondered, my pulse quickening as I heard footsteps coming down the hall. A tall, older man walked through the doorway. He was dressed in a gray suit with a blue tie and looked every bit the stereotypical attorney. He smiled and sat down before extending his hand.

"Ms. James, it's a pleasure to meet you. I hate that it is under these circumstances," he said. I nodded in agreement as I shook his hand briefly. "I have your siblings on a conference call. I will pull it up on this computer, and we can begin," he offered as he sat near me. He set his laptop out on the conference table and hooked it up to some type of projector. After tapping some keys, four separate pictures appeared on the screen at the other end of the table.

My two brothers and two sisters filled the boxes, reminding me of the intro to an old show I watched as a kid, the one about the blended family and their housekeeper. The name was eluding me, but it still brought a smile to my face. Mom would laugh at us when we watched that show.

She used to say, "I would look as fancy as the mother on that show if I had a housekeeper and cook too." It still made me chuckle, but I didn't let it creep out as I watched my siblings on the screen.

"Good morning, everyone. I was hired by your mother to prepare and present her last will. Helen worked with me over a year ago to plan out her wishes," he explained. It blew my mind to think that Mom did all of this in secret. It left me shocked to realize that I had no idea what I would learn in the next few minutes.

"Since we are all present, I will start by saying that your mother lived a frugal life. Helen had several accounts that she left untouched before her death." I looked up at the conference screen toward my brothers and sisters. They were blood, but sometimes I felt very disconnected from their lives. I had three older siblings: Darcy, Justin, and Josh. Darcy lived in California with her husband, Patrick, moving over ten years ago after they met. She had one son, and he traveled the world making documentaries.

Justin and his family had lived in Tennessee since his early retirement. Josh moved his family to Montana. He always was fascinated by the mountains out west. The last person on the screen was my younger sister, Carly. She was starting over with a new husband down in Florida. Carly always enjoyed the beach, and since finding Fred, they made the move two years ago. She was also a new mother with a baby girl. They had a blended family with her older son and Fred's teenage boy.

I had been divorced for three years, and my son Ryan was off at college. Sometimes my siblings would check in and offer support, emotionally or financially. We had been able to keep Mom at her home, and I stayed at her place more than my own. In the last three months, I had to hire a specialized dementia nurse for Mom, who required round the clock supervision.

Mr. Carter explained that Mom had divided up her assets and money evenly among all five of her children. This wasn't a surprise, as we had all discussed that we believed she would do it this way.

"Helen made one special request for an account after her passing. This account currently has a balance of fifty thousand dollars." He stopped to show all of us the account information by presenting it on the screen. I can't think straight as I view it.

What kind of plan is this?

"Helen is asking for Riley to use the money to travel out west to spread her ashes. She would like to have her final resting place be in cowboy country. Visiting there was a bucket list wish that she never fulfilled. Your mother was an avid romance reader and loved stories about cowboys." He smiled. "She has outlined in specific detail how the trip and the spreading of her ashes will go."

I could see all my siblings were taken back by this final request.

"Do any of you have an objection to this final request of your mother's?" he asked. I waited to hear what they thought. My oldest brother, Justin, was the first to speak.

"I like the idea and feel good with mom's choice to carry out her wishes," he shared. That helped ease the pounding in my heart. The last thing I wanted was for everyone to be mad at me.

"I agree with Justin. Riley is the right choice to carry this out," Darcy chimed in.

Tears welled up in my eyes. The next thing I heard was Josh and Carly agreeing with everything. I was stunned that I received this mission.

"Okay, great. Since everyone has agreed to Riley handling this directive, I will provide her with the details. Riley, are you up for this task?" He turned to me.

I wiped away a few tears that had slipped down my cheek. "Yes, I am up for the task," I replied. It seemed that any more words were unnecessary.

"Great, if you can stay right there, I will give you all the information. Thank you for your time and for honoring Helen's final testament. She instructed me to mail four letters from her directly after this meeting. You will receive them in the next twenty-four hours by expedited delivery," he tells everyone. I was going to ask about my letter, but he didn't give me the chance. "Riley, I have your letter along with the trip details."

I nodded and waited for the meeting to finish.

"Bless you all, and I am sorry for your loss. Please contact me if you think of any questions. Thank you for your time," he finished before everyone said goodbye and clicked off the meeting.

Mr. Carter turned to me and held up a large manilla envelope. "Riley, inside are all the details for the trip. Helen has one last big request from you. She wanted her ashes spread in Yellowstone on Christmas Day." He slid the envelope across the table. "Do you have any problems making this happen? I know we are only three weeks away from Christmas."

I shook my head. I honestly didn't know how I would swing all of it, but I wouldn't let Mom down.

"I enjoyed getting to know your mother, and she was very particular on this last wish. It meant so much to her for you to do this, and I wish you peace and joy along the way," he said.

I thanked him and gathered my things. I needed air. My walk out of the room and down the hall was silent, my mind racing as I wondered what she had for me in the envelope.

CHAPTER 2

$\mathcal{I}$t had been two days since the meeting at the lawyer's office. Mom's direction for this trip was meticulous, and it had taken me forty-eight hours to organize my personal life before leaving. Ryan had already made plans to spend his holiday break with his father. It was hard not to see him at Christmas, but he spent very little time with his dad. My ex-husband had remarried, and with younger stepchildren, he stayed busy. It took Ryan a couple of years to mend the relationship with his father. He was aware his dad had cheated on me with his current wife. Ryan had been sixteen when the drama happened, and he was angry at his dad for a long time.

I was glad they were mending their relationship. Ryan's happiness was the most important thing to me. He was halfway through his second year at college and loving life. His school was only three hours away, and it gave him his independence while keeping him close enough for me to visit.

I didn't have to worry about work issues for my trip since I worked from home. The decision to start my own freelance editing business allowed me the freedom to take care of Mom when she first was diagnosed. I could work on the few projects I had while out in Wyoming.

The detailed itinerary that Mom had laid out started my journey in Cody, Wyoming. She explained in her first letter that she had read about this town and its rich history. I had never been out west. The rest of the letters were in sealed envelopes and numbered. They had notes on the front, instructing me not to open them until I got to where the last letter instructed me to go. I was excited but also scared by the prospect. I was taking Mom to her final resting place, and it was hard to do. The bright spot was that I got to read more letters from her.

I picked up the first letter and read it again.

DEAR RILEY,

I know this is a shock. My love for anything cowboy or Wild West-related started when I was a young girl. I would read the dime store books about cowboys and how they ruled the Wild West. I transitioned to steamy reads as a teenager that included a hero cowboy. My dream was to one day go to Wyoming and walk the same spots as the legends. I never had the chance because I raised five wonderful kids and took care of your dad.

Please enjoy this journey because I know you need this to rebuild your soul. Don't let what happened to you smother the joy I know you have. You are my kind-hearted daughter, and I want to see that smile on your face again.

Thank you for taking me out west and checking off the last item on my bucket list.

I love you forever, my sweet girl.
Mom

THE TEARS FELL HARDER with each word I read. My mom was special, and we had a bond. I knew she loved all her kids, but she and I were the most alike. Our love for romance and reading was unmatched in the rest of the family. She always told me I should be a writer, but I never felt confident enough. I guess that is why I stuck to editing. I got to read wonderful stories and have a hand in making sure they got published.

The attached sheet with the letter explained my first stop was in Cody, Wyoming. It had me staying at the famous Hotel Irma, built by Buffalo Bill and named for his youngest daughter. I could open the next envelope after I had dinner on my first night. This experience felt like my mom was writing her own story, and I was her main character.

I checked the weather and found they had snowfall over the past few days, but the forecast showed clear skies for my trip the next day. I had packed what I thought I'd need for the trip, including sweaters and boots. It had been a few years since I had seen any significant amount of snow, and I expected it would be beautiful out there. I also thought it would be nice to see snow on Christmas.

My bags were packed, and all the essentials ready. I had received texts from family and friends wishing me good luck on my trip. Ryan insisted I call him once I landed in Cody. He loved his grandmother and thought this was a cool thing for her to do. I believed he was right. He didn't know how nervous I was about what lay ahead.

* * *

THE SIGN INDICATED a delay in my flight from Denver to Cody, so I decided to grab a bite to eat at one of the airport's restaurants. My flight into Denver was uneventful, and I had slept some on the plane. Considering I didn't get much sleep the night before, it was welcome. I had tossed and turned thinking about the trip and Mom, and woke up well before my alarm.

The airport restaurant served old-fashioned burgers, and that sounded amazing. The hostess took me toward the back to a small table for two. I was sure she was used to travelers dining alone. I thanked her and put my carry-on bag beside me on the floor before sitting down and pulling out my cell phone to let Ryan know they had delayed my next flight. The waitress handed me a menu before taking my drink order.

Ryan responded and told me to let him know when I got on the plane. I was looking to see if I had any other messages when I heard chair legs scraping the floor. I looked up to see a man sit down at the table directly across from me. He sat on the opposite side and we stared at each other. He wore a baseball cap and tipped the front. "Ma'am," he said.

I smiled at him because it is polite and because I'd had no man tip his hat and call me 'ma'am' before. My cheeks grew hot, and I knew I was blushing. Why was I blushing?

I looked away and concentrated on my menu. The waitress came back, and I ordered a good old cheeseburger without the fries. She then walked over to my neighbor and took his order. He ordered the same but with the fries. He caught me staring and smiled.

"You should always order fries," he said. "Life is too short not to enjoy." I couldn't help but laugh.

"I agree, but a girl has to watch her figure," I responded and instantly regretted it. *Why would I say that?*

He laughed, and it made me blush again. I think it was his rugged laugh.

"It's forward of me, but I don't think you have that worry."

My goodness, I thought, feeling suddenly hot. My hot flash was cut short when the waitress brought my food. I thanked her and began to eat. My neighbor was looking at his phone as I took a bite and enjoyed this luxury. I tried to watch what I ate and didn't get to have too many burgers back home.

I wiped my mouth off after my next bite and noticed the waitress bringing the man's meal. The fries did look and smell good. I loved potatoes. He caught me looking at his food.

"I told you to order fries," he said. I nodded in agreement. "My name is Rich, by the way. I'm happy to share these fries if you're okay with company at your table." My stomach flipped. I wouldn't mind a few fries.

"I'm Riley, and those fries do smell wonderful. Please join me," I offered. I moved my things around on the table to make room for him. He gathered his plate and glass. I noticed how tall he was and couldn't help but check out his boots and dark jeans. He also wore a red t-shirt and a ball cap with an outline of Wyoming on it.

"Nice to meet you, Riley. Thanks for allowing me to sit with you. It's no fun to eat alone."

"Nice to meet you too, Rich. I have to admit, it is out of my comfort zone to eat alone. I usually have my son with me." As he sat down, I felt perfectly comfortable. It was odd, but I felt as if I already knew him.

"Your son isn't traveling with you today?" he asked before taking a bite of his burger.

"No, he is with his dad for Christmas break." I reached over and stole one of his fries. Another killer smile spread across his face. This man was handsome. I also loved a good splurge, and fries were a weakness of mine.

"They are good, right?"

"Yes, and you were right; I need to enjoy life a bit more."

We sat for a minute in silence as we ate. I stole a fry here or there and happened to notice his strong hands. I guessed he worked outside.

"So, where are you headed today?" he asked, breaking the silence.

"I am going to Cody, Wyoming."

"That is your destination?" He laughed and shook his head. "That is my destination, and actually my home. I'm flying back after visiting my sister in Denver."

I think it's unusual I would meet someone heading home to Cody in this big airport.

"This is my first trip to Wyoming and Cody. It is a special trip," I revealed.

I grabbed another fry and noticed he had two large dimples when he smiled. They gave him a boyish charm despite being a full-grown man.

"Can I ask why this trip is so special?" he inquired before taking the last bite of his burger.

"I am on a trip designed by my mother. She wanted me to bring her ashes out here to spread."

He looked at me, and I could tell he was processing my words. "That is amazing, Riley. I hope it goes all according to plan."

I smiled as I thought about this trip. "I have her as my guide. She left me letters with directions for this trip. I can't open them until specific times along the journey," I explained.

His eyes grew big, and he looked excited. "That is a cool thing your mom did for you. There are many great places around Cody and, of course, Yellowstone."

I wiped my mouth one last time and placed my napkin on my plate. The food was delicious, and the company wasn't so bad either.

"Yes, I have researched the area. I'm truly excited to see everything and honor my mom."

We both stopped to listen when we heard the announcement that the Cody, Wyoming flight was boarding in twenty minutes. The waitress made her way over to our table.

"Do either of you need anything else?" she asked.

"Nope," Rich responded. "Just the check."

She pulled out a receipt, but he handed her his credit card without even looking at it. She nodded and walked away to process it.

"Rich, you didn't have to buy my meal. I could take care of it."

He shook his head. "It is my pleasure. You allowed me to sit with you, and you shared about your trip. It's a small gesture."

The heat started again in my cheeks. "Thank you so much. That is very kind of you."

The waitress brought back his card and payment receipt. He signed and then looked at me.

"I guess we need to make our way to the gate."

I agreed and grabbed my bag. It was a good meal, but having him to chat with was even better. It had been a long time since I shared a meal with anyone other than Ryan's dad, and I felt rusty in the conversation department.

We both got up and made our way out of the restaurant before excusing ourselves to the restrooms. I took my time to freshen up, worried that I must have looked a mess. I hadn't thought I would spend time with a stranger after a long flight.

I looked in the mirror and tried to add a little makeup to my face and brush my hair. It helped me feel a little more confident as I headed back toward the gate.

I noticed Rich sitting in the seats near the window and made my way over to him. He stood as I reached him, and I recognized his gentlemanly behavior.

"They made another announcement they'll be boarding in ten minutes. Which seat are you in?" he asked.

I pulled my ticket from my bag. "Looks like I am in 3A."

"I am in 10A."

It disappointed me we wouldn't get to continue our conversation on the flight.

"Thanks again for the company and for paying for my meal," I said.

He nodded. "It was my pleasure. I hope your journey is blessed with wonderful memories."

I extended my hand toward him, and he put his big hand in mine. We shook, and I got that warm feeling all over this time. I found it bizarre; I hadn't felt like a teenager in decades. I was only forty, but over the last three years, I had felt much older. It started with Mom's health, and then the divorce. I felt like they had aged me.

"Enjoy the short flight to Wyoming," he said as he pulled his hand from mine.

"You do the same." My hand felt cold and empty. They announced that the last five rows were boarding, and he smiled and walked toward the gate and then disappeared into the jet bridge. I stood waiting for my turn and thought about the past two hours. Mom sent me on this journey to bring me out of my funk. She knew me so well.

CHAPTER 3

$\mathcal{I}$ lost touch with Rich after the flight. I made my way to baggage claim and then on to get my rental car. The short drive to Cody was breathtaking. There was still snow on the ground in the lower elevations as well as on the mountain ranges. Despite getting to the hotel at 5:00 PM, the time difference made me tired. I decided that after I arrived, I would take a shower and nap before getting dinner.

Once I checked in, I found my room rustic and quaint. It gave me the feeling of being in an old saloon. My mom would have loved this.

After my shower and nap, I made my way downstairs for dinner. I felt refreshed and almost human again. When I entered the dining room, my gaze was immediately drawn to the bar area. The rich, cherry back bar was covered in intricate details. I remembered reading on the hotel website that the Queen of England had given it to Wild Bill. I was determined to sit at that bar.

I told the hostess my wishes, and she walked me over to the bar. A tall man stood with his back to us as he sorted bottles on the shelf.

"Rich, you have a customer," she announced.

Before I could register the name, my rugged lunch date turned around. I do believe my mouth fell open. He gave me his signature cool smile, dimples and all.

"Hey there, Riley. I guess the stars have lined up for us."

"I guess they have," I responded as I took my seat at the bar. "This must be a great place to work."

"It isn't bad. I work here during the winter months. I tend bar and provide handyman help."

"Only during the winter? What do you do for the rest of the year?" I asked.

He brought a glass of water over to me. "I work at the rodeo here in town. We usually work from April until September, and I spend the rest of my time here."

This is Mom's cowboy, I thought as I stared at him in disbelief.

"What would you like to have for dinner?"

I looked over the menu and knew that I would get the chicken pot pie as soon as I saw it. It reminded me of winters with Mom. She sure did love to cook, and she was famous for that pot pie. All of us kids would ask for it.

"I will have the pot pie," I answered.

"That is a superb choice. Do you want a drink tonight, other than water?"

"I'm good with water tonight."

As he entered my dinner order into the computer system, I noticed he had changed into a black t-shirt and jeans that showed some wear, but he still had his boots on.

"That sounds exciting to work at the rodeo," I said, eager to know more.

"It can be," he replied as he walked back over to me. "I help attract and manage new talent, the riders specifically. These young guys can be a handful when they first start. I have to be a brother, uncle, dad, and boss."

"I have never been to a rodeo," I admitted.

"That is sad to hear. You picked the wrong time of year to come to Cody. The summer is hopping here, and the rodeo is one of the major attractions."

A waiter brought out my dinner and handed it to Rich. He smiled as he set it down in front of me. Steam was still rising above its magnificent crust. I mused that I would gain ten pounds if all the food around here is this spectacular.

"Enjoy. I'll be back in a few. I have to help a couple who just sat down."

I spent the next ten minutes fully enjoying my dinner. The chef outdid himself or herself; it was homemade, and just like Mom's.

I wonder if she knew this hotel had pot pies, I thought as I took the first delicious bite.

"How is everything?" Rich asked after making his way back to me.

"It's amazing and reminds me of home. My mom used to make the best pot pies."

"Where is home?"

"I'm from a small college town in Virginia. Well, it can be small, once all the kids head home in the summer."

"I have never ventured that far. I've heard that Virginia is beautiful, and it's for lovers. Right?" He laughed.

"Yes, that is the motto. I wouldn't know," I responded without thinking.

Great job, Riley, I thought, immediately scolding myself.

"So, you don't have a Virginia lover joining you on this trip?" he asked. The glimmer in his eyes didn't escape my notice.

"You are funny. I told you that my son is spending the holidays with his dad. He would be the only guy I would consider for a trip like this."

"There is a lot to do here in Cody, even in the winter. I don't think you need to have someone with you to enjoy all that the town offers," he said. I liked the way he thought.

"By the way, I'm also divorced and the father of a twenty-three-year-old son. He finished up college this past summer. He is off visiting his mother in California," he shared.

"Will it be hard for Christmas, not having him around?" I asked.

He nodded. "I will miss him dearly, but he doesn't see his mom that often, and I want him to spend time with her," he explained before excusing himself to help other customers.

After I finished my meal, I realized I couldn't eat another bite. It was scrumptious. Now it was time to open letter number two.

I pulled the letter out of my purse and laid it on the bar. The fact I got to read another letter from Mom was overwhelming. I sat there staring at the envelope with her writing on top. She always hated her penmanship, but all of us kids loved to see her notes on our birthday cards.

"What do you have there? Is that one of the letters from your mom?" Rich asked as he returned again.

I nodded as I ran my hands over the top.

"I'm a bit nervous to open it," I said.

He put his hand on mine. "Riley, it's from your mom. She loved you. Don't be nervous."

His hand felt good against mine. I got the same jolt I felt at the airport. I looked at him and smiled. He took his hand away, and I lifted the envelope before opening it and pulling out Mom's next message.

DEAR RILEY,

If you are reading letter number two, then you are at Hotel Irma and just ate the pot pie. I know you picked that for your dinner. Just remember, my girl, it isn't as good as mine.

I hope your trip was good and please rest up because tomorrow I want you to ride a horse. I set up an appointment at a local place just outside of town. They will treat you right.

Enjoy and remember to laugh. You have a great laugh, and people need to hear it.

Love,
Mom

I TRIED to hold back my tears, but one slipped down my cheek anyway. Rich offered a napkin, and I took it, dabbing quickly at my eyes.

"What does your mom have planned for you?" he asked.

I gave him the letter and itinerary to read. I didn't know why, but I felt close to this man.

"This is amazing and thoughtful. Your mom truly planned a grand adventure for you. I see she scheduled you to ride tomorrow with Walt. He is a neighbor of mine."

"I haven't been horseback riding in twenty years," I confessed.

He folded the letter, then wrote directions for tomorrow's appointment and gave them back to me.

"If you like, I can meet you there. Walt is a great friend, and I would be happy to," he offered.

"I would like that very much." The thought of him being there with me was already easing my anxiety. I loved being on a horse again, but I wasn't sure I remembered how.

"Thanks, Rich. She has me scheduled for noon tomorrow. Will that time be okay for you?"

"Yes, ma'am. I'm looking forward to it."

"Well, I'm going to my room. It's been a long day. Thanks again for everything. See you tomorrow." I waved as I got up to leave.

"Sleep well and see you tomorrow."

CHAPTER 4

I slept like a rock. I didn't know if it was because I was tired from the trip or relaxed in my cozy room. I rarely slept so soundly. I got up and had a light breakfast, then made a few calls before leaving the hotel for the ranch. Ryan was excited for me and asked for pictures. I emailed my siblings and shared about my adventure so far. They all replied they were happy for me and couldn't wait to get more updates.

The ranch wasn't far from downtown Cody. I almost wished it was a longer drive so I could enjoy more scenery.

I pulled into the ranch's entrance and read the sign overhead: *The WW Ranch*. It was nestled in between two mountains, and the valley stretched on as far as my eyes could see.

I parked my rental car in front of the barn and paused, reviewing what I had worn. I had dressed in my boots, jeans, and a long-sleeved Henley. I picked up a souvenir baseball hat at the hotel to help hold my hair back and not let the breeze destroy it for the ride. I also brought my heavy coat since I was going to ride on snow-covered trails.

I got out of my car and turned to find Rich riding up on a large, dark brown horse with a honey-colored mane. He was wearing a cowboy hat and a long coat, and they made him look like a cowboy.

"Hello, Riley. I get to be your tour guide today. My buddy Walt gave me the green light," he said.

I flashed him a big smile. "That would be outstanding."

He smiled back at me and hopped down from his horse. "Let's go pick out your horse and get you introduced."

I walked beside him toward the barn.

"Did you sleep well? Any trouble finding the ranch?" he asked.

"No trouble sleeping or finding the ranch."

We entered the barn, and he directed me over to a horse.

"Her name is Sunny, and she is sweet as sunshine. You two will get along great." He walked over to her and ran his hand down her neck, then scratched a little behind her ear. I could tell they knew each other well.

He gestured for me to come closer. "Take your hand and slowly rub her from the neck down. She loves the attention."

I did as he instructed, and the mare turned, bringing her head near my shoulder to sniff me. She turned back and let me rub her. I guessed I passed her test.

"Okay, let me get her saddled, and then we'll ride," he said. I stepped away from Sunny and waited while he saddled her. The brown felt hat looked natural on him. Not the kind you see guys buy at country concerts when they are trying to be cool. Rich made everything seem genuine.

Once my horse was ready, he helped me climb on. He gave me instructions on how to guide her if needed but reassured me she knew her way around and wouldn't need much nudging.

He climbed on his horse, and we headed off. We rode through the trails along the property, and it felt like the Old West life. The incredible high-mountain scenery was something I will never forget. During our two-hour ride, he told me about Yellowstone and Wyoming. Before I knew it, we were back at the barn. I helped him rub the horses down, and we continued to talk. It was so easy with him.

I learned that he grew up in Cody and never had the desire to leave. His parents passed away five years ago, and he was an only child. He shared all of this because he understood the loss of a parent. At forty-three, he was only three years older than me.

As I watched him, I noticed the hint of a beard. It was what I like to call scruffy. The rugged look was definitely in full effect today.

"Thanks for being my guide. It was relaxing. The views here are nothing short of amazing," I said.

"Yes, that's why I bought some land near here. I couldn't pass up the views and the chance to get away from the hustle of downtown." He turned to look at me. "Do you have another letter to open?"

I almost forgot that I could open another letter once I completed my ride.

"I do! It's number three. I have it in the car."

"We are done," he said. I gave Sunny one last rub and told her goodbye. We made our way to my car, and I grabbed the third letter from my purse. I wasn't as nervous this time, but I was still excited to read another letter from Mom.

DEAR RILEY,

I hope you found a cowboy to ride with today. The WW Ranch is the best around, and I know you would enjoy it. Did you get your laugh back?

Please take your time over the next few days and enjoy what Cody offers.

I ask that you don't open letter number four until Christmas Eve.

Relax and immerse yourself in the Wild West.

Love,

Mom

HOW DID SHE KNOW? I felt like she was watching me and then sending my letters. This gave me over a week and a half to be a true tourist. I could use some time to work on edits for a few clients. I felt like I hadn't ever had this much time to myself, and I was a little out of sorts just thinking about it.

"What did your mom say this time? What glorious adventure does she have planned?" Rich asked.

"She doesn't. She wants me to guide myself until Christmas Eve. Then I get to open the next letter."

"So, you will be here for Christmas?"

"Yes, my mother directed me to spread her ashes on Christmas Day," I explained. He stepped away for a second and I watched as he cleared his throat. I guessed it might hit home for him since he lost his parents fairly recently.

He turned back to me before speaking. "I guess we have a lot to do before Christmas Eve."

I looked at him with wide eyes. "You would help me?" I asked.

"Riley, I would be honored to show you around my town. I feel like I'm part of your journey and want you to see it through."

That warm feeling came over me again. "Rich, you are kind. It would mean a lot if you helped me."

He stepped closer and pulled me into a hug. I thought he smelled like wood and leather as I realized how good it felt to be in his arms. I couldn't believe that we met only twenty-four hours ago. I was thinking maybe my mom was working her magic from up above until he pulled back and stepped away.

"How about meeting me tonight at the bar? I'm working again and would love the company."

I didn't hesitate. "That sounds great. I'm going to head back to town and look in some shops. I have several things to buy for my family."

"Have fun, and I will see you tonight."

As I left The WW Ranch, I couldn't help but think it had been a great day.

CHAPTER 5

*T*he past week was beyond words. Rich had been a top-notch tour guide and had even gotten me into places that were closed for the season. He was very well-liked around these parts. We went to the Buffalo Bill Dam, but we couldn't walk across; it was too dangerous because of the recent snow. We drove around, and I took a ton of pictures. It almost didn't look real. Rich said I would have to come back in the summer to enjoy the dam from the top.

He had taken me to Old Trail Town, which had several authentic structures and furnishings. These historic buildings were from remote locations in Wyoming and brought to the site and reassembled. There were a ton of artifacts from the Old West. It was a fun day, and I felt like I gained all this western knowledge for Mom, but I was having the best time doing it.

I spent every day with Rich, and when he worked at the bar in Hotel Irma, I was there. We talked and shared so much of our life stories. I was scared about this trip, but after this amazing week, I couldn't imagine leaving. I was even getting used to the weather. This place had such friendly people and so much history. I purchased some great souvenirs for my family, and I made a new boot purchase.

The time had flown by, and it was almost Christmas Eve. I had never spent it alone, and I was truly missing Ryan. He said he was having a good time with his dad. He checked in every day and loved the pictures I sent him. It was time for me to head down to dinner and meet up with Rich.

I spent a little more time on my hair and makeup this time, and pulled out a green top that looked good with my dark brown hair and made my hazel eyes pop. We had spent a lot of time together, and not once had he tried to kiss me. I wouldn't mind a kiss from this genuine cowboy.

I grabbed my purse and took one last look in the mirror before making my way downstairs. The dining room was quiet; only a few locals were seated at the tables.

I waved at the hostess, who by now knew my spot. There was already a drink waiting for me. Rich knew I missed Virginia, so he fixed up some sweet tea.

He is such a good guy, I thought as I approached the bar.

"Hello, beautiful. You look gorgeous tonight," he said, making me blush.

"Thank you very much," I replied as I sat down. He leaned on the bar and smiled.

"What will it be tonight?"

"I will take the steak salad."

He nodded and put my order in. I sipped my tea and started to relax. He looked great again, and even though I knew he wore the same shirt each night while tending bar, I couldn't help but notice it hugged him in all the right places. The more time I spent with him, the more handsome he became.

I have a big crush on a cowboy.

"So, you ready for the next letter tomorrow?" he asked as he walked back to me.

I nodded. "I'm ready for Christmas Eve."

"Do you have any plans for opening the letter?"

"No, I don't. I wasn't sure what might happen here."

He stepped away to assist another customer, and I hoped I didn't sound desperate asking him, but it would be nice to see him on such a special night.

"I was going to talk to you about tomorrow. Hotel Irma is having an employee party tomorrow. We won't be operating the bar or restaurant. They still make food for folks staying, but they will be eating in their rooms," he explained.

"Oh," I replied, unsure of what else to say.

"I wanted to see if you'd like to be my date tomorrow evening."

I smiled big. "I would love to be your date. What is the dress code?"

He laughed. "It's Cody. We usually wear our nice jeans and boots with a dress shirt. I think you have a choice of attire."

A server brought out my salad, and I spent the next few minutes eating my dinner and thinking about the party. I packed for the outdoors, not holiday parties. I would have to check some shops for something nicer to wear.

"How is dinner?" Rich asked, walking back to me.

"It's fabulous, like all my meals. What time does the party start? I want to make sure I'm down here on time."

He shook his head. "Riley, this is a proper date. I'll pick you up at your door."

I blushed and agreed. We spent the rest of the night talking about the holidays and what we bought for our boys. I told him I had some boots shipped to Ryan, and Rich loved that. We finally said goodnight, and he promised to pick me up at my door at 6 PM.

* * *

THERE WERE few stores open on Christmas Eve in Cody. I felt lucky to find one clothing store. I walked in hoping they had nice women's clothes. I looked around and found a rack in the far-right corner of the store. A form-fitting, red wrap, knee-length dress caught my eye. I took it to the dressing room, and I was floored by how it fit me like a glove.

I couldn't wait until tonight. I grabbed my dress after putting my regular clothes back on and made my way to the cashier.

"Hello. Did you find everything okay?" she asked.

"Yes, I found this amazing dress, but not I'm sure what shoes I should wear with it."

"The only suitable shoes in Cody are boots." She laughed. "There is a selection in the back that should work perfectly with this dress."

I walked to where she pointed and realized she wasn't kidding. They had a full wall filled with all kinds of boots. I zeroed in on a black pair that had flowers on the sides. As soon as I saw them, I fell in love--and they were my size!

I made my way back up to the front, and the cashier rang me up and bagged my purchases.

She wished me a Merry Christmas as I walked out of the shop and into the cold mountain air.

Shopping took a bit more time than I planned. I still needed to shower and dress before Rich arrived in one hour. I hadn't even opened Mom's letter yet, but I decided it was time. I grabbed the next-to-last letter. It made me sad to think that soon I would not have any more letters from her. I opened the envelope.

DEAR RILEY,

I wish you a very Merry Christmas Eve. I sure hope you have enjoyed your time around Cody. The adventure will last you a lifetime. Tonight, I want you to find something red and kiss a cowboy under the mistletoe.

You deserve to love again, and I know you will find it soon. You are living again, and this makes me happy. Enjoy a warm fire, and realize that you are special.

I will give you my last letter tomorrow when I ask you to take my ashes somewhere special in Yellowstone. I want to be in this magical place, and for you to know you can always come back here knowing it meant as much to you as it does to me.

Have fun tonight, my sweet girl.

Love,

Mom

I WAS glad I hadn't put on my makeup before reading the letter. The tears poured freely down my cheeks. She knew I would buy something red. I missed her so much in that moment. I said a little prayer to her and made my way into the bathroom to finish getting ready.

It seemed like no time had passed before there was a knock on my door. I had just put my jewelry on and slipped into my new boots. I took one last look and a deep breath before I opened the door.

Rich stood in before me looking incredible, wearing a black sweater, dark jeans, and black cowboy boots. He had shaved and smelled wonderful.

"Riley, you are drop-dead stunning. I love the red dress and boots. You make me proud to have you as my date tonight," he said.

I blushed so hard I'm sure it matched my dress. "Rich, you look very handsome tonight, and I am proud to be your date, too," I replied.

He offered his arm, and we headed downstairs.

I loved the feeling of being his date. We talked about our day as we walked, and he made talking so easy. I was going to miss him terribly, but I tried not to get sad; it was a special evening.

We entered the room, and all eyes were on us. Holiday music played while the fireplace crackled.

Mom was right.

He took me over by the fire. I enjoyed both the warmth of the fire, and the warmth of being near Rich.

"Riley, there are few times I'm at a loss for words. I can't take my eyes off you," he admitted.

I turned to reply when I realized we were standing under the mistletoe. He noticed me looking up.

"I didn't plan this," he said. I chuckled.

I know you didn't, but I think I know who did, I thought as he leaned toward me, and I accepted his kiss. The electricity between us made my heart flutter, and it felt right. I put my hands behind his neck and encouraged him to deepen the kiss. He did so, but still kept it soft and romantic. We finally pulled apart and looked at each other.

"I have wanted to do that since I ate with you at the airport," he confessed.

I smiled as I held his hands. "I felt the same way when we met. It seems like fate has brought us together," I replied. We spent the night having fun with his friends. After we danced, we had another delicious meal. Things wound down around 10 PM, and Rich walked me back to my room. I opened the door and turned to him.

"Riley, you haven't shared with me what today's letter said."

I wasn't sure I wanted to share this letter. It was too perfect.

"It was special. She wants me to take her ashes to Yellowstone tomorrow. Can you recommend a spot?" I asked.

"I know the perfect place," he quickly replied. "Is it okay if I come with you?"

I stepped toward him and put my arms around his waist.

"Yes, I would love that." He leaned down and gave me a kiss goodnight.

"I will meet you tomorrow morning at 9 AM. Merry Christmas."

"Merry Christmas," I wished him in return.

CHAPTER 6

$\mathcal{I}$ woke up early and noticed a light snowfall outside. I hoped it wouldn't give us any problems while making our way to the spot in Yellowstone. After Rich and I said goodnight, I talked with Ryan and wished him a Merry Christmas. He loved the boots I sent him and couldn't wait to see me when I came home. It was hard to believe that I would leave the next day.

I was going to miss this place. It had brought life to my soul again. My heart hurt for two reasons today: I had to say goodbye to my mom and then to Rich. It was Christmas and a blessed day, but my sadness loomed over it.

I ate a light-breakfast, then dressed for the cold weather. I also packed the gift I picked up for Rich while I was shopping. It was a special key chain engraved with his initials and the date we met. I wanted him to know how special the time I spent with him was.

I put the gift and the last letter from mom in my purse just as a knock sounded on my door. I opened it and found my cowboy standing there. He wore a felt cowboy hat with his long coat, and I loved this look on him.

"Good morning, beautiful," he said as he stepped forward and hugged me. That hug felt so good on this day. I needed it. He pulled back, then kissed my lips.

"Good morning, handsome," I replied. We both laughed, and I closed my door.

As we headed downstairs and out the back door, I found a big silver truck waiting with the passenger side door open. He helped me up into the truck, which was already warm inside. He climbed into his side and shut his door.

"There is a special meadow that I want to take you to. Of course, it's not blooming right now, but in the spring and summer, there are thousands of wildflowers. It's in Yellowstone, and I think it would be a special resting place for your mom. You can see the mountains and the water from this spot."

I got misty-eyed thinking how wonderful this place would be for Mom. She adored wildflowers.

"That will be a perfect spot for my mom," I answered. He put the truck in reverse and backed out of Hotel Irma. Over the thirty-minute drive, we talked about Christmas and calling our children that morning. His son sent him his favorite cologne and vinyl records he had been trying to find. I learned Rich had an old turntable at this house and loved collecting vinyls for it. I felt closer to him with each personal detail he shared.

We reached the spot he described, and I was blown away. I could imagine the flowers here. It had a wonderful view, even during this time of year. I felt we found the right spot for Mom.

"Before we get out, do you want to open your last letter?" he asked. I nodded and pulled the letter from my purse. My hands shook as I opened the final words from my mom.

DEAR RILEY,

Merry Christmas to you. I am blessed to be your mother. This journey was designed for you. I asked you to take this trip alone. I know your brothers and sisters have their families and lives, and I don't love them any less. They are all precious to me.

I know the last years of my life weren't easy. I want to thank you for your support and love during my final years. This is a way for you to be free and live your life now. I know it was a big burden to carry during my illness.

I asked you to bring my ashes to Yellowstone because it was a place I had dreamed about as a little girl. I know you have found a terrific final resting place, and if I know you, it will bloom with flowers in the spring.

Thank you for being special, and I love you with everything I got.

Be happy and love big.

Forever in my thoughts,

Mom

I FOLDED the envelope and wiped the tears from my eyes.

I love you, Mom, and miss you with all my heart.

Rich took my hands and squeezed them, but didn't say anything. I was glad he knew it wasn't what I needed. Him just being there with me was enough. We climbed out of the truck and walked into the meadow. I held my mother's urn with one hand, and Rich's hand with the other until we reached the perfect spot.

"I can go back to the truck if you want to be alone," he offered.

I shook my head. "Please stay."

"I'm here for you." He stood near me as I opened the urn. I said a little prayer for my mother before lifting it so I could shake her ashes and let them drift in the wind. They started to flow, and the wind took them like a river takes leaves, carrying them along the current. The ashes spread over the meadow. This resting place fit her perfectly.

I stayed in the spot for a while longer, and Rich moved behind me, wrapping his arms around my waist.

"Thank you for finding this spot," I said.

He kissed me on top of my head.

"I didn't choose this spot. It chose me. I haven't been here since I was a child."

I turned to him and was sure my confusion was apparent.

"I forgot about this location until a vivid dream brought the memory back."

I was speechless. Mom was working her magic for sure.

We stayed as long as our bodies would allow. The wind numbed my cheeks. I took some pictures as we walked back to his truck. I hoped to capture the intimate feeling of Mom's resting place. My siblings and Ryan would love this spot.

We climbed back into his warm truck, and I reached into my purse to pull out his gift. He pulled his sun visor down and grabbed an envelope. We smiled at each other as we exchanged our surprise gifts.

I waited and made him open his first. He slowly unwrapped the box and hesitated, holding it in his hand.

"Please open my gift," I insisted.

He finally lifted the lid, and the rustic-looking keychain sparkled in the daylight. I heard him clear his throat. I knew that sound.

"Rich, I put a date on the back," I told him.

He turned it over and looked at the date. "The day we met," he said before pulling me into a hug and kissing me gently. I was delighted that he liked my gift. My anxiety lifted the moment he pulled me into his arms.

"Now it's your turn."

I opened the envelope and pulled out a plane ticket. It was dated for one month from now and had my name on it. From Virginia to Wyoming. I looked at him.

"Riley, I want you to come back to me. I want you in my life. Please use the ticket. Did you notice it is one-way?"

My eyes were stinging with tears that threatened to fall on my cold cheeks. My heart was pounding, overcome with love. I looked at the ticket again.

"I have fallen in love with you, Riley, and would love for you to move out here to be near me. When the time is right, I want to marry you. You make me happy, and I want to make you happy too."

He looked as scared as I was, but I knew I had fallen in love with him too.

"I will use this ticket and come back to you," I promised. "This journey brought us into each other's lives. I feel blessed to have met you." He pulled me into another big hug.

"Merry Christmas," he said before kissing my lips. His lips were warm against mine, making the cold a distant memory now.

My mother made her last wish and helped me find love with a real-life cowboy.

ABOUT THE AUTHOR

R.K. started sneaking peeks at her mom's romance novels since middle school. She has always had her own stories in her head, but never had the courage to write them down. After one life-changing writing retreat, she began her journey. When she is not writing, you can find her exploring with her camera or discovering new music.

R.K. lives in Virginia with her two fantastic boys, Lukas and Jakob.

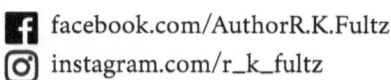

facebook.com/AuthorR.K.Fultz

instagram.com/r_k_fultz

THE PILFERED PRESENTS: A C.T. FERGUSON SHORT STORY

BY TOM FOWLER

THE PILFERED PRESENTS

A C.T. FERGUSON SHORT STORY

*M*y first week in my new office had not gotten off to a rousing start. Over the course of the initial two days, I managed to count—and triple-verify—the number of tiles in my ceiling, establish the windows afforded a fine view of the Baltimore Harbor, and doubly confirm the deli next door served a mean pastrami on rye. Other than these pursuits and a few phone inquiries, I'd done very little since renting the space.

This all changed when a man in a Santa hat walked in. The exterior of my suite opened into a small anteroom, then another door led to the business part of the office. I put a nice leather chair, a coffee table, and a few token magazines out there to make it into a waiting room. At my current pace of business, the chair would rot before anyone needed to sit in it. The fellow in the Santa hat glanced at it, saw my second door open, and kept walking. As he stepped closer, I heard him panting.

He walked through my inner door, put his hands on his hips, and bent forward at the waist. While he sucked in a few deep breaths, I hoped he wouldn't vomit. I didn't even own a wastebasket yet. After a minute of heavy breathing, the man stood up. His red face almost matched his hat, though it did not make him look like a jolly old elf. "The elevator is out," he said in what passed for a greeting.

"There's more than one in the building," I said.

He shook his head and sucked in another breath. "Didn't know where they were. Stairs were right there. Why are you on the sixteenth floor?"

"If someone comes to shoot me, I'm hoping the stairs tire them out," I said. "Gives me an edge."

"What if the elevator works?"

"No plan is perfect." I gestured toward the cushy leather chairs, thus far unused, in front of my desk. "Would you like to sit?"

A woman walked through the first door, then the second. She wore a matching Santa hat—though I guess they all matched—and sported a bright red coat atop her slim frame. She panted and gasped much like the man I guessed to be her husband. He sat, and the woman sat beside him. "Thanks. We'd like to hire you for a case you probably can't solve."

I took a seat in my high-backed executive chair. "Well, with such a vote of confidence, how can I say no?"

"I just want you to realize what you might be getting into. It's probably a fool's errand." I didn't have a snappy comeback which wouldn't paint me as the fool in question, so I let it pass. "Ron Lewis. This is my wife Cathy."

We exchanged polite-ish nods all around. "C.T. Ferguson. Nice to meet you. What's your fool's errand involve?"

"My wife convinced me to put up a bunch of exterior Christmas lights this year. We'd never done it before, but she got them for free, so I figured . . . why not? I thought they made your house more inviting to burglars. Do you put up outside lights?"

"No," I said.

"For the same reason I didn't?"

"No, I'm a competitive person. I'd feel compelled to outdo my neighbors, and then we'd all have these complex arrangements tackying up the neighborhood. If I wanted to make a scene out of my lights, I'd live in Hampden."

They both gave me funny looks, but Ron continued. "Anyway, it turns out I was right: our home got broken into. We didn't even hear a thing."

"It doesn't mean the lights invited the burglars to rob us," Cathy said.

"They might have thought we kept a lot of nice stuff inside."

"Because you hung ten-year-old lights?"

I cleared my throat to stop their bickering. "I'm not a counselor. Argue on your own time." They both looked down at the floor. "I'm going to guess all your Christmas presents got stolen."

"All of them and not much else," Ron said. "We don't own a fancy TV, so there wasn't a lot worth taking."

"You want me to track down your stolen presents?"

"I told you it was a fool's errand."

"You're right."

He bowed his head. "It would mean a lot to my kids. You have kids?"

"No."

"Want kids?"

"No."

"Oh." I watched him deflate like a balloon a child didn't pinch tightly enough. Cathy sported an impassive look. She hadn't been happy or sad since they walked in. "Well, thanks for your time."

"I didn't say I wouldn't do it," I said, interrupting his attempt to stand and leave.

"You'll help us?" Hope crept back onto his face. Cathy's eyes brightened, and she threatened a smile.

"Tell me what was taken."

"We bought the kids an Xbox One," Cathy said. "We also got them a couple games." She mentioned the games, only one of which I'd heard of.

I jotted this down as if it would make a difference. "Anything else?" They both looked at me and shrugged. "No gifts to each other?"

"We stopped doing it a while ago," Ron said. "I haven't gotten a raise in four years, and Cathy's job got cut back to part-time." As if on Cue, Cathy frowned and lowered her head. "Now we just buy for the kids to make sure they have a good Christmas."

"You realize a console and a few games will be almost impossible to track, right?" I said. "Do you know the serial number or anything?"

They both shook their heads. "No, nothing like that," Cathy said. "I know it's a long shot, but we don't have any idea what else to do. Will you help us?"

I looked at them for a moment. The clothes under their jackets had faded to more muted colors. Cathy's coat and jeans were at least two sizes too big, like she had lost weight and not updated her wardrobe. Their story was believable.

"I think it's definitely a fool's errand," I said, "but I'll see what I can do."

"And we don't need to pay you?" Ron said.

"Nope."

"Christmas special?" Cathy said.

"Sure," I said. "I just run it all year long."

* * *

THE FIRST REALIZATION TO strike me was a thief who wanted to hang onto the stolen gifts might be impossible to find. I would look for a police report, but unless the Baltimore Police uncovered a damning piece of forensic evidence, they wouldn't know who burgled the Lewis' home. This left the thief himself and what he planned to do with his ill-gotten gains. Unless he was acquainted with the Lewises, what lay under the wrapping paper was a mystery to him.

I found the Lewis' address and then searched for nearby pawn shops. If the thief didn't want the electronics, pawn shops and Craigslist were the best bets for unloading it. A real store like Game-Stop would ask too many questions. I opened a new tab and started searching Craigslist, too. A lot of people unloaded Xbox Ones, some with games, but none were advertised as being brand new in the box. I made a mental note to check later.

My phone rang, interrupting my fruitless searching. "Hello?"

"It's Ron Lewis."

"You just left not a half-hour ago."

"Yeah, there was something else I needed to tell you." He paused. "I didn't want to mention it with the wife around." I waited while he paused. Inevitably, he filled the conversational gap. "I got Cathy a present. We said we don't do it anymore, and we didn't for a few years. But this time, I broke our rule."

"What did you get?" I asked.

"A Swarovski tennis bracelet."

I knew the brand. "Pretty expensive considering the financial picture you painted earlier."

"Sure, if I paid retail. I snagged it at a pawn shop."

His choice of store could prove helpful. "Do you still have the receipt?"

"Yep."

"Good. I need to get it from you."

"I can stop back down in about an hour. Maybe you can meet me in the lobby, so I don't need to take the stairs again?"

"Can't you just take a picture and text me the image?"

"Oh," he said. "Sure. I'll do it right away."

"Whenever you can," I said. Because I wouldn't have another client until next month at this rate.

* * *

I MADE copies of the receipt and drove to the pawn shop where Ron purchased the bracelet. I didn't possess a wealth of experience with these stories, but it looked like a typical entry in the category. The shelves brimmed with detritus and things once valuable to someone. Behind the counter, a tall, slender bald man with a gun strapped around his waist surveyed the store, vigilant for miscreance and malfeasance. Three people browsed the shelves, probably looking for a last-minute gift for the non-discriminating folks on their list. I walked to the counter. The man with the shaved head frowned at me.

"Can I help you?" he said, sounding like he had little interest in the pursuit.

"I hope so." I showed him my ID, then slid a copy of the receipt to him across the counter. "A man bought the bracelet recently. You remember him?"

"Maybe."

I looked at the shop owner. His head had been freshly shaved and I couldn't see a single nick or imperfection. His nails were short and neat. He wore a polo shirt tucked into a pair of dark khaki pants. Everything about him suggested order. "You don't strike me as the type to forget too easily," I said.

He looked at me, then the receipt. "OK, I remember him. So?"

"The bracelet he bought from you got stolen last night."

"Tough break," he said, wincing in what I hoped to be sympathy.

"Yeah, it is. The family also had the rest of their presents stolen." I gave him a copy of the gift list I had written down earlier. "I don't have the slightest idea who stole these things yet. If he doesn't want to keep them, he might come here to unload them."

"And you want me to keep an eye out for him?"

"Would you remember the bracelet if someone tried to sell it to you?"

"Sure."

"Good." I gave him a business card. "Will you call me if someone does?"

"Yeah." He looked at the card and put it on a shelf under the counter. I could only hope he would call me. At least he knew the bracelet. The next five pawn shop owners I visited didn't, even though they all claimed an intimate knowledge of the Swarovski tennis bracelet line. I left each owner with a copy of the receipt, a list of stolen gifts, and a business card.

When I got back to my office, I looked for the police report. During my days as a nascent investigator, my cousin Rich, then a uniformed sergeant with the Baltimore police, left his computer unattended with me on the other side of it. I repaid his foolishness by swiping his IP and physical addresses. From there, getting the BPD's network to accept my computer as one of its own had been easy. Officer Jennings, whom I knew a little, wrote the report. I discovered nothing new in it, which I expected. I needed the pawn shop angle to pan out.

* * *

"WHO ARE YOU, the patron saint of lost causes?" Rich said. We sat at his desk in the precinct. Rich wore a tweed sport coat straight out of the 'seventies and paired with a much more modern pair of khakis. All his suits must have been at the cleaners. This constituted a sartorial crisis for him. All told, he handled it better than I would've. A cup of coffee looking stale and smelling worse sat neglected in front of him. At least he possessed the good sense to ignore it.

"Do I get a church built in my honor?" I said.

"If you find those presents, you just might."

"You wouldn't have taken the case?"

Rich shrugged. "I think you might've given these people hope you can't deliver on."

"Normally, I might take issue with your assessment of my skills," I said, "but even I think this is hopeless."

"You said the husband called it a fool's errand?"

I nodded. "He did."

"Sounds about right."

I wondered if Rich meant to paint me as the fool. Probably. I ignored it. "Any insight as to how to work a fool's errand, Sergeant Ferguson?"

"Nope," he said.

"I'm glad I came here for your pearl of wisdom."

"No harm in taking the case, though. You might even work a Christmas miracle."

"Now I just need an office on Thirty-Fourth Street."

"You wouldn't want an office there."

I thought about it. "Neither East nor West 34th," I said.

"I figured," Rich said.

* * *

THE NEXT MORNING was December 23rd. My father called it "Christmas Eve Eve," and my mother chuckled dutifully every time he said it. I grimaced at the idea of enduring another round or two of my father's annual attempts at holiday humor. I grimaced anew when I got to the office and realized I still had nothing in this case. Maybe I would need a miracle, after all. It would probably help if I believed in them.

An hour after I arrived—and fifty-nine minutes after I had a productive thought about the case—my phone rang. It hadn't made much noise since I moved to this location. "Hello?" I said.

"Is this C.T. Ferguson?" said a male voice.

"It is."

"You were in my pawn shop yesterday. Downtown Pawnbrokers."

It was my first stop, the same place from which Ron Lewis had bought the Swarovski. "Yes. Did the bracelet turn up?"

"Sure did."

"You're positive it's the same one?"

"I sold the damn thing in the first place. Of course, I'm positive."

"All right. I presume you have the seller's information."

"Sure do."

"I'll be there soon," I said.

* * *

I HAD to buy something to get a copy of the receipt. One tennis bracelet later, I walked out with a copy in my bag. I looked it over while I sat in the car. Zachary Cross sold the stolen goods to the pawn shop. The receipt listed an address. I wondered if Cross gave his real one. A smart criminal wouldn't. Either way, the phone book would not be awash in Zachary Crosses. I would find him.

Google told me the address he provided was real. So much for being smart. He lived in a part of Baltimore called Gardenville. I sort of knew the area, but not well enough to find his house, so I plotted a course with my GPS. Twenty minutes later, I entered the neighborhood. It dated from around World War II and featured a lot of old houses, many of them ranchers, interspersed with two-story dwellings and the occasional Victorian. A network of side streets composed the community. The houses were almost all old, but the local businesses had sprung up more recently. Some were obviously in repurposed buildings, like the McDonald's shoehorned into what I remembered as a bank.

Thanks more to the GPS than my knowledge of the area, I found Zachary Cross' house with ease. He lived in an L-shaped rancher begging for a fresh coat of paint, a new roof, and a new fence. The car in the driveway rolled off the assembly line the same year I did and didn't look nearly as good. I parked on the street and walked up to the door. Azalea bushes on either side lay in wait for the warmer spring months to spark their flowers to bloom again. I rang the doorbell. A short, slender man opened the door and pulled his sweater tight against the chill in the air. "Can I help you?" he said.

I showed him my ID. "I think we need to talk about some presents you have," I said.

He recoiled as if I'd struck him, then frowned. "I got nothing to say. I don't have to talk to you." He tried to close the door, but I shoved my foot in the way.

"I think talking is in your best interests," I said.

"I could call the police."

"You could. In fact, why don't you? We'll start with the receipt I have proving you sold stolen merchandise to a pawn shop." I held my phone out. "Wanna make the call?"

He looked at the phone, looked at me, and then shook his head. "Maybe you should come in," he said.

"Maybe I should," I said. Might as well be agreeable. It was Christmas Eve Eve.

* * *

CROSS MADE us each a cup of hot cocoa. I'm OK with drinking it from the packets if I must, but I need the little marshmallows to take my mind off the fact I'm drinking chocolate-flavored water. Cross purchased the marshmallow-free variety. I frowned and took a sip, anyway. All I could taste was water and not quite enough powdered cocoa. Cross sat on his shopworn sofa, opposite the recliner I occupied. The Xbox sat out in full display. Two smaller wrapped packages the size of games lay beside the console.

"You're aware I stole these gifts," he said. It wasn't a question.

"I am," I said.

"I saw the guy buy them and followed him." Cross was confessing without any input from me. I decided to sit back, sip my extremely mediocre hot chocolate, and let him keep hanging himself. "I'd never done anything like it before. This has been . . . a rough year, though."

"For a lot of people," I said when he paused.

"For me more than most. Wife left a few months ago. I have to pay her alimony because she works such a lousy job. Mine's not much better, but I make more, so I owe her some." He shook his head and scowled. "Don't get divorced in Maryland, whatever you do. This state sucks." He paused again and sipped some hot chocolate. I didn't say anything. He was on a rant, and my participation was superfluous at this point. "We got two kids. They're with me more than her, but of course, the judge didn't consider the circumstances. I wanted to give my kids a good Christmas because they ain't getting one from her."

I regarded the presents on the floor. They hadn't yet been moved under the artificial tree, but it wasn't for a lack of room. Only one other box currently occupied the space. The carpet needed as much work as the outside of the house did. Cross owned furniture whose fashion and utility expired a decade ago. He looked like the type who might need to steal someone else's presents to make a good Christmas.

"You have pictures?" I said.

Cross smiled for the first time since I met him. "Sure do," he said. He leaned back, wrestled an old iPhone out of his pocket, and queued up some photos. "Tommy and Sally." They were cute kids, and both looked at least somewhat like Cross. Tommy had his eyes and nose and Sally had the same chin. I wondered what their mother looked like.

"Nice kids," I said.

"They are." He smiled again and put his phone away. "They deserve a nice Christmas. You gonna sit there and tell me they don't?"

"No, I'm not."

Cross sat back down on his sofa and sighed. "Now what?"

I looked at the presents again, then looked at Cross. His kids deserved a good Christmas. So did the Lewis family. Zachary Cross confessed to theft when I arrived, and I possessed ample evidence proving it. I even obtained it legally. Mostly. I could have Cross arrested. Then the gifts he stole would get seized as evidence, and who knew if they would get returned to the Lewises? Tommy and Sally would get to visit their father in jail for Christmas. The Lewises would still be left staring at an empty tree. Nobody won in this scenario.

"Now you get to give your kids a nice Christmas," I said after a moment of thought.

Cross' eyes brightened like someone threw a switch. "Really? You mean it?" He beamed.

I nodded and couldn't help a smile. "I mean it. Merry Christmas."

"Wow." Cross' eyes welled up. "You don't know what this means to me and my children, man."

"You're probably right." I downed the rest of the hot cocoa in one swig and stood. "But your theft escapades end here. I'll be watching."

"How you gonna watch me?"

"I found you once," I pointed out. "I'm smarter than you. Make sure your life of crime stops here, and you won't see me again. But if I have to come back here, those cute kids you showed me can visit you in prison if your ex decides to bring them."

He bobbed his head. "OK. No more. I'm done."

"I'll hold you to it."

"What are you gonna do now?"

I'd already decided on my next course of action, as much as it pained me. "Go shopping," I said.

* * *

I CALLED Ron Lewis before I showed up at his house. It was late enough the Lewis children should have visions of sugar plums dancing in their heads. Ron sounded tired on the phone but insisted I didn't wake him. When I parked at their place, he came outside to meet me. I popped the trunk of the Audi and took out a large bag. Ron watched me with expectant eyes.

"You got our presents back?" he said.

"More or less," I said. I handed him the bag. He looked inside.

"I see the Xbox and some games. What's in the smaller box?"

"A certain Swarovski tennis bracelet."

He looked up at me and beamed. "You found it!"

"It was the key to the case," I said.

"Wow, I can't believe this." Ron paused his smiling to wipe at his eyes. "We're actually going to have a good Christmas after all." He put the bag down, started to go for a hug, then thought better of it and stopped. We bumped elbows instead. "Thanks so much," he said. "You've really made our holiday."

"Glad I could help," I said.

I didn't want to tell him he also made mine. He might've tried to hug me again.

* * *

"YOU BOUGHT THEIR PRESENTS AGAIN?" Rich said over breakfast the next morning. We ate at Lenny's Deli before his shift began on Christmas Eve.

I took a sip of my coffee. "I did," I said.

"You're a sucker."

"I could have arrested the fellow who took their stuff."

"And you probably should've."

"Maybe. But this way, two families get to enjoy Christmas, and zero kids had to visit their parents across a Plexiglas window."

"And you're just out some money. It's not like you don't have more."

I shrugged. "It seemed like the best way to handle it."

Rich polished off his bagel. He wiped the cream cheese from his lip, checking his reflection in the window to make sure he presented a professional appearance. "It probably was," he said. "In your place, I probably would have done the same thing."

"Wow. I can't remember hearing something so complimentary."

"It's Christmas," he said. "Must be something in the air."

* * *

AFTER BREAKFAST, I did an interview with a local news station about the case. It would air on their noon telecast. When one operates a free private detective business, one must whore oneself out to the press to spread the word. After lunch, I got the phone call I'd been expecting. "Hi, Mom," I said.

"Coningsby, your father and I just saw the news," she said. "What a great thing to do for those families."

"I might even need to get a Santa hat."

"It might be a good idea, dear. I think Saint Nicholas would approve."

"Both families get a good Christmas out of the deal. The outcome would've been different if I'd had the thief arrested"

"You don't think he'll steal anyone else's gifts?" she said.

"No, he's happy to have a big package of freedom under the tree."

"You did well, Coningsby. Your father and I will wire five thousand into your account when the banks open again."

"Thanks, Mom."

"You be here for Christmas dinner tomorrow," said my mother. "It starts at four o'clock sharp. None of your usual foolishness about showing up late."

"Wouldn't dream of it," I said, knowing I would be my usual ten minutes delinquent. It's not like they would start without me.

"Are you bringing Gloria?" my mother said.

"Yes. She'll need to do her hair, though. Might make us late."

"She's a nice girl, Coningsby. I'm sure she'll keep you on schedule."

"My other line is ringing, Mom," I said, even though it wasn't. "I'll see you tomorrow."

"Have a happy Christmas Eve, Coningsby."

"You too, Mom," I said.

ABOUT THE AUTHOR

Tom Fowler is a mystery and thriller writer. He was born and raised in Baltimore and, even though he now lives in the DC suburbs of Maryland, still considers Baltimore his home. His full-time job is in the field of computer security.

Even from a young age, Tom wanted to write. He was about seven or eight, so the stories were brief and awful. Among them was a "murder mystery" in which no one died (and, in fact, everyone recovered quite nicely in the hospital). In the intervening years, Tom has gotten over this problem with killing characters in his stories.

Tom's first series of books focuses on unconventional private investigator C.T. Ferguson. His other series stars former special operations soldier John Tyler, who can never quite settle into a career as a classic car mechanic The stories are, of course, set in Baltimore.

Tom Fowler writes stories featuring flawed heroes, action, and plenty of snark. He's also a proud indie author who learned from a lot of smart people and is happy to pay it forward. Visit his site at www.tomfowlerwrites.com.

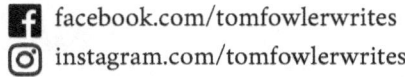

facebook.com/tomfowlerwrites

instagram.com/tomfowlerwrites

CHRISTMAS, COCOA, AND KEYCHAINS

BY N. TERRY

CHAPTER 1

12 YEARS AGO: ARIA

"*A*ria!" I heard my mother yell from downstairs.

"Coming!" I yelled back as I looked at myself in the mirror one last time. As a 14-year-old, I wasn't great at makeup or dressing up, but I wanted to leave an impression. An impression on one person in particular. Or one boy in particular, really: Jay.

Jay was visiting my family's bed and breakfast with his family for their holiday vacation. Today was Christmas Eve and they planned to leave late tonight so they could be at their home for Christmas Day.

This was the second year their family had visited, and this year I just so happened to notice that Jay was, in fact, a boy… a very cute boy that made my heart flutter and my cheeks turn red. Not to mention, he caused me to stutter like a bumbling idiot. My J-Pop magazine said 'Our love is written in the stars.' Whatever that means.

None of it really mattered. Who knew if I'd ever see him again after today, or if his family would ever come back.

Which brought me back to my hair, makeup, and outfit for the day.

I tried to mimic the girls in my magazine, but calling it a disaster was putting it nicely. So I stuck with something simple. I just hoped it was enough.

What impressed sixteen-year-old boys anyway? I had no boobs, which I hear they like, and I was as curvy as a two-by-four. It was times like this I wished more than anything that my parents had given me a sibling, someone-- anyone--to ask. All I had were my teen magazines.

I sighed once more before rolling my eyes. Christmas was my favorite time of year and I wouldn't let some silly crush ruin it for me. Nothing could ruin the smells and sounds of Christmas. The cookies, the decorations, the movies, the snow; it was just too magical.

At least that's what I told myself as I walked down the stairs towards Jay and his family. But as Jay turned around and smiled at me, my heart nearly climbed up my esophagus and out of my mouth.

"Hey Aria," he said as his parents followed mine towards the den.

"Hey Jay, what's up?"

"Did you bring your camera downstairs?"

I pulled my digital camera out of my back pocket and smiled bashfully. "Never leave without it."

Jay smiled again and I had to do an internal check to make sure all my organs were still functioning.

"Great! Let's go outside and see what photos we can take today. I want to check out that old barn again and get some good shots. I need your help to get the angle right."

"Kay," I replied. It was all I could manage, and I followed him to the door where we put on our winter gear.

Jay was the one who introduced me to photography last year when he visited. He showed up with his Canon in hand and I was obsessed. I saved all summer to finally buy a small camera of my own. It was our thing, what bonded us together.

That's how we spent the rest of our final day together. Taking photos of anything and everything around us and laughing. It wasn't until we sat in front of the fireplace in my family's den that I realized this was goodbye.

We sat huddled together in front of the fire on a worn flannel blanket, but I had never been more comfortable.

"Do you think you'll come back next year too?" I asked as our knees rubbed slightly.

Jay sighed, which wasn't a good sign. "My parents said this was going to be the last time we'd be able to make it up for a while. They are trying to push for a full ride at Michigan for basketball, which means adding more training. So they plan to put me in basketball camp next winter break."

I tried to fight the disappointment as I stared into my cup of peppermint hot cocoa, but the idea of never seeing him again caused a pain in my chest so intense I felt it down to my very bones.

"So this is it. I'll never see you again after tonight." My words came out just barely a whisper.

Jay chuckled, bumping his shoulder into mine. "Who can say?"

I smiled to myself. It was so like Jay to try and make the best of a sucky situation.

"I do have something for you though." He reached into his pocket and pulled out a small gift wrapped in Christmas paper. "Merry Christmas, Aria."

I took the package that looked like it was wrapped by a two-year-old and laughed. "Did you let your little brother wrap it for you?"

Red flushed his cheeks as he pouted. "Just open it."

I delicately unwrapped the package and gasped when I pulled out a keychain. It was a silver camera, one with a spot to place a photo in the back. It was so simple, but it meant everything to me.

I looked up at Jay, the light from the fire casting dancing shadows onto his face, but not even that could dull the shine of his baby blue eyes. My body was warm, too hot even, but not from the fire.

"Jay, it's beautiful... perfect. I don't know what to say. Thank you."

We were so close, our faces inches apart, so close we could kiss.

"I'll make you a deal," he said quietly. "If we meet again after today, that means we are fated to be together. If we find each other again in the big, big world, you'll just have to marry me."

Jay's words caused my world to tilt ever so slightly, and I had to pinch myself to make sure I wasn't dreaming.

"Jay, hunny. It's time to get ready to go," his mom called from the kitchen, breaking our connection.

With our moment broken, I became embarrassed and was unable

to look Jay in the eye again. We stood, putting our untouched peppermint hot cocoas on the coffee table.

We walked towards the staircase together, but Jay grabbed my arm and pulled me just under the opening of the den. He hugged me and whispered in my ear, "I'll miss you, my little Christmas Elf."

I couldn't help but grab onto his shirt and squeeze back. "I'll miss you too, Scrooge."

Jay pulled back slightly and looked up. I followed his eyes and my heart skipped a beat. He raised an eyebrow playfully and leaned down to place a kiss on my lips. We were standing under the mistletoe, which was now my new favorite flower, or plant, or whatever.

Jay's warm lips were on mine for only a second, but it felt like time had been suspended. I was sure my heart was going to fail from the erratic beat it was kicking out, and my brain was dizzy from his touch.

As he pulled away, he flashed his signature smile and said, "Don't forget: fate." Then he turned to leave and walked out of my life forever.

I couldn't stop the grin that spread on my face as I walked up the stairs to my bedroom. The keychain burned in my hand, and my cheeks hurt from smiling. It was the best Christmas Eve I'd ever had, with only one setback: I didn't know when I'd see Jay again.

In my heart, I knew fate would follow through.

CHAPTER 2

PRESENT DAY: ARIA

*C*hristmas in New York.
      The Rockefeller Tree.
The Rockettes.
Ice skating and cocoa.

All things I used to love about New York. Keywords: "used to."
Now the carolers drove me up the wall. All the decorations around
the city made my heart hurt. They were just a constant reminder that
I couldn't afford to decorate my tiny studio apartment with anything,
let alone holiday decorations.

I sighed as I passed yet another giant snowman on the sidewalk.

I was on my way to a job interview, as close to my dream job as
I've come since being in New York: advertising photographer for
People Magazine. It was still early afternoon and I had to leave my call
center job a little early to make the interview time. I planned to pick
up a shift at the bar tonight to make up the regular hours of pay I was
missing. I could only hope that this would be worth it and I would
finally get to start my career as a real photographer.

I was trying to keep my mood from dropping as I walked block
after block through downtown New York City. I almost had a smile
on my face, despite the chill I felt in my bones from my worn thin

coat and thrift store heeled boots. But this was it; this was my big break. Things were going to get better.

At least that's what I was telling myself before the cab drove by too close and splashed puddle water onto my boots, soaking my feet through the suede fabric.

"Hey watch it!" I yelled at the tail lights as they traveled past me.

I shivered as if someone was walking across my grave, realizing in my effort to avoid getting wetter from the cab, I had stepped off the sidewalk into a pile of shoveled snow.

Great. Just great.

The snow clung to my wet boots as if the fabric was its savior and I quickened my pace to ensure I didn't catch my death outside.

So much for holiday cheer.

CHAPTER 3

JONAH

*B*ored. That's how I was feeling when I saw a petite girl with long sandy blonde hair practically fall out of the elevator. I was waiting in a small sitting area for my name to be called as the next interviewee when she decided to take a tumble into the little space.

She sat down beside me with a loud huff, and I couldn't help the grin that threatened to peak from my lips. I pulled my phone back out and tried to focus on my social media pages, but my attention was drawn to her.

I studied her out of the corner of my eye, calling it a severe case of 'nothing better to do'.

She was shivering, pulling the lapels of her coat closer together, and bouncing her knees to generate warmth. Her shoes were soaked. No wonder she was cold. The black tights she wore under her red pencil skirt couldn't be providing much warmth either.

For a moment I felt sorry for her, and I felt the desire to do what I could to help alleviate some of her uncomfortableness.

But then she opened her mouth.

"Take a picture, it'll last longer."

For the first time, I looked into her eyes. Despite being hunched over and shaking like a leaf, there was a fire that showed in her grey eyes. A fire that said 'don't screw with me,' and I fully believed in her fighting spirit.

However, where she was all hot and bothered, I was indifferent and uninterested in most aspects of my life. I guess that is what happens when everything is easy-you get to a point where everything is just... blah. Nothing truly caught my attention anymore and everything was pretty lackluster.

Which is the reason I'm telling myself I can't stop wanting to engage with her. Hoping her drive and passion will rub off on me a little.

"Well, I was debating on if I should call security after you made your grand entrance. Beggars aren't normally welcome here, but I can see how cold you are so I thought I'd do the right thing and look the other way." I flashed my most genuine smile, knowing I was being a complete jerk and loving every second of it.

And she didn't disappoint.

First, her mouth opened slightly in utter shock, then her eyes narrowed as her pure, unadulterated anger rose to the surface. My fiery little nymph was ready to play.

She turned toward me and opened her mouth, but we were interrupted by the receptionist.

"Mr. Cross?"

I cleared my throat. "Yes?"

"Ms. Smith is ready to see you."

I stood up, grabbing my portfolio from the seat on the other side of me.

"See you later, train wreck," I called over my shoulder as I followed Ms. Receptionist into the inner offices.

I could see how much it killed her to bite her tongue, how much she wanted to unleash her anger on me... how beautiful she was with her eyes lit up with passion.

It had been a long time since I found someone attractive in more than just their looks. Women didn't come on to me because they wanted to have an intellectual conversation. No, they came onto me because of my last name, because of who my family was and what they thought it would get them.

Maybe after the interview, I could ask her for her name and number.

"Mr. Cross?"

Startled, I had forgotten where I was and what I was doing.

Get your head in the game, Cross.

"Yes, I am Jonah Cross. It's a pleasure to meet you, Ms. Smith." I shook her hand confidently and sat down. *Time to crush it.*

* * *

CHAPTER 4

ARIA

I sighed as I shut the door to my apartment and slid the deadbolt home. It was just past 2:30 am, which is exactly what time you get home when you work in the bar scene. Most of the other bartenders didn't have to get up and work an 8-5 job either though.

My eyes were heavy and my feet felt like ten-ton bricks, but I smelled like alcohol and greasy food. Not exactly what you want to smell like as you climb into your clean bed.

I spent more time than usual in the shower with my eyes closed and the hot water running down my skin, caressing the day's troubles away.

I still couldn't believe that guy, that Mr. Cross, and the way he had talked to me. I hoped now more than ever that I snagged that photography job just so he wouldn't get it. I hoped I never had to see him again.

Nevermind the fact that I hid behind a large plant in the small lobby when he came out of the interview just so I didn't have to speak with him again. I didn't think my blood pressure could handle the confrontation and I needed to be on my A-game for the interview. But it still wasn't one of my finest moments.

I shuddered, goosebumps raising all over my skin despite the heat from the water.

For a moment, he had me captivated with his eyes. They were a light shade of blue and I found myself being pulled into them. It made me forget the awful things he had said for just a second.

There was no doubt he was handsome. When he stood I was surprised at how tall he was, and as he walked away his fitted suit left little to the imagination. His ebony hair stood out in contrast to his baby blue eyes.

I shook my head slightly to clear the fog that had settled. There was no way I'd ever see him again, and good riddance. No one needs that type of toxic person in their life.

I finished my shower and followed my nightly routine before climbing into bed. I grabbed my old phone, the kind that was hanging on by a very small thread, and my heart nearly beat out of my chest as I saw I had a missed call and had a new voice message.

With trembling hands and a silent prayer to the big man upstairs, I put my phone to my ear.

"Ms. Parker, This is Ms. Katie Smith with People Magazine. I'd like to offer you the position of advertising photographer and we hope you can start as soon as next Monday. It was between you and another and we couldn't make up our minds, so we decided to hire you both. I know it's getting late so please give me a call back tomorrow and we can discuss the fine details. Congratulations, Ms. Parker. I look forward to working with you."

The phone cut out, but I couldn't get my arm to move. I did it, I got the job.

Yea, you and someone else.

But it didn't matter, I got the job. This would allow me to quit one of my part-time jobs and hopefully lead to an actual career in photography.

I closed my eyes, unable to process the emotional overflow I was feeling. Finally, after so long, there was a light at the end of the tunnel.

I set my phone down on my nightstand and plugged it in before opening my nightstand drawer. From its depths, I pulled out my most sacred treasure. The metal was cool and smooth in my hand. So familiar and comforting. I didn't fight the smile as I thought of the boy who gave it to me. I wished I knew how he was doing and if he was able to become a professional photographer too. I slid down on my pillow, clutching the keychain to my chest.

Memories of a fourteen-year-old love-struck girl lulled me off into a deep, exhausted slumber.

* * *

THE FOLLOWING Monday came a lot quicker than I was prepared for. My call center job was gracious about the notice I gave them even though it was less than two weeks. I even managed to hit up the thrift store and splurge on a few nice items for my very first professional job.

I stared at myself in the mirror, running my fingers through my long sandy brown hair one last time. Scanning over the maroon blouse tucked into my black pencil skirt that I paired it with black pumps, I believed I looked the part.

Take that, Mr. Cross.

A thought had bothered me all weekend though. Ms. Smith had mentioned that two people were hired. I didn't want to sound too nosey on the phone when I spoke with her, but part of me wondered if that other person was going to be the one and only pompous jerk himself.

I couldn't and wouldn't let that deter me though. I had just received another past due notice on my electric bill and I needed the money, pompous jerk or not. I'd have to suck it up even if it was him.

Sure, I could ask my parents for help and they would in a heart-beat. But I moved to New York City with a dream of becoming a professional photographer. I put myself through college at NYU, only taking out student loans when completely necessary. With my grades, I was lucky enough to qualify for many scholarships and grants which kept my loans to a minimum.

When I graduated, however, things got bad. It wasn't my parents' fault that I decided to move to one of the most expensive places to live. Things weren't really bad until recently. I had worked for a financial advisor as their assistant and when they retired I was out of a job. It wasn't my dream job, but it paid decently and the hours were super flexible. After losing that job, I had to scrounge around for another, which landed me at the call center, but not before having to take out credit cards and missing a few bills.

This job had to work. I was determined to make it work no matter what. It was a friggin' Christmas miracle that I got the job in the first place!

I walked to my little kitchenette in my studio apartment and looked over the space. When I first moved in, I did everything I could to celebrate the holidays on my budget. I went and picked out the cheapest, smallest Christmas tree I could find, and the thrift store I frequented had decorations all the time. I just hadn't been feeling in the spirit the last couple of years.

When I was a kid, Christmas was my favorite time of year. Everything about it felt special and magical, like anything could happen.

Now, the magic was gone.

I finished off my cup of coffee and placed it in the sink. Grabbing my coat and purse, I paused. This day wouldn't be happening if it wasn't for Jay, and I felt like I needed a piece of him to help me get through it. I ran back into my bedroom and grabbed the keychain and threw it into my purse. I locked up and headed out into the frigid December air, my skin prickling with goosebumps instantly. The commute to People Magazine wasn't terrible. I took the subway, and then made the rest of the way on foot, making sure to avoid all cabs and puddles this time. I walked into the building at almost exactly 8:45. There was nothing wrong with making a good first impression and being early.

I let the receptionist know why I was there and sat down by the windows to watch the hustle and bustle of the city below. I looked around the lobby to see if anyone else was sitting there waiting like I was, trying to figure out who my mystery counterpart would be, but I was alone for now.

At 8:58, I heard a scoff behind me that sent chills down my spine. Whether the chills were from delight or rage was yet to be determined.

Are you kidding me?

I turned to look into the blue eyes of Mr. Cross himself. I smiled sarcastically,

"Are you here to beg for a second chance or to apologize for being the biggest prick in New York?"

"Actually, honey pot, I'm here for the job. They decided to go with greatness instead of mediocre, second-rate photography."

I rolled my eyes. "Hate to break it to you, Mr. Great, but they hired me as well."

This time it was Mr. Cross who was interrupted as Ms. Smith stepped into the small lobby to greet us both.

"Good," she said with an enthusiastic smile. "It looks like you two have met. You'll be spending an awful lot of time together."

I flashed my best 'I Told You So' smile at Mr. Cross and he looked... fine. Actually, he didn't look unhappy at all. If anything, he seemed intrigued. He squared his shoulders, and held his hand out to me.

"I believe we haven't been properly introduced. My name is Jonah Cross."

With Ms. Smith standing next to us, I couldn't muster a sarcastic response. "I'm Aria Parker."

A small flicker passed through his eyes so quickly I wasn't sure if I was imagining it.

"Nice to meet you, Ms. Parker." His voice was deeper now, and his gaze penetrating.

"Likewise."

"Perfect! Now, if you two would follow me, I have some initial paperwork to have you fill out before we dive in. We have a full plate with Christmas next week and we haven't finished our Christmas issue!"

We followed Ms. Smith into her office quietly, but as soon as we sat in front of her desk, whatever weirdness had overcome Mr. Cross... *Jonah*... was gone. He charmed the pants off Ms. Smith, and had her completely smitten with him by lunchtime. I sure as hell hoped he had actual talent and didn't just charm his way into this job.

For the next couple hours, Ms. Smith went through all of our new hire paperwork, and explained the company's rules and expectations.

"Now that we have all the HR stuff done, let's get to the fun part." Ms. Smith smiled warmly at both of us. "We loved both of your portfolios and it was truly amazing how well each complemented the style of the other. It was the reason we decided to take you both on. Ms. Parker, your attention to tiny details is exactly what we are looking for, and Mr. Cross it is your unique point of view that made your photos stand out."

She paused, appraising us both once again.

"Our Christmas issue will be put on the press in a week, just in time for Christmas. So that only gives the two of you until Friday to get the shoot done and complete the final edits ."

"That shouldn't be a problem, Ms. Smith," Mr. Cross said confidently, and I nodded my head in agreement.

"Great. The article is in our lifestyle section and is about the perfect Christmas. It's going to have traditional family recipes, neat gift wrapping hacks, and of course, the latest and greatest in Christmas decor and kitchen appliances. What we are waiting for in this article is a few key photos to encompass the joy of Christmas Day. Your job is to set up a shoot to give our readers the illusion of the perfect Christmas celebration. I really want to see some Christmas spirit and traditional pieces."

Crap. A photoshoot all about the perfect Christmas when I can't even stand the sight of the Salvation Army Santa on the corner. I hid my groan as Ms. Smith went on about how excited she was to see us work together and how she hoped it would be the best Christmas issue ever. I wanted to place my head in my hands and rub my temples. Somehow this didn't sound as easy as Ms. Smith was making it out to be.

"Why don't you two go and grab some lunch, and when you come back I'll take you to the studio."

Mr. Cross was the first to stand and I followed his lead. All of my earlier confidence and fight seemed to have left me, and all that remained was the outer shell of Aria.

"Why don't we go grab a sandwich, partner, and we can brainstorm what we think our perfect Christmas is like. I know a good place right down the road."

"Yea, sure."

Mr. Cross gave me a curious look, like he was surprised I agreed so easily, but said nothing as I followed him into the elevator and back out into the busy New York streets.

CHAPTER 5

JONAH

To say Aria was acting weird after our meeting with Ms. Smith was an understatement. I didn't know her that well, but from our few interactions I could tell that she was acting completely lost. Gone was the spiteful minx who wanted to fight me on every word. While we ate our sandwiches, I tried to goad her into bickering with me once more, but she didn't take the bait. I even tried to talk work with her and she still wouldn't come out of her shell.

It wasn't long before I figured out the problem.

Back at the office, Ms. Smith took us to the studio to set up our shoot, and gave us everything we needed.

I had a few ideas myself. My family wasn't super into the holidays, but my mom made a mean Christmas dinner. So I wanted to see a genuine Christmas dinner set up and ready to be served on a styled table, ready and waiting for the family to come in and spend some quality time together. Then I had an idea for having a family around a well-decorated Christmas tree.

I turned toward Aria to start our brainstorm session for real, or to just tell her what I wanted at this point when she finally spoke.

"Why Christmas? Why did the first job have to be about Christmas?"

I frowned, a bit taken aback by the question. "Well, it *is* Christmas time."

Aria let out an exasperated sigh. "Yea but not everyone likes Christmas that much."

I scoffed. "What do you have against Christmas?"

She laughed, taking a step toward me. The light in her eyes was finally returning. "Right now? Pretty much everything. The expectations, the decorations, the fact that I haven't been able to buy my parents a proper Christmas present in years. The whole holiday is just shoved down your throat at every turn. No matter where you go in New York... BAM! Christmas. You know during the holiday season, more people turn to drinking alcohol than at any other time of the year? That should tell you! Not everyone wants to be reminded it's Christmas."

She was talking animatedly with her hands and subconsciously moving closer and closer to me. It was like she was being pulled into me as she ranted on and on, just like I was being pulled to her. By the time she finished, she was less than an arm's length from me and I could see every fleck of white that shined in her grey eyes and every freckle that colored her cheeks. She really was beautiful, despite her homely attire, which I would guess based on what she told me, was because she couldn't afford much else.

I must have been staring, because her cheeks reddened and she turned away from me.

"Sorry, I just haven't had much Christmas spirit lately."

I shrugged, trying to gain back my nonchalant attitude. "It's not a requirement to love Christmas. In fact, most people just endure it. I don't have much to say about Christmas. It just happens and I go see my parents, and then it's done."

Aria turned her head toward the window, a look of longing on her face as she watched the snow begin to fall. "I haven't seen my parents in five years. We used to have the best Christmases."

Now that was odd. "So, you hate Christmas, but you used to have great Christmases with your family? That doesn't make much sense."

Aria turned toward me again, a tight smile on her full lips. "Sorry, I don't want to talk about it anymore, okay? Let's just focus on the shoot."

Of course, I didn't want to stop talking about it. I finally had her talking and I didn't want her to shut me out again, but what else could I do?

"Sure."

Aria sighed deeply. "So, any ideas?"

I nodded. I told her about my plans and she didn't exactly see my inspiration. We went back and forth until both of us were pretty worn out. It wasn't that we exactly disagreed, it was just that neither one of us could say we loved the other's ideas. Everything was just so... generic, already done.

I rubbed my eyes for the umpteenth time in the past hour.

We needed a plan, and stat. This shoot needed to be completed and turned in Friday.

When 5 o'clock hit I was ready to take myself to the nearest bar and have a nice glass of whiskey on the rocks. I wondered if maybe Aria was onto something about drinking and Christmas.

At 5:30, Aria stood abruptly and knocked over her purse along the table we were sitting at.

"Oh shoot," she cursed as she scrambled to pick up the items. I reached a hand out to help her pick up her items and froze as something caught my eye.

"I'm sorry, I've got to go. I have to make it to my second job."

And just like that, she was gone. I didn't even have enough time to say goodbye.

Then again, I felt glued to my seat and unable to form any kind of words.

There was a reason I thought her name sounded so familiar, a reason why I felt I was drawn to her. A reason for the way she brought a light to my dull life. It wasn't the first time her light had poured into me and woken me from my dazed life.

The keychain. The camera keychain.

I turned my head toward the door Aria had just walked out, knowing she was gone, but unable to stop myself.

Fate. I told her meeting again would be fate,and now we had. I had a promise to keep.

Later that night, I sat on my couch with my whiskey chilled to my liking in my favorite glass as I thought about Aria. The Aria I knew as a kid was so different. She was happy all the time. The sweetest girl I'd ever met, she was genuine and pure, and always brought a smile to my face without even trying. It didn't matter that she was two years younger. Plus, they say girls mature faster than boys anyway, but I definitely had a thing for her. After our first Christmas at her parent's bed and breakfast, I begged and begged my parents to take me back.

There was just something about Christmas at that bed and breakfast. Everything felt hopeful and magical.

It is hard to imagine that the same Aria who adored all things Christmas back then now seemed to despise all things Christmas. But life could be tough, and from the sound of it, Aria hadn't walked an easy path like I had.

I looked around my Upper East Side three bedroom apartment and wondered what her home looked like. Was it decked out in holiday decorations? After her rant this afternoon, I'd guess not, but it should be. The Aria I knew would do everything to celebrate her favorite holiday. Maybe that was what she needed, a holiday spirit recharge, like jumper cables on an old car battery.

I smiled to myself as my plan formed. I knew just what to do to get Aria's love for Christmas back.

CHAPTER 6

ARIA

*O*nce again, my alarm woke me too soon. Or should I say, my
bartending job kept me out too late again, and my alarm had
no mercy for my sleep-deprived self? I wasn't supposed to work past
eleven last night, but the bar got busy and the idea of good tips kept
me working into the wee hours for the second night in a row.

At least it had kept me from thinking obsessively about Jonah. If
our first interaction had me on the hook, the second was the 'line and
sinker' part. After our official meeting yesterday morning, he had
opened up a side of him I didn't think existed in a man like him. His
ideas for our shoot weren't terrible, and when I complained about
Christmas, he seemed genuinely interested in what I was saying. His
baby blues had just about penetrated every wall I had built up around
myself. I almost felt bad about running out of there without much of
an explanation. It was the strangest thing: he seemed to break down
walls so easily even though I barely knew him. Not only did I know
nothing about him, but I had also only spent hours with him. It made
no sense. Being alone in New York must have finally gotten to me.

I glanced at my phone and shot out of bed. If I didn't hurry, I'd be
late! I showered quickly, but spent a little extra time on my hair and
makeup because... Why not? Sometimes a girl just wanted to look

nice, right? It didn't have anything to do with spending all day with a good looking man who seemed to send the butterflies in my stomach into a frenzy.

I was out the door and on my way in record time, even with the splurge on my beauty routine.

I made it into the lobby at 8:55 AM, and this time I went directly to where the shoot would take place. To my surprise, Jonah was already there. I had just assumed he always flew by the seat of his pants and didn't care much for being on time.

But he was on time for his interview wasn't he? That was how we had our chance to spar.

He smiled at me when I walked in the door. It was a real genuine smile that lit up his entire face, like seeing me was all he needed in the entire world. I nonchalantly looked over my shoulder. There was no way that smile was meant for me. It was too familiar and raw to be a smile for a stranger.

But it *was* for me.

"Hello Aria. How is your morning so far?"

I was speechless. Who was this man and what did he do with Mr. Stick-up-his-butt? Someone pinch me, because I was absolutely certain I was dreaming.

"Uh… fine?"

Jonah started to walk towards me, and I had to control my fight or flight instinct. Once again he completely surprised me by holding out a Starbucks paper cup. I gave him a questioning look before he nodded to me to take a drink.

Before my brain could throw around the 'you don't know this man, don't drink anything from strangers' lecture, I raised the cup and took a sip.

The taste of warm, chocolatey goodness melted down my throat and I had to stop myself from moaning out loud. The hint of peppermint at the end really did me in, and I closed my eyes to try and savor the taste. Peppermint hot chocolate. One of my all-time favorite drinks. But how did he know?

I opened my eyes and watched him drinking from his own cup.

"How did you know I liked peppermint hot cocoa? It's not a normal go-to drink."

"Lucky guess." He smirked at me and I couldn't muster the energy to argue as I took another drink of my heaven in a cup. It was the best cup of cocoa I'd had in a long time. I couldn't afford fancy Starbucks on my budget, and even the Swiss Miss packets just don't compare to actual peppermint syrup and a professional-grade machine.

Jonah gestured to the table in the corner of the room. "Why don't we sit and get started. We have a lot to do."

I nodded and set my stuff down before sitting. "Thank you for the cocoa," I said quietly, smiling.

Jonah looked up and our eyes met, freezing us both in place. "Of course."

As I looked into his bright baby blue eyes, a small prickle of aware-ness settled in the back of my mind. I studied his face openly, brazenly even, and I couldn't help but feel like I was missing something. His dark hair, his smile, the way he carried himself. I couldn't put my finger on it.

I mentally shook the ridiculousness away. I was totally losing it.

"So," I started, breaking the spell. "I was able to think a little more about our project last night."

Jonah nodded.

"Well, your idea of having the perfect Christmas dinner set up sounds great, but it also sounds sterile. I think we need to add more of a realistic feel to it."

Jonah nodded again.

Just like that, we started brainstorming and sketching out ideas for the rest of the day. As the 5 o'clock hour rolled around, we were still not 100% set on our plans.

"Ugh!" I groaned in frustration. "Why can't we figure this out?"

I had lost Jonah. He was staring out at the snow that was beginning to cover New York in a silent, white blanket. Unfortunately for him, I wasn't in the mood for spacing out ,and watching him just sit there made my blood boil.

I stood and placed my hands on my hips. "Um, hello? Earth to Jonah?"

He snapped his head towards me, his sudden movement taking me by surprise. "That's the first time you've ever called me by my real name."

"Geez, sorry. I didn't realize it was taboo." I rolled my eyes exaggeratedly.

Jonah never broke his eye contact with me. "Let's go ice skating."

CHAPTER 7

JONAH

*M*y name on her lips. It was like heaven had opened up and God's angels were singing sweet angelic music in my ear. She had always called me Jay before, just like my parents, and more recently she was stuck on Mr. Cross. But it was never Jonah.

She was still giving me the 'WTF' look after I suggested we go ice skating, and there was no doubt in my mind that I could sit and watch her expressions all day and be completely content.

"Well," I said, trying to sound confident and not at all like the words were just blurted out "you kind of hate Christmas right now, so why don't we try to get back some of that Christmas love? It might allow you to break through your creative block for this shoot."

I was spouting off complete nonsense, but she didn't seem to notice.

She moved from one foot to the other while she pondered the idea. Her silence was brutal, and I felt like I was at a guillotine just waiting for the blade to come down.

"It's my only night off this week." She looked down at her feet, a blush creeping over her skin. "I planned to just go home and sleep."

I jumped out of my seat a little too enthusiastically. "I'd say that settles it then. Let me take you ice skating and buy you dinner. To, you know, get your creative juices flowing once again."

Aria sighed, seeming to finish her come to Jesus moment, "Fine. But it means nothing. Just two co-workers needing to get this shoot design finalized."

We grabbed our stuff and were out the door. Rockefeller Center was just a block away, but it didn't make it any less cold of a walk. We hunched down and made our way through the sea of people.

"Any particular requests for dinner?" I asked as we waited for the crosswalk to signal our turn.

Aria thought for a moment, scrunching her face up in thought. "Why not stop in for a burger at Bill's?"

I smiled. That sounded just like her. Nothing fancy-schmancy for this girl. Living away from home hadn't changed her too much, it would seem. "Sounds great."

It was only about a five-minute walk, but we were both shivering from the cold by the time we stepped into Bill's Bar and Burgers. We had beaten the dinner rush and were seated right away at a cozy little two-top in a back corner.

A cute waitress came up to our table. "What would you two like to drink?" she asked.

"Do you have Sam Adams Winter Lager on tap?" I asked, scanning the menu.

"We do. Small or large?"

I glanced up at Aria. "Large, please. I have to remember how to ice skate in the very near future."

Aria smirked, trying to hide her laugh. "You know, I'll have the same, please."

The waitress nodded, and we went back to sticking our noses in the menu, both hiding our smiles.

As we looked over our menus, I allowed myself to sneak a peek at Aria. Her dark blond hair was tucked behind her ears as her grey eyes scanned the selection. She had put makeup on this morning, more than she had yesterday, but it looked natural and beautiful.

This was the first time we were truly alone since we were kids. Not that she seemed to realize who I was yet. But us being together again brought warmth to my chest, a feeling that I hadn't experienced in years. Or, more accurately, since I gave her that keychain twelve years ago.

Too soon the waitress was back, dropping off our beers and taking our orders.

Aria took a sip of her beer, wiping the foam from her lips before I could poke fun at her. We chatted easily, falling into a comfortable conversation. She had always been easy to talk to, and it seemed that hadn't changed either. Only her love of Christmas seemed to be the one major difference between adult Aria and my childhood Aria. That, and she grew into the attitude she had sported as a kid.

"So, when was the last time you made it home to see your parents?" I asked, wanting to learn more about her life now without seeming like a creep.

She sighed. "Too long. It's been about five years, I'd say. I just..." She paused, a look of genuine anguish flashed over her face.

"It's okay, you can tell me," I pressed

"I can't afford it, okay? I work three jobs right now to keep my head afloat and I just can't spot the extra cash to take the train up to my parents."

"Three jobs?"

She nodded. "Yeah, I just quit my call center job to work this one with People. I also work at a bar, and I pick up shifts cleaning houses with my neighbor when she needs an extra hand, or when I'm strapped for cash and desperate."

I tried to hide my surprise. Who knew she was working so hard just to have two pennies to rub together, meanwhile I'm over here just coasting through life trying to keep myself from being bored. It made me feel guilty, and more in awe of Aria than I had been before. She had always been a strong person; she could handle anything, but I never imagined she'd be handling this, and doing it alone.

"Your parents won't help you?"

"Of course they would!" she said instantly. "But I refuse to ask them. I'm not their responsibility, and I'm the one that moved away."

Our food was placed in front of us and I ate without tasting much, processing the new information.

"So," I said between bites of my burger, "does that have anything to do with your scrooge attitude?"

She shrugged her shoulders noncommittally. "Probably. It doesn't make you feel good when you can't spend money to go see your parents or buy them the gifts they deserve. It also doesn't make you feel good when you can't even partake in most of the celebrating. I don't have cable to watch movies, and I even stopped getting a tree because I couldn't put anything under it, and that extra thirty bucks came in handy. It just stopped being fun."

Again, we fell into silence and I mulled over her words. Christmas was no longer fun for her. Well, we would be changing that. She had me now, and now that we found each other after twelve years meant our fates were intertwined.

We finished up our meals with lighter conversation. I skirted around a lot of her personal questions about myself, not wanting to give too much away. I wasn't ready to come clean about who I was just yet. My alter ego felt like a shield of protection, and I wasn't ready to let it go just yet. When I did, I knew it would be over for me and I'd fall for this girl completely.

Down at the ice rink, I rented our skates and we strapped ourselves onto the blades with the anticipation of children. I hadn't skated since I vacationed at her parent's bed and breakfast but with my adrenaline pumping, I was more excited than I thought I would be.

Our first few laps around the rink were rough for both of us, but it didn't take long for either of us to find our groove and soon we were skating like pros. I watched as Aria unwound next to me. Her body relaxed and she threw her head back to laugh at my clumsiness when I fell. She was becoming *my* Aria before my very eyes, and I couldn't look away. I was completely entranced.

Unable to stop myself, I reached over and took her hand in mine. Aria looked up at me, startled, but then rewarded my boldness with a smile as she interlaced her fingers with mine. Warmth spread all over my body from her touch.

When did I become bewitched by this girl? For years I never felt anything for another woman, and now I felt like a teenager going through puberty. But there was only one simple answer: it had always been her. No one else could penetrate the space in my heart because it was already occupied by the girl who I promised to marry when I was sixteen years old.

Soon, our session was over and we made our way off the ice. I didn't want to say goodbye, I *couldn't* say goodbye yet. So I offered to ride with her in the cab to her apartment, promising her my apartment wasn't too far away. It was a complete lie. My apartment was in the opposite direction.

I had to stop myself from reaching for her as she climbed out of the cab. I was screwed. I was wound so tight around this girl's finger and she had no idea.

But a 'thank you,' a wave, and one of her sweet smiles was all I got from her. That was enough. For now.

I had a promise to keep, and I intended to follow through.

CHAPTER 8

ARIA

*L*ast night was unexpected. Unexpected in a good way, and unexpected in a kind of amazing way. I hadn't expected to have as much fun as I did, and spending time with Jonah turned out to be easy and enjoyable. Easy like two old friends just picking up where they left off after years of being apart. It was odd how comfortable I felt with him after knowing him for such a short time. If I believed in all that past life stuff, I'd wager we knew each other before.

If Jonah's goal was to jump-start my love for Christmas, it was working. I woke with a smile on my face, feeling well-rested for the first time in a long while. I even hummed a Christmas carol or two in the shower. Our little excursion had also given me a few ideas for our photo shoot.

Arriving at the office, Jonah greeted me once again with a cup full of delicious peppermint hot cocoa.

I smiled, "Thank you. You know you don't have to keep bringing me cocoa."

"I know," He said, returning my smile. "I enjoy sharing my morning coffee with you."

My heart did a weird skip thing, but I didn't dare dwell on it. It was Wednesday morning, and our prints were due Friday.

I sat down at our brainstorming table ready and extremely eager to get to work. It was funny to me how I had become eager to work on a project I was dreading just two days ago.

"So," I said, flashing my I've-got-a-plan devious smirk. "I think I've come up with the best idea yet for this shoot."

"Oh?" Jonah said, lifting his eyebrows. "Let's hear it."

"So, my parents run a bed and breakfast and one of our favorite times is Christmas. Our customers love coming in for the holidays because my family does such a good job of making the home comforting, cozy, and homey for Christmas. My mom goes all out for our dinners leading up to the big holiday, and everything is just--" I paused, unable to explain it.

"Magical. Like anything could happen."

"Yes, exactly."

How did he know exactly what I was trying to say?

I cleared my throat to keep my voice from cracking. "So, I suggest we incorporate homey, cozy, magical Christmas into this shoot along with showcasing the holiday's latest and greatest. Let's set up a table full of Christmas dinner on nice china, but keep the rest of the decor homely. By bringing in a more traditional, lived-in feel, we can keep the photos from feeling sterile. Then we can set up a Christmas tree next to a warm and cozy fireplace, get some nicely wrapped presents to set under the tree. We can decorate the tree and mantle with exclusive decorations from our sponsors. Stockings, garland, and beautiful ornaments, all with the feel of home. What do you think?"

I was sitting on the edge of my seat after explaining my pitch and I could see the excitement behind Jonah's eyes. I didn't need to ask how he felt. This was it. This was our shoot.

"It's perfect."

I smiled proudly. "Then let's get started."

We spent the rest of the day pulling props and setting up our cozy but sleek displays. We ended up working until six, and I had to call my boss at the bar and tell them I wasn't going to make it in tonight or tomorrow night. It was worth it though; this shoot was turning out perfect.

Jonah surprised me again as I put on my coat and grabbed my purse.

"Don't be mad," he started, "but I made plans for us tonight, too."

I rolled my eyes. Anytime anyone said 'don't be mad,' it meant they did something that warranted that exact response.

"Okay, and they are?"

Jonah pursed his lips together. "It's a surprise," he glanced down at his watch, "and one that should be showing up at your apartment in about twenty minutes. We should go."

Was he for real? "Jonah, I don't know--" I didn't get to finish my sentence before he grabbed my hand and pulled me toward the door, a huge smile spread across his face.

He looked so excited about whatever it was, and I didn't have the heart to crush that smile. Not only that, but his hand in mine felt like home. Like a missing puzzle piece to the chaos that was my life. I sighed and let him lead me to a cab.

When we pulled up outside my apartment, a delivery truck was there. Jonah greeted them immediately and gave them directions on where they would be putting "the goods."

It wasn't until the gentleman opened his delivery truck that I realized what was going on. Jonah had brought a tree--a beautiful Christmas tree--to my apartment.

I had no words as I unlocked my door and told the men where I wanted them to set up the tree. I stood there, mouth open, as I watched them work. I felt Jonah next to me, supervising their work and letting them know at which angle the tree looked best. Next, they brought in plastic totes, but they just set those on the floor next to the tree.

Then, they were gone. Just like that. Leaving behind the most amazing smelling tree in all of New York.

"Jonah, this is too much."

"Nonsense. I didn't have a chance to decorate my apartment this year so I figured we could do it together at your place where you'd appreciate it more than me anyway." Jonah started to open the plastic totes and pulled out various decorations. "Although, we should order some take out. I'm starving."

"Fine, but I'm buying this time." It was the least I could do after everything. "And I won't take no for an answer. I can be very stubborn."

Jonah rolled his eyes, "I know. Fine. Then I'll order the wine."

"Wine?"

"Can't decorate for Christmas without some wine! And actually, it's just a friend dropping some off." Jonah chuckled as he continued to pull things from the containers.

We ordered our Chinese takeout and started working on the tree. It wasn't long before we had both the lights and garland up. It was clear Jonah had never decorated a tree before, and after nearly knocking over the tree he decided assisting was better for him. Every brush of his hand on mine, every time our bodies skimmed each other, it pushed my blood pressure up another notch. I was getting used to the irregularity of my heartbeat around Jonah, but a girl could only take so much.

Our food and wine were delivered, and we sat down on my couch to admire our handiwork. My apartment was meager, but it didn't feel rundown. My coffee table was the perfect spot to enjoy our food. The wine Jonah had picked was a sparkling white that fit the taste and spirit of our night. His friend had even brought Christmas sugar cookies for dessert.

After we finished eating, we refilled our wine glasses and began hanging the ornaments on the tree. Everything between us was effortless and pleasant. In fact, after that first day of work we got along better than I ever would have expected. The lingering glances and constant closeness of our bodies told me he felt the same way. There was no need to pretend to be anyone other than who I was, and that was liberating.

After putting the finishing touches on the ornaments, we stepped back to see the finished product.

"It's beautiful," I said, slightly in awe.

"Yes, you are."

I looked over at Jonah and rolled my eyes before giving him a gentle elbow to the side.

He laughed as he turned toward me. "So, we've checked off ice skating, decorating a tree, peppermint hot cocoa, and I think listening to that awful couple singing at the rink counts as hearing carolers. What's next?"

I paused to think. "Christmas movies." I glanced at the clock, it was after 10 PM. "Well, I guess we don't really have time for that."

"Of course we do!" Jonah declared, plopping down on my couch again. He leaned over and refilled our glasses of wine before sitting back and getting comfortable. If that man didn't make it in the photography world, he could make a living as a couch model. He looked so at ease with his dress pants and loosened dress shirt. I'd buy the couch in a heartbeat.

I sat down next to him and turned on my TV. I only had streaming capabilities, but I was able to find a movie we both agreed was our favorite. I grabbed my blanket off the back of my couch and got comfortable.

I didn't wake when Jonah got up and tucked me in on the couch or when he picked up our mess. I didn't stir when he placed a kiss on my forehead before he locked up on his way out.

CHAPTER 9

JONAH

oday was the day. I decided it was time to come clean to Aria about who I was. I had stopped at every gas station and trinket store on my way into work this morning to find an almost identical keychain to the one I had given her all those years ago.

I greeted her once again with her peppermint hot chocolate, and I couldn't help the butterflies in my stomach as I thought of how this day might go.

We had a lot to do though and we needed to put the finishing touches on the shoot. Tomorrow morning, we would have our gear and do the actual shooting and spend the editing before turning in our final photos before close of business.

The day went by in a whirlwind, but that didn't stop the butterflies from turning into eagles by the time 5PM came around.

We had set up a gas fireplace display and set up the space around it very similar to what Aria's parents' den at the bed and breakfast looked like. I don't know if she realized it yet or not, but Aria associated her childhood home with her happiness. The more she pulled away from home, the more troubled she seemed. She needed that place and her parents in her life more than she knew. Not only did the setup break Aria of her Christmas Scrooge-ness, but it also created the perfect place for me to come clean. To tell her who I really was.

I had asked Aria to run down for some bogus errand. I didn't have much time, but then I didn't need much time.

I set up a blanket on the floor in front of the fireplace, turned on the Christmas tree, and set out our cups of cocoa. Everything we had had that night so long ago.

I sat down on the blanket and waited.

A few minutes later, I heard Aria's footsteps and then her voice. "Well that was a waste of time. Mark didn't even know what I was talking about."

I chuckled to myself. "Aria? Can you come in here for a second please?"

"Sure, I--" She stopped as she stepped into the room. "What are you doing?"

I tapped the spot on the blanket next to me. "Come sit?"

Aria narrowed her eyes, but her legs moved anyway. She folded herself slowly on the blanket, still skeptical about the whole thing.

"Jonah. What is this?" Her eyes darted around her, picking up the subtle similarities I would imagine.

I handed her a cup of cocoa "I have something for you." I began to pull the keychain out of my pocket that I had wrapped so terribly in Christmas wrapping--again--when I saw the first tear fall down her cheek.

"I..."

"Just open it."

Her tears were flowing freely, my only indication that she had finally figured it out. These last couple of days had been the best days of my life. This was why the two of us went together so well, and why it was so easy to fall back into our relationship once again.

Aria's hand shook as she peeled back the paper. "You really are terrible at wrapping."

I couldn't help the laugh that escaped. It was like I was reliving that night twelve years ago.

Finally getting the keychain free, she closed her eyes, the metal camera hanging from her hand. Her shoulders shook slightly, and I couldn't take the silence anymore.

"Aria, I..."

She flung herself at me, wrapping her arms around my neck. I nuzzled my nose into her hair, breathing in the scent of her. This was all I needed: Aria, in my arms and in my life.

When Aria did finally pull away, she wiped the tears from under her eyes "How did you know?"

"The day you spilled your purse, I saw the original keychain."

She chuckled. "It was supposed to be my good luck charm."

I tucked a loose strand behind her ear. "I'd say it worked."

"But I thought your name was Jay?"

"Just a nickname my parents use. You picked up on it and I never thought to correct you. It made me feel like you were closer to me." I grabbed her hand, caressing the back of it with my thumb. "Aria, I have never forgotten about you and our promise. These past twelve years have been lukewarm without you in my life. I knew at sixteen we were fated to be together, and now that we have each other, I couldn't handle letting you go again."

Aria nodded. "You have always been the piece I needed to feel whole again."

"I have something else for you." I pulled my hand away as I pulled a small box out of my other pocket. Her eyes widened in surprise.

"It's not what you think. I mean, I intend to uphold my promise, but I figure we should at least date a little before any proposals are made. We only just found each other again, but... "

I snapped open the box and it did indeed have a ring nestled inside. I took the ring out, a small diamond surrounded by a diamond halo, and slid it onto her ring finger. "This is a promise ring. Last time I promised on a keychain, and now I'm a big boy who can afford something a little nicer. With this ring, I promise our future, our happiness, and everlasting love."

Aria's tears were once again flowing down her cheeks as she looked deep into my eyes. "I love it. Thank you."

"There is one more thing."

I pulled a sprig of mistletoe out from under the corner of the blanket and held it up between us. Heat blossomed as we leaned in close, our lips touching softly at first, then harder as our kiss deepened. I dropped the mistletoe and ran my fingers across her wet cheek and into her hair, pulling her closer.

Aria broke the kiss suddenly, holding my gaze. Her grey eyes shined with feeling and life, so different from the eyes I saw just a few days ago.

"I've always loved you, Jay, ever since that night. You stole my heart under the mistletoe, and you've had it ever since."

"And you've had mine."

I pulled her back into my arms, showing her just how much I loved her with my kiss.

CHAPTER 10

ARIA

*T*he shoot had run so smoothly that I was anxiously waiting for disaster to strike somewhere. Jonah and I were able to get great shots of a 'Perfect Christmas,' and Ms. Smith ate up the final prints. She was so happy with our photos that she jumped up and hugged us both. I couldn't help but hug her back. She had given me so much more than she would ever know.

We decided to end our night in front of our Christmas tree watching Christmas movies and eating take out again.

I took another sip of my wine and snuggled deeper into Jonah's side. I couldn't remember the last time I had felt so incredibly happy. So content.

"I have another surprise for you."

I chuckled. "I don't know what you could possibly give me at this point since you have already given me everything I need, but shoot."

"I booked us a vacation."

I raised an eyebrow, urging him to keep going.

"At your parent's bed and breakfast."

That got me. "What?"

"For Christmas."

Emotions bubbled up inside and caught in my throat. Tears threatened to spill and I couldn't seem to form any real words. This man was everything. He knew what I needed most and made sure I had it. So, I did the only thing I could to let him know how thankful I was.

I kissed him.

ABOUT THE AUTHOR

N. Terry has always been passionate about writing, creating stories as a little girl and into adulthood. She also enjoys reading and crafting in her very little free time.

N. Terry is a military spouse and happily married to her biggest supporter for over 10 years. They have two sons together and two fur babies, a Calico and Bengal cat. Their family enjoys spending time traveling and exploring when they can.

facebook.com/authornterry

THE SMALLEST OF GIFTS

BY K. MCCOY

CHAPTER 1

THE HOPEFUL CROWD

*W*atching as the people shuffled around her in the chilly afternoon weather while she took a sip of her warm honey and ginger tea, Jetti tried to stop the corners of her mouth from turning upward as she sat across from her lunch date, Ricardo, at the outdoor cafe.

The change in weather--from the crisp orange and brown leaves to soft white snow--was quite possibly her favorite time of the year since deciding to make Krakow, Poland, her home away from home two years ago.

After finishing up another productive lunch date, Jetti felt rejuvenated.

I cannot wait to see this finished product! I just know that it is going to be amazing when it goes to print next quarter, she thought as she began to bounce her crossed leg excitedly at the table.

"You know, it has been a few weeks since you and Ximena have met to catch up, has it not?" he asked while finishing up his espresso.

Ricardo then cradled the tiny cup into both of his calloused hands and carefully placed it back to rest on its matching serving plate before he continued.

"We would love it if you stopped by our holiday party this weekend. You know what they say: the more, the merrier. Right?" Ricardo asked.

Jetti's foot halted mid-bounce, and she slowly brought it back to the ground after hearing the invite that she was hoping to avoid today.

Seeing the hopefulness in Ricardo's eyes only made Jetti feel more like a grumpy Grinch as she began to turn down the offer.

"Thanks, but I do not think that I would be good company this weekend."

Feeling the subtle glare from his sudden yet thorough assessment of her physical and overall presence, Jetti rushed to add, "And I really do need to recharge my social meter before the new year hits and we are all swamped with work again."

Jetti's smile did not quite reach her eyes, but Ricardo accepted it all the same. As the two slowly stood up from their table, Ricardo reached behind him and picked up his large work messenger bag. Peering at the bag for a second longer than Jetti thought was normal, her friend looked to be mulling a complex thought over in his head before turning his attention back to her with one of his classic Cheshire cat grins.

So, he is not going to keep trying to sway me into going to their party? she asked herself hopefully.

"If you say so, mi amiga."

Hearing Ricardo speak again and confirming her last thought made Jetti's day even brighter.

Once the bag was securely placed over his shoulder, Ricardo held out his arms and grinned again as Jetti lowered her eyes and timidly walked into his warm bear hug.

Slightly swaying before parting, he chuckled.

"Well, should you change your mind, let me give you our new address. I do not want my Mrs. Claus to be cross with me this close to the big day and all."

Giggling in agreement, Jetti added, "I totally understand. We for sure would not want you to wake up with coal in your stocking this year."

They shared another laugh before Ricardo turned around the thick strap to his messenger bag and unzipped the opening. He reached inside and removed a round object wrapped in gold gift paper. She took the small package from him and began to gingerly remove the wrappings to reveal a shiny, clear bulb ornament with fine cursive script written in blue ink on each side. Jetti's name shimmered on one side while the other had the lovebirds' new home address written on it within a hand-painted, intricate border pattern.

Raising a playful eyebrow his way, Jetti teasingly asked, "What is all this? Are you trying to secure your spot on Santa's 'Nice List' this year or what?"

"I told you, Ximena is really going all out this year for the holidays. She even took extra time off from her last assignment to make these invitational ornaments for everyone."

Hearing that news tugged at Jetti's heartstrings.

Ximena really wants me to be there, she thought.

Seconds before she could tell Ricardo that she had changed her mind and would be happy to show up for their housewarming holiday party, images of everyone else there in the tiny space filled Jetti's thoughts.

She imagined loud laughing,, drinks flowing, and multiple eyes all staring at her minus a plus one.

No way! I cannot deal with that mess again. Sorry, Ximena, but I am just not ready.

Jetti could still recall the stares she saw in the mirror as the lights danced at rapid speed during her last work New Year's Eve party three years ago. She remembered a woman twice her age all but digging her talons into her husband's arm as she threw her head back and laughed with the other women from her creative marketing department. They pointed and shook their heads at Jetti when they thought she would not notice after she excused herself to refresh her drink.

But she did notice.

Because I do not want what they have, do they think that it is okay to behave this way behind my back?

Before she lost her temper--or her holiday bonus--Jetti tracked down her boss and, thanking him for the 'lovely evening,' made a note to start looking for a new job elsewhere as soon as possible. As luck would have it, her passport had arrived the next week, and she took it as a sign from the universe to finally start traveling around the world like she had always dreamed of when she was growing up.

No way can I continue to work around these people and pretend not to know what they really think of me. They must think that I am some freak to show up to a place like that without a partner, especially since everyone else there is romantically attached.

After a few more months of biting her tongue and refusing to go to any other company gatherings, she had squirreled away a little more into her savings and purchased her first one-way ticket to Poland. Jetti had met Ximena at The Dark Elixir Coffee Shop soon after her arrival in Krakow, and the two had hit it off instantly!

Their shared passion, love of traveling, and encouraging others to see the world led them to work together on a small company's freelancing campaign that same year. Ricardo, that company's Public Relations Manager, was smitten with Ximena from day one, and Jetti worried his feelings for Ximena would soon affect their new work relationship. Over time, as she saw that they did not, her fears of working with more people who would only shun her privately were slowly swept away.

As much as she loved collaborating on projects with the two, she still struggled to accept their offers of going out to social events, so much so that she finally had to share with them what happened at her last company gathering. They understood, and the trio reached an agreement: they would only mention networking events to her, and if Jetti could attend, she would let them know. They never brought up the subject again, and Jetti was thankful for that.

The holidays were now the one time a year where she could feel them wanting to invite her to non-work-related events, but the two never did.

Until now.

Jetti could feel her heart tighten while envisioning herself having to entertain the group of folks with her 'happily single routine.' She quickly shook the images out of her head before bringing her full attention back to Ricardo.

Seeing and catching up with Ximena will have to wait until the new year, I suppose.

Trying to take the focus of the conversation off of her, Jetti held up her invitational ornament and tapped it gently with her index finger, watching it lightly twirl and shine from the tealights surrounding the cafe.

"I love this little guy! As soon as I get back to my place, I will make room for him on my tree."

She stared at Ricardo again, noting how his eyes softened as he looked at the ornament within her hand.

Ximena is never far from his thoughts. I am really happy for them.

And Jetti meant it.

Just because she was happy not having a partner did not mean that Jetti wanted her friends to be without one in their lives.

"Please thank the missus for me. It really is a wonderful invitation," Jetti told Ricardo once more.

"I will, but you know you could tell her yourself in person. Just say that you will be at our house tomorrow and wear something glittery and super festive."

Of course he would not give up on me that easily. Not with the possibility of making Ximena happy on the line.

Jetti beamed up pleasantly at her friend.

"How about this: I promise to wear my best festive sweater when I call to send you two all of my love by video chat this weekend," Jetti replied.

Ricardo wrapped her up into another hug, this time kissing Jetti on her forehead before he let her go.

"Alright. You take care of yourself, okay?"

"Always," she replied before the two went their separate ways.

Before calling it a day, Jetti made sure to pick up some groceries on the way to her apartment. With the biggest day of December only hours away, she knew that this weekend everything would be closed, and she needed to stock up for her action-packed streaming weekend.

Taking the stairs two at a time, Jetti was almost breathless when she reached her apartment and let herself inside. After putting away her food and ordering her holiday evening meal from the new soul food restaurant in the neighborhood, Jetti showered and put on her favorite onesie.

Smiling and content to be alone in her cozy apartment, Jetti turned on the decorative lights covering her miniature tree and watched as hues of pink, gold, green, and blue lit up the walls. Remembering her gift from earlier, Jetti retrieved the tiny ornament, making sure to hang it with care just below the mahogany angel that sat on the top of the tree.

She stood back and looked at her tiny tree in awe.

It is not the biggest or brightest, but as far as Jetti was concerned, it was just right for her.

Feeling the need to share this moment with her online friends, Jetti took out her phone and snapped a picture to post to her favorite social media account.

A short message was all that was needed in the caption, and it was all Jetti had time to type. The doorbell rang, and she suspected her food delivery was waiting for her on the other side.

"Great gifts do not need to be grand, for even the smallest ones can say so much. Thank you, XR!"

Jetti spent the next few hours streaming her favorite seasonal movies and sipping mulled wine over her ever-so-yummy holiday mini-feast. Just as she began to turn off her laptop and call it a night, an idea came to her.

It had been some time since she had played it, but Jetti was sure that with a quick refresher, she still could remember the classics. Or at least Ximena's favorites.

Making her way into her tiny bedroom, Jetti went to the closet and pulled a soft baby blue gig bag from the top shelf.

"Well, hello there, Fretter. It has been far too long since our last session."

Sitting on her bed, Jetti unzipped the gig bag and saw that her cherry oak ukulele was just as fine as the day she bought it from Stings and Things.

After a quick tuning, she strummed it lightly to check the sound. The stings echoed harmoniously throughout the room, putting a twinkle in Jetti's eyes.

She was going to love this. Jetti just knew it!

Excitement shot from the crown of Jetti's head to the tips of her toes as she leaped from the edge of her bed and grabbed her laptop. While waiting for it to come back to life, she thought back to all the songs that Ximena would put on repeat last year when the two worked together on a new traveling apparel campaign. As her computer lit up, so did her eyes as she remembered one key detail from that time.

Oh, Dios mio! Almost all of those songs were in Spanish!

Refusing to let a little language barrier stand in the way of her plan, Jetti logged in and quickly typed in the name of the first song that she could remember. As the soft strings and the performer's voice filled her room, the memories of that time spent working and getting to know her close friend and Ricardo kept her up practicing each song.

Before long, Jetti could see the beginning of a new day outside her bedroom window. The warm orange and blush-like hues were steadily beginning to spread across the sky. Exhausted, she finally put down her ukulele to fully take in the view.

Jetti was so glad that she recorded the last few tracks before noticing this. She would be even happier to be able to share these cover songs with Ricardo and Ximena! Getting comfier in her bed, Jetti uploaded the recordings to her email account and sent them to Ximena's primary email address before shutting off her laptop again.

Before the sun had made its grand entrance from behind the clouds, Jetti's head had already made contact with her favorite fluffy pillow, and she grinned as she drifted off into a well-needed sleep.

CHAPTER 2

THOSE SERENDIPITOUS SURPRISES

*X*imena felt as though she was walking on air. Her Saint Nick really made all this happen today, and Ximena could not be happier! She stared at Ricardo with adoring eyes as he ushered guests into their new home.

Thinking back to when they first met, she still could not believe how everything turned out now. She had almost missed this blessing. She was glad that Jetti had convinced her to stay in Poland and to give freelancing another try.

* * *

WHEN XIMENA first arrived in Krakow, everything was one big adventure after the next. Until she was unexpectedly let go from her job and then couldn't find work elsewhere. Her family back in the States, worried about her well being, started to tell Ximena that maybe it was time to come home. All her friends were quick to remind her how the market for expats in the popular city was simply too saturated, but Ximena was not one to quit when things got tough. She decided to try her hand at freelancing with her digital art degree. When that did not work out as she had hoped, Ximena had to get real about her situation.

So, as she was sipping coffee on what she had thought would be her last visit to her favorite coffee shop, The Dark Elixir, Ximena fought the tears that threatened to fall. Why did things have to end this way for her?

Grabbing a napkin to catch a tear that was about to slip down her face, Ximena spotted Jetti.

It had been some time since she had seen another foreigner, and this woman's cherry and midnight-blue smattering of shoulder-length locs caught her eye. Ximena listened as the woman softly ordered her drink in Polish. Ximena hoped that the woman would have better luck in Poland than she had.

Getting up from her seat, Ximena reached to grab her bag. As she turned around, she found herself face to face with the stranger she had been admiring only moments ago. The two gasped, but when Jetti smiled at her, Ximena returned it in kind.

"Hola! Lo siento, señorita."

In Poland of all places, hearing her mother tongue was what set off the onset of tears that Ximena had managed to keep at bay all day.

This stranger probably thought Ximena was crazy! Why was she crying over something like this anyway?

Instead of leaving her in the middle of her sob fest as expected, Ximena was shocked to feel soft, comforting hands rubbing in a circular motion in the middle of her back.

"Was my Spanish that bad?"

Ximena opened her eyes and found this stranger's kind ones staring back at her, with a tiny smirk pulling at the corners of her lips. Seeing this made Ximena smile again. She cleared her throat and spoke.

"No, your Spanish was not too bad. But your Polish..." Seeing the woman giggle made Ximena laugh as well.

"My name is Jetti," the woman introduced herself.

"Ximena. It's nice to meet you."

"You too, Ximena. Are you leaving now, or can I join you?" Jetti asked.

If she only knew, Ximena thought to herself.

She then remembered her landlord had said that they would not be able to pick up her keys until later that afternoon. Ximena reminded herself that she could stay a little longer before answering Jetti.

"I can join you for tea."

* * *

THE TWO TALKED over tea and tears, and along the way, they became the best of friends. Combining their talents and connections in a country far away from their homes, Ximena and Jetti became known as the freelance travel media tag team, the ones everyone wanted to work with in Krakow.

Then came her insanely charming Ricardo, and soon so much more. Gently caressing her stomach, Ximena thought her heart would burst from the news she received during her doctor's visit yesterday.

I can not wait to tell him the news tonight!

She was so caught up in how she wanted to share the news with Ricardo, she was surprised when her husband casually strolled up behind her and wrapped her into his embrace.

"I would love to know what you were thinking about just now. Everyone says that you are just giddy with the holiday spirit, but I know you, my gordita. What is really on your mind?" Ricardo asked.

Ximena leaned into his chest and smiled. "I was thinking about you and how we got here."

Not easily convinced, Ricardo pressed on further. "Really? Is that all that is on your mind?"

Of course he knows there is more. I did not marry him just for his good looks, Ximena thought while shaking her head.

"I was also thinking of our work wife." Ximena sighed. "Before making her invitation, I prayed that she would say 'yes.' But it seems that I got all the miracles I was allowed this year."

Feeling her husband kiss the top of her head as the two swayed back and forth slightly, Ximena closed her eyes and listened to Ricardo's rich tenor voice vibrate soothingly against her back.

"I tried. And for a second, after I gave her the ornament, I thought we had succeeded in getting her to come today. But you know how she feels about these kinds of get-togethers."

Ximena squinted, and heat flooded her nostrils as she thought about what Jetti told them a year ago.

"I wish I could have seen those hyenas myself! Making Jetti feel like crap because she is happy and unattached. I would waste no time at all clawing out each of their eyes--"

Hearing Ricardo's chuckle caused Ximena to stop talking as she pulled away to look up at him.

"Just what is so funny?" she demanded.

Ricardo tried to bring her back into his arms, but she swatted him away and pouted.

"You say that every time this topic comes up, so much that Jetti can mimic your little speech from memory by now."

Arching an eyebrow at this new information, Ximena stared hard at her husband. "So, you and Jetti mimic me during your little work lunches? I knew that I should have gone with you this time! I know for sure that she would be here right now if I had."

Imagining Jetti chatting and laughing merrily with others interrupted Ximena's mini-rant. Ricardo must have known where her mind went to as he took her hands into his, kissing each of them gently.

"It is okay. She is okay. I promise," he reassured her.

Not trusting herself to speak as she now felt both her nose and throat begin to sting, Ximena only nodded.

"Hija! Hija!"

Ximena could make out her mother's shrill voice anywhere and almost hid behind Ricardo from the sound. Before she got the chance to try, her mother quickly approached them, waving her phone in the air.

"Your phone is buzzing! Oh, Dios! Just who do you work for that would call you on this day? It is not right, hija!"

Taking her phone, Ximena began to check her messages with Ricardo looking over her shoulder.

"It is from the wifey! Open it already!" Ricardo urged her.

Ximena clicked on the message, and as they read the email together, she could feel her tears threaten to fall once more.

That Jetti! Always doing something to make me cry!

"What does she mean, 'The Spicy Special Seasonal Mix'?" Ricardo asked with a smirk.

Ximena tried not to cry and laugh all at once as the two found space on their couch to sit.

"I almost forgot about that," she replied.

Clearly not satisfied with her answer, Ricardo tilted his head, so Ximena explained.

"Last year, when we worked on the Travel Chic Coolest Campaign, I was feeling super homesick and created a playlist of all my favorite holiday songs. Jetti must have remembered. Now that I think of it, how could she not? I played that playlist almost all day, every day for a week straight."

And she never once complained or said that I was being too extra. Ximena thought back to that time and beamed at those memories. She and Jetti worked around the clock while everyone else was away visiting loved ones. They had food delivered, and Ricardo would show up, cracking jokes as he checked up on them to make sure they were still eating and resting when they needed to.

Looking at him fondly, Ximena let a tear slip from the corner of her eye.

That was when I started falling for him, she silently admitted.

"Well, if you are already crying, we should watch these clips, huh?" Ricardo joked.

Ximena nodded and pressed play on the first video. The two held each other close as Jetti's face showed up on the screen, with the ukulele that Ricardo had talked her into buying a year ago.

Hola mi amors!

Thank you, Ximena, for such a thoughtful gift.

After I got home, I realized that I did not get you two anything this year. And I know that if I called you right now and said that, you two would say something oh-so cheesy about how I do not have to give you two anything.

. . .

THEY CONTINUED to watch the screen as Jetti straightened her back and started to mimic Ximena.

YOU GIVE me the gift of friendship all year; what else could I possibly accept better than that? How did I do that time, Ricardo?

XIMENA SAW Ricardo doing his best not to laugh as the video continued.

SO PLEASE ACCEPT THESE PERFORMANCES, from the bottom of my heart to both of yours.

Thank you for being my friends, the best colleagues ever, and just the most all-around awesome people that a girl like me could ever ask to have in my life.

I LOVE YOU BOTH.

Happy Holidays!

THE FIRST CHORDS were a little slower than the original, but hearing Jetti singing with her whole heart in Spanish, Ximena's all-time favorite song warmed her inside and out. This time, she did not bother with wiping her face as the tears fell quickly. The room grew quiet, and the sound from her phone was heard by more people than just her and Ricardo.

"Hija! Who is that singing?" Her mother asked as she stepped around a few guests to get closer.

"My best friend, the one I told you about earlier," Ximena answered, not taking her eyes off of her phone screen.

"Hmmm. She is not too bad. Hija, you have to help her with her R's some time! They are shaky."

Ricardo chuckled loudly, but Ximena was not sure if it was because of what her Mom had just said about Jetti's pronunciation or from the look on Jetti's face in the video after belting out her grito at the end of the upbeat Classic that she chose to cover from Ximena's playlist.

Either way, more people were making their way over to the sound, and soon there was a crowd in front of the two of them, clearly interested in what they were watching on her phone. Before they pressed play on the next clip, Ricardo looked out into the crowd.

"Does anyone know how to connect this phone to the flat screen?"

A few minutes later, the entire house was filled with the sound of Jetti's happy singing and strumming to several more seasonal songs. Some folks were even dancing, while the others simply nodded their heads along as they watched her perform in her bedroom on the couple's TV screen.

Ximena sat on the couch next to her husband, watching the scene around her. She tried to remember the last time she felt so much joy all at once.

Feeling a soft vibration on the couch, Ximena looked at Ricardo as he took his phone out of the back of his jean pocket and looked at the incoming message.

"Our Jetti did not want me to feel left out, I suppose."

Curious, Ximena leaned over to look at the message and broke out into the biggest smile ever.

THANK you for loving my best friend. I think back to when we first met you, and I honestly cannot think of a better man to walk this life's journey with her.

I wanted you to know that I almost said 'yes' when you invited me to the party yesterday. Someday I will, but for now, I want to thank you from the bottom of my heart for accepting and respecting my choice to say 'no.'

Also, I did some online shopping when I woke up this afternoon and thought that I should get you something super fancy.

. . .

"OUR JETTI IS REALLY something else! I have been waiting to try this cologne for a while now. How did she know?"

Ximena saw Ricardo scroll down on his phone to a picture of *Into the Wild*, a well-packaged cologne noted for being full of an earthy yet bittersweet smell. She tried not to let her mind wander recklessly about how delectable he would smell with a splash or two of it on his deep caramel skin when it arrived after the holidays.

Now is not the time for those thoughts, and you know it, hotpants! Especially not with your Mom in the room anyway, Ximena chided herself.

Ricardo kissed her cheek, ridding Ximena of her latest thought.

"She could not resist, could she?"

"Curious," Ximena asked. "What? Is there more?"

Her husband nodded. "For you, not me."

Ricardo handed her his phone and kissed her check as Ximena read the last message from Jetti.

I saw these and just had to buy two pairs; one for me and the other for Ximena. Do you think she will like them?

Ximena stared at the pair of simple yet chic gold hoop earrings that Jetti had bought and could not shake the feeling of blessed fate that came over her.

Screw timing. I will tell him now! She decided.

There is no way I cannot. All the signs are here. Gold, Myrrh, and Frankincense?! But what could they mean...

The name was out of her mouth before Ximena could stop herself. "Jesus!"

Ricardo looked at his wife and laughed. "Come on, Ximena! I know that you are trying to cut back on all your cursing, but do you have to throw His name out in vain right now?"

Ximena shook her head as she stared at her husband, more tears welling up in her eyes.

"No, I did not mean it like that," she said with a calmness that she had never heard in her own voice before.

"Jesus... As in the name of our son." Thinking quickly, Ximena added. "Or Jesusa, if it turns out to be a girl instead?"

Seeing Ricardo stunned into silence, Ximena realized that he was starting to understand what she was trying to tell him.

"Are you saying, th-that you are... Really?"

When she nodded, Ricardo reached for her and pulled her close, covering Ximena in a quick session of sweet kisses, from the crown of her head to Ximena's cheeks before capturing her full lips.

"I knew that you were right about what you said earlier. We got all the miracles that we could have hoped for this year, my sweet gordita," Ricardo whispered gently against Ximena's ear.

The two held each other close as they listened to Jetti sing with soft reverence. She gently fingerpicked the ukulele along to the ballad of how the one they were celebrating that day was brought into the world, and Ximena's heart was beyond full.

With her best friend, husband, and a new addition of love coming into their lives, Ximena knew that no other gifts would ever compare to the ones now etched into her heart.

ABOUT THE AUTHOR

K. McCoy wants to live in a world where the LGBTQA community is allowed to live and thrive in peace. As an Independent Writer, she has just finished her first novella, MAGIX, and is now looking for some-place sunny to celebrate before scheduling her next soap opera and hallyu infused story.

When she is not baking or practicing a new Yoga pose, you can find her writing down new ideas and concepts somewhere sunny or discovering new music online. Visit her online at www.krealmccoy. wordpress.com.

facebook.com/KRealMcCoy
instagram.com/krealmccoy

MIRACLE DAWN

BY MYRIA WILD

MIRACLE DAWN

The glint of fake firelight on an etched crystal snowflake ornament caught Stacy's eye as she wandered silently around the aisles of the Hallmark store. She reached out and gingerly lifted the snowflake from the branch of a giant, forest green plastic tree. The crystal was heavy and cool in her hand as she traced the frosted etchings with one finger.

"What's that?" Cameron asked as he walked up behind her, peering over her shoulder.

"An ornament," she replied simply, her voice barely audible over the sound of "Oh, Christmas Tree" playing on piano in the background. The din of conversation buzzed around them in the packed store.

"It's pretty. Do you like it?" He reached around and flipped over the tag attached to its string. He whistled as he read the price. "So, that's the cost of Swarovski crystal."

"I guess it's all right. Not really my style," she lied. She didn't want him spending any more money on stuff. For a moment, she was thankful her mask hid her face. She wouldn't have to feel guilty for faking a smile. Even though money wasn't a problem for them, it bothered her a little that he had already paid for their entire trip and insisted that she spend her own paycheck purely on self-care. It hurt her heart too much to tell him, but she couldn't think of a single thing she wanted.

Stacy had stopped painting her nails and reserving hair appointments three months ago, rarely making much effort to take care of herself. Any "self-care" beyond the basics like showering and dental hygiene was too much effort. It was all simply too much after her miscarriage.

The physical and emotional pain had dimmed the light in her life, despite Cameron's unwavering love and support. Their April wedding had been a dream come true, but after losing the baby in June, she had struggled to enjoy her time as a newly-wed. Although she could see the deepening lines of worry marring his bright face, Cameron asked few questions.

"Come on," he challenged, his immediate disbelief apparent. "This is exactly your style."

She didn't bother replying as she carefully placed the ornament back on the tree. "Do we have everything we need?"

"We've always had all we needed. I've got you, and you've got me." He pulled her into a hug and kissed her cheek.

"I love you, even when you're corny," she whispered.

It was true. Even if she was emotionally unavailable these past six months, Cameron was still her partner, her best friend, and her guardian. She knew that what they shared was special, and she prayed she could find her passion for life and love again before he started to give up on her.

"Are you sure you don't want anything?"

"I'm sure." She nodded and started to walk out, but he pulled her hand.

"I'm going to grab a few things to decorate our room, okay?"

"Don't spend too much, Cam," she warned. "It's not about things."

"I know, I know," he huffed, rolling his eyes. "How about you grab us some Auntie Anne's for the ride. I'll meet you in the food court after I check out."

Stacy smiled and squeezed his hand before walking away. She was sure he would buy too much, but she hoped she had convinced him not to get the ornament. Truthfully, she loved it, but some part of her fought the idea of actually having the things she wanted. As much as she had wanted the most precious thing life could offer, fate had denied her. Objects were simply lesser things; they didn't have a heartbeat, didn't have a soul, and she didn't *need* them.

She was anxious to get back on the road. They had reached the city of Winchester after a nerve-wracking drive north on I-81 and decided to take a break and stretch their legs. The traffic was brutal, and the roads were wet. After being caught in standstill traffic for two separate accidents, they needed to get out of the car and take a break from the incessant traffic. Unfortunately, the feeling of being surrounded by people was only exacerbated by the crowded mall.

Grinding her teeth, she held herself together as she waited in line at Auntie Anne's. As much as her floral mask increased her anxiety, the prospect of catching COVID was far more frightening to her. When she reached the front of the line, she ordered two pretzels with cheese and honey mustard dips.

She didn't have to wait long. A worker quickly handed her the bag of pretzels and dip, and she smiled under her mask before turning toward the center of the food court.

Cameron stared at her from one of the open tables. He stood as she reached him and lifted too many shopping bags for her liking. Although he wouldn't be able to see her mouth, she knew he would notice her raised eyebrow.

"What's in the bags?" she asked impatiently as she tried to peek.

"Nunya," he replied with a laugh and pulled the bags away from her prying eyes.

"Cam, seriously. You didn't get that ornament, right?"

"Relax," he said before sighing. "I just got a few things to make our stay a little nicer."

Stacy said nothing as she fixed her gaze on her husband, not trusting that he didn't buy a bunch of things they didn't need.

"Let's get back on the road." She hooked an arm in his, her anxiety lessened by their closeness. He kissed the top of her head before leading her out of the mall.

The forty-minute drive to Harper's Ferry from Winchester was far more relaxing than the drive to Winchester from their home near Lewisburg. Once they were finally off of I-81 and driving on the county roads, the traffic was lighter.

Stacy had believed no scenery could surprise her after all she had seen of the Allegheny Mountains. However, she was stunned by the beauty of the drive into Harper's Ferry. The mountain pass featured a highway bridge and rail bridge spanning the Shenandoah River before its confluence with the Potomac River.

Katie, the fiance of Cameron's best friend Clay, had passed through the little mountain town when she had moved from Philadelphia to Fairlea. She had raved about the town's tranquility and natural beauty. So when Cameron brought up the idea of getting away for Christmas, Stacy remembered Katie's experience in Harpers Ferry. It didn't take long to find a B&B in the historic town that could provide parking and was within walking distance of all the shops and restaurants.

It was too far from Fairlea and Lewisburg for anyone to come and bother them for Christmas. Besides, it was a famous historic town in the region, and she had never visited before. More than anything, Stacy wanted a break from the sympathetic looks and prying questions from their friends and family.

There was no better place to lose oneself than somewhere new. Stacy could only pray it would give her the peace she hadn't felt since June.

Joy would be a bonus, but it was a hope she didn't dare count on. She would smile for Cameron because she loved him, but the idea of feeling real joy seemed abominable still, even after all these months.

"Wow," Cameron said, breaking through the blur of Stacy's depressing thoughts. "This place is incredible." He pulled their car into one of the three spots in the parking lot as they examined the bed and breakfast. The grayish stone building seemed to glow in the winter's late afternoon sunlight.

"It's so pretty," she muttered softly as she took in the green garlands strung along the windows and the red and green wreath hung on the blue door. A little sprout of hope sprang up from the depths of her heart, and she wondered if a getaway had been what she needed all along.

Cameron turned off the engine and grabbed her hand, stroking the back of it softly with his gentle thumb. "I hope you love it."

"You picked it, so I'm sure I will," she reassured him, smiling broadly before leaning over to kiss his cheek.

After donning their masks, they grabbed their luggage from the car and locked it. Walking up to the door, they were startled when it opened before they reached it. A tall, middle-aged blonde woman stood in the threshold, a weak smile stretched across her tired face.

"Stacy and Cameron?" she asked.

"That's us," Cameron replied, waving his free hand. Stacy was glad Cameron was extroverted. She struggled when meeting new people, but he easily took the edge off these situations.

"I'm Amanda. It's nice to meet you. I'll show you around and get you settled, but I'm a bit busy. I hope you don't mind." She finally looked to Stacy as if seeking approval.

"That's fine," Stacy said, barely avoiding a stutter as she held the woman's gaze. "It was a long, crazy drive on eighty-one, so I think we're ready for dinner and sleep."

"Great," Amanda replied. "As mentioned during registration, I'll provide breakfast, but I'll need you to fill out your breakfast request as soon as you can. The cards are in your room, on the bed," she explained as she led them inside.

The entryway was small but bright and expertly decorated for Christmas with Santa statuettes, graceful gold reindeer figurines, and miniature ceramic pine trees. As Amanda led them to the right of the entryway, they walked through another threshold, and Stacy spotted the stairs. Green garlands made to look like evergreen boughs were wrapped through the banister and dotted with red, velvet ribbon. Red, gold, and silver bulbs glittered from the greenery, reflecting the light from a fireplace in another room.

"There are a few places open for dinner. I highly recommend the Cannonball Deli; their gyros are delicious."

"I think we'll get settled right quick, and then take you up on that recommendation," Cameron said as they followed Amanda up the stairs.

"I've got three kids, but they'll leave you alone and generally be out of sight."

Stacy caught Cameron's eyes, and they shared a questioning look.

"We don't mind," Stacy said softly as they reached the top of the stairs.

Amanda was quiet as she led them through the tight hallway, stopping at the farthest room. "Well, here it is." She opened the door and gestured inside before passing a key ring to Cameron.

Cam held the door open and let Stacy enter first.

"Thank you," she called over her shoulder before losing sight of their host. She heard Cam thank the woman too before he followed Stacy inside and shut the door.

The room was more spacious than she imagined for a bed and breakfast in a historic building. Dropping her luggage by the dresser, Stacy studied the bed, its four-poster frame stained a deep, chocolate color. Her visual exploration moved to the matching headboard, hand-carved with intricate details.

"It's beautiful," she whispered as she moved closer to examine it.

Cameron laughed. "I'm glad you like it. I guess that means I get a couple brownie points for picking a nice place?" he asked, joining her to look at the carvings on the headboard.

"You guessed right," she said, turning briefly to give him a wink.

After exploring the rest of the room and admiring the antique furniture, they unpacked their things into the dresser in the corner, then completed their breakfast cards before locking up their room and heading back downstairs.

A chorus of children's voices greeted them as they reached the bottom of the stairs. Stacy led the way, following the sounds to a cozy, old-fashioned parlor where she found three children stacking presents under a thick, exquisitely Christmas tree.

"You found us," Amanda said as she walked into the parlor with a silver tray of sugar cookies in hand, holding it out in offering.

It all seemed so surreal, so perfect. It was harder every year for Stacy to hold onto the memories of Christmas with her parents, who had already passed on. Of course, she didn't have siblings like these children did, or like Cameron had.

"Thank you," Cameron said before Stacy could as they each plucked a green, sprinkle-covered, tree-shaped cookie from the tray.

"Are you heading out to explore?" Amanda asked as she set the tray down on a coffee table. The couch beside it was another antique, but it looked perfect for cuddling near the fireplace with Cameron. If they needed anything during their vacation, it was some quiet time together doing nothing.

"Yeah, we're going to walk around, explore the park, and check out some shops. We'll probably get dinner before we come back."

Stacy flipped her wrist and looked at her watch. It was already five o'clock. "Does it matter when we return?"

"Your keys work for the front door too. Just be sure you're closing the door tightly and locking up when you come in. We go to bed around nine, so if you come in late, please try to be quiet."

"Of course," Stacy reassured her, peeking at the woman's children. The little ones were all eagerly whispering their arguments about where they believed each gift should be placed around the tree. "How old are your children?" she asked before she could stop herself, nervously twisting her fingers around each other as she finished her sentence.

"Five, eight, and ten," Amanda said softly as she allowed her gaze to fall on them. Her tired look turned soft and contemplative for a moment as she watched her children. Stacy wondered if the woman was on the verge of a nervous breakdown.

"You have a beautiful family." Stacy smiled broadly as the woman turned back to her, but she watched in sadness as the woman's tired appearance returned at full force.

"Thank you," Amanda replied, her eyes glassy. She started to speak, then shook her head. "Well, if you go to the Cannonball, be sure to tell the guys I sent you."

"We will," Cameron promised. He grabbed Stacy's hand, and she interlaced her fingers with his as they walked out the door and into the crisp winter air.

"It smells like snow," Stacy noted as they followed the sidewalk down the hill and toward the heart of Harper's Ferry.

"No," Cameron argued. "We get snow this time of year down in the mountains by us, or up by Wheeling, but the Panhandle doesn't usually get snow before Christmas. Well, not for the past several years, I think. It's a little too warm here."

"I'll bet you," she challenged.

"Bet me what?"

She shrugged and tried to hide her smirk. "I want to look in all those bags you got at the mall."

"Nope," he enunciated loudly, the word echoing off the weathered bricks of the buildings around them.

"What? Why not?" she pouted.

"I ain't stupid." Cameron laughed and put his arm around her shoulders, hugging her close before kissing her head. "I'll bet what you bet. So if you say it's gonna snow, I guess we'll be makin' snow angels. Betting against you is a trap."

"You're no fun," she chided, but she didn't really mean it.

"The longer you have to wait, the sweeter the surprise'll be."

"You might be right," she conceded with a dramatic sigh before standing on her tiptoes to kiss his cheek.

After a short walk around Harpers Ferry National Historical Park to build a plan for the next few days, they made their way to the Cannonball Deli. The gyros and French fries were delicious, belying the comfortable and relaxed atmosphere of the tiny eatery. When they had finished every last bite, Cameron took their plates up to the counter and ordered ice cream cones.

"Only three more days until Christmas," Cameron observed as he returned. He handed her a small paper bowl filled with her favorite: chocolate chip cookie dough.

Stacy sighed and nodded, taking a bite of the cold, delicious ice cream so she wouldn't have to answer.

"I wanted to make this trip really special for us," he said softly. "For you."

She looked up and found him staring into his mint chocolate chip, his usually bright eyes dimming. Reaching over, she ran her fingers over the stubble on his cheek.

"Hey, don't look so sad. We're here together, and this place is amazing. The room is beautiful, the food is delicious, and I have the most wonderful husband a woman could dream of asking for. It's already special."

His green eyes met hers, and she felt a tingle in her stomach. He still had that effect on her, no matter what she was going through.

"You don't have to pretend you're okay if you're not." He held her gaze and reached out for her free hand, squeezing her fingers gently. "You're not alone anymore. I got you, honey."

She wanted to tell him he was overthinking everything, reading too much into it, but she couldn't bear to look him in the eyes and lie. Her eyes stung as she looked down at the table. She squeezed his fingers in return as the first tear slid down her cheek. There wasn't any strength left in her to hold them back any longer.

Cam didn't wait for an invitation. He sprang from his seat and took the chair beside her before wrapping his arms around her shoulders. Pulling her into his chest, he rubbed her back gently and kissed the tears from her cheeks.

"It's okay," he whispered softly into her hair. "You're going to be okay. We're going to be okay."

Stacy pulled back slightly to look into his eyes. "But what if it happens again?"

"You mean Daniel?" he asked, using the name they had chosen for the son they wouldn't meet until they passed from this life.

She nodded before leaning into his shoulder again.

"How about we walk back now? Let's get some fresh air and head down to the water. There's a beautiful spot, and I'd sure like to catch the sunset with you." He rubbed her back for a second before standing to clean up their table. "Do you still want this?" He gestured to her ice cream.

"I can't eat anymore." She shook her head. Dinner had stuffed her, and the ice cream had already been an indulgence. Once she became upset, her stomach quickly threatened revolt.

She watched as Cameron threw away their cups and thanked the man staffing the counter before meeting her at the door. They walked hand-in-hand to The Pointe, the little stretch of land that jutted out into the Shenandoah River before its convergence with the Potomac. They sat as close to the edge as possible and said nothing as they watched the water. The swift-moving current rushed over and around the various rocks and boulders scattered across the river's shallows.

The sounds of the river before them imparted a calming effect that surprised her. The weight of the year was finally falling on her. All the feelings she had pushed away were now bubbling to the surface, and she couldn't ignore them anymore. She couldn't keep pretending that she was over it, that she had moved on from the loss of the little one they had so desperately wanted to welcome into their lives.

"What if it happens again?" she repeated the question, her mind unable to release the thought from its grasp. She leaned her head on his shoulder and closed her eyes, wishing away the images that flooded her mind's eye.

"Well, that depends. I don't want you to hurt, Stacy. I love you too much to put you through that hell again if you don't want to go through it. But if you did want to try again, I'd be happy that way, too. Either way, I'm with you one-hundred percent."

"What if I can't have kids, Cam? Can a relationship survive that?" she challenged, opening her eyes to stare up at the mountains across the river. To her surprise, he laughed and hugged her.

"Honey, kids are a beautiful gift, but they won't define us. I said I wanted to be with you no matter what. That means I'm here for all of it. I'll be by your side as long as you'll have me, and if you want kids, then we'll keep trying. If you don't, then that's fine too."

"I always wanted a big family," Stacy whispered, frightened she would sob if she said it any louder.

"If you want to, then we'll keep our arms and our hearts open to a baby — or five."

She laughed through her tears and slapped his arm playfully. "I don't want five! Maybe just two or three."

"Does that mean you wanna keep trying?"

The memory of all their hopes dashed, and the pain that ensued screamed in Stacy's memory.

"I'm so scared of failing again," she admitted, snuggling deeper under his arm as she gazed out over the roaring rapids.

"Failing?" he asked incredulously. "Stacy, you didn't fail. Please do not for a second let that word ever come into your head again. Call it fate, or God, or whatever, but it simply wasn't meant to be. We'll never forget Daniel, but you can't let what happened determine the course of the rest of your life. If you want to try again, we have to do it with open arms, knowing the risk and accepting it for the potential reward of growing our family. The doctor said you're fine, right? She's not worried about you trying again?"

Stacy thought it over and shook her head. "She said to mourn and heal emotionally, but there wasn't anything physically wrong with me."

"Then let's heal together, and once you're ready, then we'll talk about it again. I mean, we haven't exactly been careful, but if you want, we can be. Until you're ready to make another decision."

"And you're sure you can live the rest of your life like this?"

"With you? One-hundred percent."

"With this uncertainty, too, Cam. With never knowing if we'll get to have the family that we've dreamed of, that you've dreamed of?"

"I don't want to sound like a hero in a movie, but I never even thought I'd want a family until I met you," he confessed. "I go where you go, and we can foster or adopt if it's too much risk for you. Or, if you want, we can be the cool aunt and uncle that give the best gifts and travel the world with their extra money."

Stacy felt her lips curling into a smile before she could stop it. "That actually sounds like a pretty good deal, too. I've always wanted to go to Morocco."

"Now that sounds like a helluva trip." Cam knelt in front of her and took her hands in his. "Whatever you want, that's what we'll fight for. You don't have to decide anything right now. Heck, life is full of surprises, so we'll never know what could be waiting for us right around the corner. Whether it's babies or international trips, all I know is that I want to be with you through it all."

Stacy threw her arms around his neck and hugged him, nearly toppling them both. The lump in her throat was painful as she fought the tears, denying them purchase on her cheeks until she simply couldn't anymore. They flowed down her cheeks, and she sobbed into Cameron's shoulder as he held her and whispered sweet comfort into her ear.

OVER THE NEXT TWO DAYS, Stacy and Cameron relaxed and unwound, both from the ache of loss and from the daily grind of the life they had left back home. He encouraged her to enjoy the Christmas music playing incessantly in every building in town. They explored the shops, museums, historical buildings, and the scenic spots scattered throughout the tiny village.

The temperature continued to drop. Stacy was praying for snow, but not just because she liked being right. Her fondest memories of Christmas involved family trips to the snow-covered mountain hollows of West Virginia.

As she woke up on the morning of Christmas Eve, she spotted the geometric patterns of frost on the glass just beyond the window curtains. It would snow today; she was sure of it.

Rolling over, she snuggled up to Cameron and kissed his shoulder, anxious for him to awake. She had felt lighter since her revelation and their talk, and she was starting to see the colors again in the world around her. All that had been dim for the past six months became vibrant again. Even her appetite was coming back. It was difficult to see how toxic it had been for her to hold in all the pain of loss, keeping it to herself. It was equally difficult to accept that she could share her pain with someone else, even if he was her husband.

"What time is it?" Cameron groaned as he rolled over and hugged her.

"I have no idea," she whispered, gently scratching his back with her nails.

"Tomorrow is Christmas Day. Are you ready to be blown away by the best gifts you've ever gotten?"

"Sure, honey. Just be ready to bow to the queen of gift-giving."

"Why are you so competitive?" he asked, squeezing her tightly before kissing her on the neck.

"I can't help it," she said as she slipped from his arms and rose from the bed. "Let's get breakfast."

The pair flirted as they got dressed, and Stacy realized she was more in love with Cameron than ever before. Her love had simply grown over time, and she hoped this was what their marriage would look like for the rest of their lives.

As they arrived downstairs and entered the kitchen area, they found Amanda preparing breakfast.

"Good morning," she greeted them, looking up from the stove as they sat down on the barstools at the bar-height island counter.

"Good morning," they returned in unison, giggling like kids afterward.

"Y'all are in a good mood this morning," she observed as she returned her attention to the pancakes and bacon.

"It's Christmas Eve," Stacy replied, unable to stem her own excitement.

Amanda laughed and shook her head. "Well, I hope you have a beautiful day and a wonderful night."

"What will you and the kids do?" Cam asked.

Amanda shrugged as she filled two plates with bacon, eggs, and pancakes. "I'll let the kids open one present each in front of the tree tonight, and then tomorrow--after Santa comes--they can open the rest. I'll make them cookies and hot cocoa tonight and cinnamon buns tomorrow. It's our own little tradition."

"What about you?" Stacy asked. "Will you open something tonight too?"

Amanda shook her head, her smile tight. "The kids weren't able to get me anything this year, and that's okay. Their dad was supposed to take them shopping for me like I take them to shop for him, but he took off for Christmas this year and..." she let her words trail off as she put the plates in front of Stacy and Cameron.

"What?"

"I've said too much. It doesn't matter." Amanda grabbed two sets of silverware wrapped in cloth napkins and set them next to the plates. "Sometimes, once you have kids, you don't get presents for Christmas. But we already know that's not what's important. I have them, and they have me, and I'm lucky. I'm lucky that I get to have them for the holidays this year, instead of spending it alone like I thought I would."

The air felt heavy around them, and Stacy watched helplessly as the woman's eyes glittered, on the verge of tears.

"If you need a break, we can hang out with the kids," Stacy offered, the words spilling out before she had time to think them over. She didn't know too much about kids yet, but she wanted to help.

"I couldn't possibly ask--" Amanda started to say.

"Stacy's right. Let us work on Christmas projects with them, and you go get a nice latte. Just take a little time for yourself," Cameron insisted. Stacy squeezed his hand, grateful they thought so much alike.

"Are you sure?" Amanda asked, gnawing on her bottom lip as she mulled over the possibility. "It *would* give me a chance to get a few more stocking stuffers."

"We're sure." Stacy nodded and offered a gentle smile.

"And you have our driver's licenses, our home address, everything you need to check us out if you need to. We wouldn't want you to worry about them being safe or anything. Just take a little break, get a little treat for yourself, and finish up that shopping."

"That would be incredible," Amanda conceded, a tear escaping one eye and falling down her cheek. "I have them full-time, and I love it, but I don't get any breaks and I'm so tired. There isn't anyone nearby who can watch them, so it's just been me this month. I've had to order everything online because I couldn't even go shopping."

"Go," Stacy insisted, reaching over and squeezing Amanda's hand. "Tell me what projects we can get them started on, and you go do what you need to do."

"Taylor has been begging for a gingerbread house, but I just haven't had time."

"Done," Cameron said between bites of his breakfast. "What else?"

"Breakfast, but they'll probably just want cereal."

"Easy," Stacy responded. "Anything else?"

Amanda sighed as she thought about it. "Anything to keep them busy and off their devices."

"Alright, go on then," Cameron said. "Go get ready, and be sure to tell the oldest--"

"Mason," Amanda informed him.

"Tell Mason that you're letting us hang out with them while you go to the store."

"Wow, this is so unexpected." Amanda paused, studying them both.

"It's the least we can do," Stacy reassured her.

"All right," she said, an excited smile brightening her weary face as she surrendered. "I won't be gone long. I'll just get everything I need right there in Charles Town--including that elusive cup of caffeinated heaven. Then I'll be back, and you two can go enjoy your day."

"Sounds like a plan," Cameron said before returning his attention to the fluffy, warm pancakes he had drenched in West Virginia Maple Syrup.

"Thank you," Amanda said, holding Stacy's gaze. Stacy could feel the woman's gratitude buzzing in the air around them, and it warmed her spirit to know she could do something, anything to help.

After getting ready and letting Mason know she was heading out-- and instructing him to be "gentle" with the guests--Amanda was out the door. Stacy and Cameron listened to her car's engine roar to life as they sipped their coffee and finished their breakfast. It wasn't long before Mason came out, his brown hair brushed, teeth cleaned, and properly dressed for the day.

"Good morning," Stacy greeted him.

"Good morning," he returned, eyeing her and Cameron as he made his way into the kitchen.

"Do you want anything to eat?"

"Cereal. Could you get it out of the cupboard for me, please?"

She was grateful for the boy's good manners. "Sure," she said as she got up to grab it from the cupboard he pointed to. "Anything else?"

Mason shook his head as he took the cereal and poured it into a bowl. As he was getting the milk from the fridge, Stacy looked to Cameron, gesturing with her head for him to say something.

"Are you excited about Christmas?" Cameron asked.

The boy shrugged. "I'm ten already. I know Santa's not real."

"You didn't tell your sisters that, did you?" Stacy asked as she sat down next to Cameron again.

"Of course not. They love Christmas."

"Don't you?" she inquired, worried over the way he didn't seem to want to make eye contact.

Another shrug. "It was fun when I was younger." He paused as he capped the milk and put it away. "When it was all of us," he added softly. She guessed he was referring to his father.

"It looks like your mom put a lot of work into making it special. I hope you can still have fun this Christmas," Stacy offered, eager to change the direction of the conversation.

"Yeah, she's gone all out on these decorations," Cameron agreed.

"She always does," Mason said, smiling proudly before climbing on the stool next to Stacy and sitting down at the counter.

He ate for a few minutes, and they all sat in silence. Stacy and Cameron only moved to refill their coffee cups.

"I just..." Mason started, but then seemed to think better of it and didn't finish his sentence.

"What?" Cameron asked before Stacy could.

"I couldn't get her anything this year. We're doing virtual school this year because of COVID, so we didn't get to do the Secret Santa shops. And Dad forgot to take us shopping before he left on his trip."

Stacy's heart ached for the kids. Not only would they miss seeing their father on Christmas, but they also missed out on getting something for the mother they loved.

Cameron turned to Stacy, and his eyes widened before he nodded toward the kid. She shook her head, not understanding his unspoken question. He widened his eyes again and mouthed something, but she still didn't understand.

"What?" she mouthed back before sipping her coffee, trying not to laugh at Cam's antics.

"Hey, Mason. What would you think of sending me to town to get something for your mom from you and your sisters?"

"Huh?" he asked through a mouthful of cocoa rice, startled at the idea.

Stacy was impressed with Cameron's thoughtfulness and how well it matched the inkling of a plan that had been forming in her own mind.

"That's a great idea," she agreed, turning to Mason. "What do you think? We'll look online and see what gifts you and your sisters would like to get for her, and then Cam will go and pick them up while we do some Christmas projects."

"But I don't have any money," Mason said, shaking his head. The boy looked dejected, and it stabbed at Stacy's heart.

"That's okay," she reassured him. "We'll set a little budget, and you can each choose something within that budget."

"I don't know. Mom might be mad," he argued, but she could see the light of hope emerging in his deep brown eyes.

"You know, bud, I don't think she will," Cameron assured the boy. He pulled out his phone and moved to the other side of the counter to show Mason the local stores they could peruse. "If we turn on the 'pick up today' option, we can see what Walmart has available. Do you think fifty dollars each is enough for you and your sisters?"

"Fifty!" Mason exclaimed, pulling back in shock. "That's too much!"

"Okay, up to fifty. But don't feel bad if it's fifty. Just take a look, pick something out, and then have your sisters come pick out their gifts and I'll run out and grab them before your mom gets back. Then you'll all have time to wrap them. Sound like a good deal?"

The boy hesitated, looking to Stacy and nodding vigorously only after she gave him a reassuring smile.

"Thank you so much, mister," he said as he pushed his cereal bowl away to look at Cameron's phone. He made his selection: a stylish gold heart with a diamond in the center, dangling from a delicate gold chain.

"So that's the one you want to get for her?" Cameron asked.

"That's the one," Mason confirmed, his eyes bright and face alight with a broad smile as he nodded.

"Great. It's in the cart. Now go wake up your sisters so they can pick out their gifts for your mom. I have to get going if I'm going to beat your mom back. She's already out there, and I don't know how long she feels comfortable leaving her kids with a couple of strangers."

Mason nodded abruptly and raced off to wake up his little sisters.

"Cam, you are the most wonderful man--"

"Bah," he said, interrupting her. "We both know it's the right thing to do. See? We're already doing the rich aunt and uncle thing." He hugged her before refilling his and Stacy's mugs.

As he rounded the counter with two full mugs of steaming coffee, Mason came racing back into the kitchen with his little sisters in tow. Charlotte, the eight-year-old, was first, her dark wavy hair flying around her. Taylor, the five-year-old, was right on her sister's heels, her short dark hair bobbing just above her shoulders. Both girls were still in their pajamas and wore bright smiles to match the joy and excitement in their eyes.

The girls picked their gifts quickly. Charlotte chose an ultra-soft, oversized throw blanket, while Taylor selected a sixteen-piece bake-ware set.

"The order is in, so I'm off," Cameron announced as he stood. "It should be ready by the time I get there."

"Did you remember gift wrap and tape?" Stacy asked as she washed their coffee cups and plates.

"I knew I forgot something," he exclaimed, groaning as he looked up at the ceiling.

"It's okay," Stacy said as she dried her hands and hugged him. The kids had since moved into the living room. Mason let the girls take their cereal to eat at the coffee table while they watched cartoons. "Just grab those first and then get your pick-up order."

"Good idea," he said before kissing her goodbye.

After Cameron left, Stacy washed the dishes and contemplated the idea of having a house full of little ones like this with her husband. Of course, Amanda's situation as a single mother was a sobering reminder that marriage didn't always play out the way people hoped it would. The mere thought of going through the trouble to start a family and then be left all alone with children after a divorce was terrifying. It was enough to make Stacy lean toward the other scenarios Cameron had suggested.

Amanda had looked worn and exhausted from the moment they arrived. She had worked hard to manage the bed and breakfast while also caring for her children on their two-week break from school. Still, with virtual school the rest of the year, she hadn't experienced much of a break since the beginning of the pandemic.

As Stacy opened the mostly-premade gingerbread house box and set everything out on the counter, she wondered if she could be as strong as Amanda. Could she raise a family alone if things didn't work out between her and Cameron? She would never confess that her mind had wandered into doubt about their relationship, but she had to consider reality.

The whirlwind of thoughts overwhelmed Stacy as she imagined herself in Amanda's position, and she suddenly felt nauseous. She ran to the bathroom and closed the door before splashing cold water on her face. As she leaned over the sink, she thought about all that she had been through with Cameron. They had a strong bond, a bond created through hardship, and an unusual shared experience created when they unexpectedly volunteered for flood relief together.

That short time spent together had felt like far longer than the few days it had actually been. Being with Cameron wasn't just comfortable; it felt right, like it was meant to be. They had been through so much emotional growth to end up together that she couldn't easily imagine splitting up with him.

After Stacy turned off the water, she looked at herself in the mirror, examining the curve of her jawline, her jet black hair, and her deep, dark eyes. She had to be honest: doubting what she had with Cameron wasn't an authentic thought or feeling. It was inspired by seeing another woman struggling alone, just like she had seen during the floods.

Seeing others' experiences couldn't predict her own, she decided as she dried her face and returned to the kitchen.

"Who's ready to make a gingerbread house?" she called into the living room.

"Me!" The girls called in unison. They raced into the kitchen, their big brother trailing behind, but Stacy was glad to see he was finally relaxed and smiling.

"Do you think we can finish before your mom gets back?"

"Yeah," little Taylor yelled excitedly, bouncing up and down on her tiptoes. The girl's excitement overflowed in the room, and Stacy was sure it was contagious. She couldn't help but smile as she got all the kids settled at the island counter.

They spent the next hour building and decorating the gingerbread house. Stacy helped them work together to put up the walls, add the roof, and cover the scene in snowy marshmallow. Each of the kids added their candy details to the house to create windows, a door, and then decorated the mini-lawn in front with candy canes and gumdrops. When that was finished, the two older children let the little Taylor shower it in sprinkles. The sprinkles scattered across the counter and onto the kitchen floor, but Stacy and the kids only laughed as they chased after every tiny piece.

The scene felt like a dream to Stacy, or a glimpse into a possible future. Her heart was softening, and she could see why Amanda didn't complain, even if she was exhausted. Her children were full of light and overflowing with love.

Just as they finished cleaning the kitchen, the front door opened and closed, and they all froze, listening as the footsteps came closer to the kitchen. When a head poked around the corner, Stacy was relieved to see it was Cameron. His hands were full of shopping bags and a roll of wrapping paper was tucked under one arm.

"Help!" he demanded jokingly.

Stacy took a couple of the bags and placed them on the bar stools. Together, she and Cameron helped the kids wrap and label their presents to their mother. She couldn't help but admire Cameron's choice of wrapping paper: the shiny, silver paper was dotted with gold stars and white snowflakes of varying sizes. It was eye-catching and beautiful.

"All right, girls," Stacy called when they had placed their gifts with the rest of the presents under the tree. "It's time to get dressed before your mother gets home. Mason, can you turn on some Christmas music?"

"Yep," Mason agreed before jetting off to the living room as his little sisters ran to their room.

"We're almost alone," Cameron said, winking as he pulled Stacy close for a kiss.

She gave him a peck on the lips before pushing him away with a playful smile. "Not now," she chided. "Behave."

"You're no fun," he declared before opening another shopping bag.

"I also got these." He pushed the bag toward Stacy, and she found toys and goodies inside. "For Amanda and the kids," he said, shrugging as if he couldn't explain why he had bought more.

He didn't need to explain; Stacy knew she would have done the same if she had been the one to go.

"You want to wrap these, or should I?" he asked, tying the bag closed again.

"You should," she said. "I'll hang out with the kids. I figure it'd be best if I keep a close eye on them until Amanda gets back."

"Yeah, you're probably right. I'll be back in a jiffy." He sped off, his footsteps thudding up the stairs as he raced to wrap the new gifts for their host family.

Stacy busied herself with double-checking that everything was tidy before helping the girls put red bows in their hair. Cameron returned and placed a big box under the tree, expertly covered in that pretty, silver wrapping paper. She grinned at him knowingly, and they turned up the Christmas music before starting the kids on drawing Christmas cards for their mother.

When Amanda returned, shopping bags in one hand and a coffee cup in the other, she looked surprisingly refreshed. Stacy was over-joyed to see it. She could only hope that the surprise gifts would be happily received. Saying nothing, Amanda pointed up the stairs, and Stacy nodded, understanding the look of someone wanting to wrap presents in secret.

Stacy and Cameron helped the kids finish their Christmas cards and place them in the branches of the tree just as Amanda returned with nothing but a paper coffee cup in one hand. There was a glimmer in her eyes that was missing before.

"Thank you so much," Amanda said softly as she and Stacy watched Cameron play and color with the kids.

"I don't have kids, but I think I get it. We all need a break from time to time." Stacy shrugged. "That's kind of why we're here in the first place. We just needed a little break."

"I hope you're getting a good break. It makes me feel bad that you watched the kids--"

"No, no, no," Stacy interrupted. "Don't feel bad at all. The kids were great. Besides, Cameron and I really enjoy helping other people. It's kind of what we do. So what did you do while you were out? I mean, besides getting those few extra things." She referenced the shopping bags that she had suspected were full of gifts.

"I went to Starbucks, indulged with a venti Eggnog Latte, and then sat in my car and called an old friend. It felt so good just to have that much. I could breathe again, and yet I couldn't stop thinking about my kiddos. So I got them a few more things. I couldn't help it," Amanda admitted with a laugh.

"It sounds like a good morning out, and I'm glad you could get a few more things before the stores closed for the night. I'm also glad you got a second latte," Stacy whispered, smiling as she tipped her head toward the new cup.

"I decided to treat myself. I can't remember the last time I got a real latte. What did you do with the kids while I was out?"

"We set up the gingerbread house, cleaned up after breakfast, and they created Christmas cards for you."

"Awww!" Amanda's eyes lit up with surprise. "That's so sweet."

"Your children are very sweet, and they love you so much," Stacy confided. Tears welled up in Amanda's eyes, and she turned away to fan her face. "I think Cam and I are going to walk around, so we'll leave you all to the holiday fun."

"Okay," Amanda said, her voice shaky as she faced Stacy once more. Her eyes glittered with tears on the brink of falling, but she successfully held them back. "Again, thank you."

"You're so welcome," Stacy replied, placing a hand on the woman's shoulder and squeezing. Cameron returned to them, stretching his back after sitting on the floor to color with the kids.

"Ready for a walk?" he asked Stacy.

She nodded before smiling at Amanda once more.

When they left the B&B, Stacy and Cameron walked around town, grabbing large hot chocolate drinks from Battle Grounds Bakery & Coffee before walking down to The Pointe. It had become one of their favorite places to relax together. For a few minutes, they laughed and talked about the morning, with Cameron sharing how he picked the gifts for Amanda and the kids. Stacy told him about the gingerbread house and having the kids create Christmas cards for Amanda.

"What a perfect morning," Cameron observed as he interlaced his fingers with Stacy's.

"Absolutely perfect," she agreed, giving his hand a squeeze as she sipped her hot chocolate. The air was frigid, and the wind blowing across the water nipped at their exposed skin. "I think it's too cold to be out much longer."

"You're right!" Cameron laughed and stood before gently pulling her up with him. "What do you want to do?"

"Maybe read a book in bed," she suggested.

"Your wish is my command," he replied dramatically as he bowed.

Stacy kissed his cheek and didn't fight the giddy, warm feeling that was returning to her after months of dormancy. After getting back to the B&B, they crept upstairs to avoid disturbing Amanda and the kids. They now surrounded a board game while the sweet sounds of Auld Lang Syne gently filled the house.

When Cameron opened the door to their room, he froze. Stacy clasped one hand over her mouth in surprise when she peeked past him. A miniature plastic Christmas tree stood atop the dresser in the far corner of the room. Its soft branches and bristles poked out over the curtain of the window that overlooked the train station. The lush, dark-green plastic tree branches were wrapped with gold garland and sprinkled with red and silver balls. A little angel with feather wings caught the light from the window and glittered from the top of the tiny tree.

"Cam!"

"Wow," he muttered, astonished.

A folded card sat on the dresser next to the tree. Stacy opened it and began reading aloud with Cameron huddled close.

"Stacy and Cameron, I didn't realize how much I needed a little time out of the house. Thank you so much for watching my children and helping them have a good time while I was out. I hope this little tree adequately represents the sense of Christmas spirit you have shared with me. Enjoy your Christmas, and thank you for sharing your love and joy with those around you."

"And she doesn't even know that Santa's coming tonight." Cameron laughed, trying to hide how much the gesture and card had affected him.

Stacy wiped the tears from her eyes and hugged her husband.

"Cam, this is so sweet," she said, sniffling against his shoulder.

He hugged her close before pulling back so he could kiss her deeply. In the still of the afternoon, with muffled Christmas music playing just beyond their door, they held each other under the soft blankets of their borrowed bed.

In the evening, after sharing Christmas dinner with Amanda and the children, Stacy and Cameron waited until they believed everyone was asleep. Tiptoeing downstairs, they carefully placed the presents from 'Santa' under the tree and hid them behind the family's presents. Cameron suggested that the extra gifts would be a pleasant and unexpected surprise if they were the last gifts found. He loved creating dramatic surprises.

After ensuring the presents were tucked beneath the farthest branches of the tree, Stacy led Cameron back upstairs. Just as he closed the door behind them, movement on the silvery angel atop the tree caught her eye. She looked closer and realized the light coming through the nearby window was moving ever so slightly.

"Cam," she whispered. Pulling aside the curtain, they watched as giant, fluffy snowflakes fell through the orange glow of the streetlights.

"Well, I'll be a--" Cam started, but Stacy cut him off with a deep kiss. He kissed her back, and they embraced. She could smell the spice of his cologne as she melted against his warm body.

She finally leaned back and looked up into his eyes. "Let's go," she said excitedly.

"Wait. Outside? Now?"

"Yes! It's the first snow," she argued, unable to control the smile that overwhelmed her face and the warmth that overflowed from her heart.

Stepping softly, they left the house and shut the door without a sound. Stacy tipped her face toward the sky, opened her arms, and closed her eyes as a cold but gentle breeze washed over her. Snowflakes kissed her cheeks and melted against her skin.

Cameron surprised her, picking her up and spinning her around until she laughed with glee.

"Okay, stop spinning me," she commanded through her laughter. He set her down but held her close and planted a soft kiss on her lips.

Stacy ran her fingers through his short-cropped hair and kissed him back before stepping away. She held his hand and pulled him along, striding down the street. At the bottom of a crumbling, cut-stone staircase, she pointed up.

"What?" he asked, suddenly hesitating.

"I want to see a snowy Harpers Ferry from St. Peter's," she declared, gripping his jacket with both hands and bouncing on her toes.

"That's a lot of stairs." He sighed as he looked up to the next street. "The things I do for love," he said.

Together, they climbed the steps and walked the steeply inclined streets before climbing yet another set of stairs to reach the church square. They took a few seconds to catch their breath before turning.

When Stacy looked up, it was all she could do to hold back a delighted squeal so she wouldn't break the silence of the square. The town, wrapped in the orange glow of its street lights, slept peacefully beneath the swiftly falling snow. She sucked in a breath of the wintry air and filled her lungs, reveling in both the peace and the energy of the moment. Suddenly feeling heavy in her abdomen, she took a seat at one of the stone benches along the low stone wall.

"Are you all right?" Cameron asked, rushing to her side and putting an arm around her.

"I think we took those stairs too fast," she told him. "I just need to sit with you for a minute. Just look at this sleepy little town."

"I'm right here with you, Stacy," he reassured her. "I go where you go."

She smiled and leaned against him as she looked out over the town. Her eyes danced between the cozy buildings. A blanket of Christmas snow quickly covered the town and the lighted rail bridge over the river. As charming as it was, she found herself hoping she wouldn't hear the train running on Christmas Day.

They stayed like that, quietly watching the town and the river until Stacy couldn't stop sniffling. She pulled a pack of tissues from her pocket and offered one to Cameron before using another. Her cheeks and nose were numb with the cold, and her toes were beginning to protest her thin boots.

"Let's call it a night, beautiful," Cameron suggested. She nodded her agreement and looped her arm through his when he offered it. The night air was too cold for arguing, even playfully.

When they returned to the B&B, they entered and locked the door behind them as quietly as they had when they left. They made their way to their room and got ready for bed. As Stacy slid under the covers, her stomach felt heavy again. Dinner had been delightful, so she was sure it hadn't made her sick, but she knew the quick burst of cardio in the freezing air hadn't done her any favors.

She fell to sleep cuddled up to Cameron, savoring the excited but sleepy moment and the way he held her.

In the morning, Stacy woke to kisses and sweet whispers from the man she loved. As she rose, she noticed the one corner of the frame of the window was filled with snow. After quietly squealing her delight, she raced to get ready to open gifts with Cameron. It didn't take the pair long to dress, and soon after, there was a knock on the door. They opened it to find a breakfast tray waiting for them with a note:

Enjoy breakfast in bed this morning. :) -- Amanda

Before Stacy and Cameron ate their breakfast, they pulled wrapped gifts for one another from their luggage and placed them under the tree Amanda had so generously provided. A breakfast of pancakes, eggs, and bacon followed, with orange juice and coffee to drink. They were about to finish their first cups coffee when Stacy's stomach suddenly felt heavy again. She froze and thought of the one thing she had packed that she hadn't planned to tell Cameron about.

Ever since they had started being intimate after the miscarriage, she had been worried about the possibility of getting pregnant again.

She had stocked up on pregnancy tests for peace of mind. She took one every week, wanting to know as soon as possible if she was pregnant. Out of that obsession and fear, she had brought a single test with her for their trip.

No, Stacy scolded herself. She was simply paranoid because of the breakthrough she'd had with Cameron. After that emotional revelation with him, combined with the time spent with Amanda and her kids, her secret hope for a family had sprung back to life in her heart.

Ignoring the feeling in her stomach, she poked Cam in the ribs just as he was reaching for the carafe to refill his coffee cup.

"It's time," she stated, holding her cup forward for a refill.

"I guess there's no putting it off anymore," he joked as he refilled their cups and set his down on the table next to the bed. He pulled two presents from under the tree and handed one to her.

"You first," she insisted, excited to see his reactions to her gifts.

The first gift he unwrapped was a pair of black leather riding gloves. He raised an eyebrow and looked at her.

She laughed at him. "You can't complain about your hands being too cold to go riding anymore." Shrugging, she rubbed his shoulders. "Those horses are getting lazy!"

"You got me," he dramatized, clutching the gloves to his chest. "We'll ride as soon as we get home." He lifted one of her hands and kissed the back of it before gazing up at her and grinning. "Your turn."

"Okay," she started, but Cam pulled a long, wrapped box from beneath the bed and passed it to her before she could open the smaller gift he had first passed to her.

"I've changed my mind. Start with this one," he commanded, a mischievous twinkle in his eyes.

"Sneaky!" She tsked at him as she carefully unwrapped the box and opened it. A pair of dark brown winter riding boots rested inside. Stacy nearly jumped out of the bed, squeaking with joy before sitting again to put them on. She pulled the zippers over the legs of her fleece pajama pants. "They fit perfectly," she marveled as she walked around the room to test them out.

"They look great too," Cameron declared, giving a soft whistle as he watched, his grin cemented into his cheeks.

Stacy grabbed a small present from beneath the tree and handed it to Cameron before unzipping her boots and replacing them in the box.

"Wait," she said, stopping him before he could begin shredding the wrapping paper. "I have to use the bathroom."

"Fine," he said, turning his attention back to his coffee cup. "Hurry, though. I can't promise how long I can wait."

"Hush," she commanded, patting his leg before reaching into her bag and sliding the test into her palm. If he saw her take it, he said nothing. When she glanced over her shoulder, he was pulling the tags from his riding gloves and trying them on.

In the bathroom, she took the test and set it on the sink counter before washing her hands and returning to Cameron. The test took a couple minutes to process, and she didn't want to waste her Christmas morning in the bathroom waiting for another negative test.

When Stacy emerged, she found Cameron sitting patiently with the wrapped box in his hands.

"Okay, you can open it now." She grabbed another present for him and sat down on the bed again.

Cameron unwrapped it to reveal a new FitBit, complete with replacement bands in a variety of cold colors Stacy had selected for him.

"You didn't have to do all this," he exclaimed, but she could see the appreciation in his eyes.

"Do you like it?"

"Of course I do! I love it, and I love you!" He planted a kiss on her lips and gave her a hug before turning it on.

"You said you wanted to be healthier, so I thought this might help," she offered, loving the way his face lit up as he examined his new piece of technology.

He paused only to get another present for her. This one had initially escaped her eye. It wasn't wrapped like the others they had brought with them; instead, this small box donned the silver wrapping paper they had used to wrap the surprise presents for Amanda and the children.

Raising an eyebrow, Stacy looked at her husband. "That's suspicious," she declared, pointing at the wrapping paper. "That's weird."

Cameron laughed nervously and waved his hand. "Just open it already."

She pulled the paper from the box it concealed and then lifted its gold lid from the beige bottom. Nestled in a bed of silver tissue paper was the crystal snowflake she had seen at the Hallmark store on their way up from Lewisburg. Tears fell down her cheeks before she realized she was crying.

"Cam," she said softly, her heart bursting at the seams with her love for a man who would never give up on her. He knew what she wanted, what she needed, and even if she tried to stop him, he refused to let her down.

He said nothing in response, only kissing her and pulling her into his embrace.

After several days of emotional evolution and the unexpected rekindling of her joy and hope, the delicate ornament was even more beautiful than the first time she saw it. It glittered with the bright, natural morning light streaming through the window, its brightness bolstered by the fresh snow that blanketed the quiet town.

"Need a tissue?" he asked. She nodded, and he strode into the bathroom to collect them from the vanity.

She was cradling the ornament in her hands and admiring the etching when she heard his voice again.

"Uh, Stacy?" he called. Her head jerked upward, and she looked toward the bathroom. "Is this yours?" Cameron stepped into the doorframe and held up the pregnancy test she had left on the counter and forgotten.

Heat rose to her cheeks, and she nodded. "Obviously. Unless it's yours," she joked, trying to relieve some of the tension.

"Okay. Well, what does a plus sign mean?"

Her heart thudded in her chest, but before she could answer, there was a knock at their door.

"Stacy? Cameron? We found the presents," Amanda called out to them. It sounded like she'd been crying happy tears. "Would you join us downstairs? The kids are begging me to thank you all and Santa for the gifts."

Cam nodded, his eyes wide and his smile broad.

"Yes," Stacy called back, fighting the lump in her throat. "We'll be down in a minute."

Without waiting another moment, she leaped off the bed and raced to Cameron. With a glance, she confirmed the positive result on the test before throwing herself into his arms.

They cried tears of joy and sent thanks to heaven for all of the unexpected blessings and little miracles that graced them this Christmas.

ABOUT THE AUTHOR

Myria Wild has been writing since she could tell herself stories, and once she hit high school, those stories involved wild romances. Although she never considered herself a romance writer in the beginning, the seed had always been there, planted by her love of seeing perfect partners in film, books, and in real life.

When the pandemic hit, she knew she needed more happy endings, so she began writing sweet but steamy romances to bring more light and joy into her life. She now hopes these stories will help bring joy, hope, and love to others' lives as well.

Follow Myria on Facebook or Instagram to be the first to know when her Wild and Wonderful Mountain Love series is ready to read.

facebook.com/myriawild
instagram.com/myriawild

KINDNESS AND
FRESH SNOW

BY KATRINA ROSEMOND

KINDNESS AND FRESH SNOW

"This is the time of forgiveness, a time we forgive not only the people that wronged us, but we forgive ourselves. Does anyone want to share a story this week?

This was usually the part of the meeting where Marcus tuned out. He didn't like hearing everyone's sob stories. It went against the image he was raised to have for a man to share any feelings other than aggression. He looked outside at the snow as it drifted to the ground. The sidewalk and the trees and the light posts were all dusted in a light covering. This was his daughter's favorite time of the year.

"Yes, Marcus. What would you like to share with the group?"

Marcus stood, suddenly aware of the oversized fit of his clothes. He kept his eyes down, hoping to will away the butterflies in his stomach.

"My name is Marcus, and I'm an alcoholic." Six months of Alcoholics Anonymous and that was the first time he had said that out loud. "I've been sober for fifteen years but only recently started coming to meetings. I, uh, I had the perfect life. At least I thought it was perfect. It was far from perfect for those that were around me. My wife, she tried her best to get me to stop drinking, but nothing could get through. She was a teacher, had the patience of a saint, and never raised her voice to me or the kids. Then I had to go ruin everything."

* * *

IT WAS CHRISTMAS EVE, and I had been drinking since I got off work that morning. I managed to hold it together long enough to get home. The house was empty, but it smelled like my wife had been baking all day. I was focused on getting to my bed. I didn't care that the house was cleaned and put together. Why would I care? I was drunk.

I didn't bother taking a shower or even taking off my work clothes for that matter. I collapsed, face first, into the soft down comforter and completely blacked out. I don't know how much time had passed, but I woke up with my wife standing over me as she pulled my boots off my feet. Instead of being grateful that she was looking out for me, I kicked her. I kicked my wife because she was doing something for me that I couldn't do for myself. She went flying into the dresser and knocked over an antique silver picture frame that held our wedding photo.

"Get the hell off me!"

"I was trying to help you get-"

She stopped herself, causing me to look up. She was standing again with a shard of glass sticking out of her palm. She didn't cry. She didn't scream. She speed walked out of the room and out of the house. I blacked out again, waking up to the sound of my daughter calling for me.

"Daddy, Aunt Lisa is on the phone for you."

She handed me the cordless phone before bouncing to the edge of the bed. The recoil was enough to send waves of nausea through my body. The sun was finally down but every light in my bedroom was on, making it harder to focus my vision.

"Hello?" My voice was thick and groggy, not at all like my normal voice.

"I am calling to let you know that CPS is on their way to come get the kids and the police are on their way to come get you."

"Wait, what? Why?"

"My sister is done with you! She's having a four inch shard of glass removed from her hand that's going to take seventeen stitches to close. That's something that would interest law enforcement."

"No. You gotta convince her to change her mind."

"I don't 'gotta' do anything, Marcus. She has enough evidence to make any charge of child endangerment and domestic violence stick."

I sat up clutching my head. I stamped my foot down in an attempt to make the room stop spinning. The only thing that did was snap everything back into focus. The one foot that still had its boot landed in the many shards of glass that were still on the floor in front of the dresser. She hadn't had time to clean up the glass before she left. She managed to pick up the frame before she left, laying it face down on the dresser.

"Lisa, please talk to her. Don't take my kids from me now. Not today."

"Do you think she likes having to make up stories about her injuries, Marcus? Don't you think she's tired of covering for you all the time?"

I saw something out of the corner of my eye but I wasn't sober enough to react to it in time. Thank goodness my little girl was there. She stopped my infant son from swallowing a piece of glass. I would have had a hard time explaining how much of a good father I was if that had happened. She scooped him up and brushed the glass out of his hand before it could reach his mouth. She bounced him and cooed softly to soothe him as he started crying.

The sound of my son crying and my sister-in-law yelling at me widened the crack that I felt forming in my head. She was seven years old but somehow had already become a better parent than I would ever be.

"Marcus! What the hell is going on? Why is MJ crying?"

"I gotta talk to my wife. I gotta change her mind."

"Marcus don't you dare get in the car with those kids. Marcus! I am calling the police if you-."

I dropped the phone and herded the kids to the front door. I had nothing else on my mind other than getting to my wife. If I could just explain to her what happened, why I came home in the shape that I did, I could make her understand why the cops didn't need to be called. I wanted to keep my family together for as long as possible.

I didn't know where I was going. I just got in the car and hoped that the adrenaline coursing through my veins would be enough to sober me up. I could hear my kids crying from the backseat. I didn't stop until I reached her best friend's house first. I knocked and knocked but no one came to the door. I went to her sister's house next but the driveway was empty. That meant that she had to be at her parents' house.

Her parents never liked me. I was the man that got their darling daughter pregnant at nineteen. She was on the fast track to being a doctor when I came around. She was the most beautiful woman I had ever seen in my life and knew that I had to have her. It was more than her beauty that attracted me. It was her spirit. She calmed me in ways that alcohol never did and I never appreciated her for it. I never told her that.

I parked a block away from my in-laws' house. I figured I could intercept my wife before she got into the house. That's when the headache started. It was a dull ache at first, growing into a driving pain that I couldn't shake loose. I searched my pockets and the center console, finally finding my stash of miniature whiskey bottles in the glove compartment. I had gotten the cap off and brought the bottle to my lips when she spoke up.

"You're not supposed to do that, Daddy." Her voice was small from the backseat but felt like a punch in the stomach. "You're going to get in trouble and Santa doesn't want to put you on the naughty list."

I thought about putting it down. I thought about pouring it out the window. I thought about climbing into the backseat and begging for her forgiveness. Instead, I downed the bottle in one shot and hoped she would understand. I was too far gone to register the disappoint-ment on her face.

I was digging through the glove compartment again when I heard the door open. She was out of the car, holding my son, and running toward my wife's car that had just pulled up in front of my in-laws' house. My daughter was barefoot and my son was just in a diaper as she sprinted to the house. I got tangled in the seatbelt as I went after her. My wife, wide eyed, ran to meet them on the sidewalk.

"We gotta go," I said breathlessly as I caught up with them.

My wife was kneeling on the icy pavement listening to my daughter as she tearfully told the story of how we got there. There was no detail spared. I grabbed my wife up by her arm and started pulling her toward the car.

"I am not going anywhere with you, Marcus."

"We can talk about this later. Now we gotta get the kids home."

"What are they even doing here? I can't believe you drove them here like this." She knelt down to talk to my daughter again. "Go inside with your brother. Nana and Pop will be happy to see you."

I recognized the smile she plastered on her face. It was the smile that she put on to make it seem like everything was okay when she was really coming apart on the inside. This was another opportunity for me to walk away, sober up, and fix things when I could be more rational but I chose to stand there and fight.

"Let's go!"

I pulled my wife with one hand and my daughter with the other. They fought against me but I managed to get them to the car when my father-in-law came to the door. He had a phone to his ear and a shotgun in his other hand. I couldn't make out who he was talking to over the sound of my blood rushing in my ears and the police sirens that were flooding the neighborhood.

My wife put up a fight at first, squirming out of my grip and attempting to get back to the safety of her parents' house. I couldn't let her go for no other reason than I knew I wasn't going to see her or my children again if I did. I admit that I was selfish but I didn't know how to live without my family. I don't think I was prepared to find out what that felt like either.

She finally relented, getting in the backseat with the kids. I peeled away from the corner a moment before the street was filled with police cars. As I rounded the corner, I could see my father-in-law motioning wildly for them to follow me. I was almost out of the neighborhood when I saw the lights flash behind me. It was a police car that had been diverted on their way to the house.

I knew then I was defeated. I stopped at the stop sign with my hands on top of the steering wheel. I rested my head against the horn and waited for the inevitable. I could see the officer in the side view mirror as he walked up, hand on his holster.

"Marcus, you have to let us out of the car."

It was a simple statement that cut through the alcohol fog I was in. I turned to see my wife, stoic and calm, as she clutched our infant son to her chest. She had learned over time that was the way she needed to speak to me. I just needed a few more minutes to explain, to make things right.

Before the officer could make it to my window, I slammed on the gas pedal and sped through the intersection. I could hear my daughter screaming and my wife trying to calm her down. I couldn't focus on the words because traffic was getting thicker the closer we got to the expressway. The one police car that was behind us became three then became seven. It was wild.

I couldn't tell you what I was thinking except that I needed to get back to my home. I didn't care about the curbs I jumped or the cars I side-swiped. I needed to get away. I got off the expressway and took a turn too fast. That's when the panic started to seep into her voice. She clawed at me, reached for the steering wheel, anything to get my attention.

"Marcus, look out!"

Those three words broke through the noise in my head but it was too late. Without realizing it, I ran a red light straight into the path of a pickup truck.

People say their lives flash before their eyes during a near death experience, that the world slows down and then speeds back up again. I didn't have that particular pleasure. I didn't get to see the day I met my wife or when our children were born. All I saw was the terrified look on the pickup driver's face when she realized she wasn't going to be able to stop. The impact knocked the breath out of my lungs and then, everything went black.

I could hear my daughter crying and the crunch of glass under foot as the officers swarmed the car. Then, nothing. I don't know how long I was out. I just remember waking up to Christmas music. I tried to get up but I was handcuffed to the bed. There was no one there to tell me what the hell was going on. I tried calling out to a nurse as she passed by but my voice came out dry and raspy. My eyes felt like sandpaper and every muscle in my body hurt.

Once my head cleared a bit, the only thing I could think of was my family. I fought hard to grasp on to the fragments of my memory. Did I miss something? Were they safe?

"Mr. Miller, my name is Detective Harrison. I'm here to talk to you about your accident."

"Is my family okay? Can I talk to my wife? I need to talk to my wife."

"Before I ask you anything, I need to advise you of your Miranda Rights."

That's when reality hit me. I was handcuffed to the bed, I was being mirandized. Something bad happened and it was worse than the DUI I was facing. Detective Miller finished reading me my rights and took the seat at the end of my bed. He looked at me, and I could tell everything was going to be different.

"You were in an accident while fleeing from the police. You ran a red light and were t-boned by oncoming traffic. Your daughter is okay but your wife and son didn't make it."

The words coming from the detective sounded so clinical, like it was something he had said a hundred times before. Maybe he had but why was he saying it to me?

"You're being charged with felony Driving While Intoxicated, felony Child Endangerment, felony Fleeing and Eluding, two counts of Vehicular Manslaughter for the death of your wife and son as well as three counts of assault with a deadly weapon for the people in the pickup you wrecked. Is there anything you don't understand?"

The question was just a formality. I could see the thinly veiled contempt for me in the detective's eyes, not just for what I had done but for pulling him away from his family on Christmas eve. His words were moving too fast in my head for me to latch on to. I shook my head as he stood to leave.

"You're being discharged in the morning. I'll be back to transfer you to the jail where you'll be booked in. Don't hold out hope for getting bonded out anytime soon."

The door clicked closed behind him and it was the loudest sound I had ever heard. I couldn't piece together what had happened save for a few flashes of my children crying and my wife speaking to me. I remember her voice being calm and level but loud enough to cut through the noise in my head. I remember the light touch of her hand on my shoulder as she tried to convince me to pull over. And then, in an instant, there was nothing.

The next day, as promised, Detective Harrison took me into custody. My hands were cuffed in front of me as to not aggravate the shoulder I had dislocated. Across the parking lot I could see my father-in-law staring me down as I was placed in the back of the waiting police car. He made no attempt to hide his disgust of me as I was driven away to be booked into jail. The booking process was as horrible as anyone could have imagined. I was stripped of my clothes and my dignity with all the invasive searches and interviews.

I was housed in the medical wing of the jail and placed on suicide watch my first week. Killing myself was never an option for me because it was all a mistake in my head. A cruel practical joke my wife cooked up to teach me a lesson about drinking and driving. It was only after my first few days that I realized it wasn't a joke. I talked with my public defender who wanted me to admit to being an alcoholic and explained how that was an illness that should be taken into consideration. The more she talked the more I wanted to be locked away for what I had done. She was trying to excuse away the damage I had done to my family, to everyone that knew and loved my wife and my children. I may have wanted to get out, but what I wanted didn't matter anymore. It never mattered. Putting my needs before my family's got my wife and son killed.

* * *

"I SPENT the next fifteen years in state prison sitting in my cell, not really doing much. I got a couple of letters from my daughter while I was in there, but I was too much of a coward to open them. Whatever it was she wanted to say to me, she was better off not having a loser like me as her father." Marcus looked around the room and saw few dry eyes. "I guess thank you for listening," Marcus said as he sat back down.

He resumed looking out the window. The sharp ache of loss replaced the numb, hollow feeling that had kept him alive. He watched the snow falling, thicker snowflakes blanketing the street below, and thought about how his daughter would beg him to play outside. She loved the sound her boots made as she crunched through the grass. There were many memories like that hidden away in his mind because he was never worthy of them to begin with.

The sound of chairs scraping against the stone floor snapped Marcus back to reality. The meeting was over, and he needed to get back to the halfway house before the snow got too bad. He stacked the chairs nearest to him against the wall and gathered some cookies in a napkin before leaving.

Marcus walked with a deliberate stride through the crowds of people doing their last-minute shopping. He kept his head down, attempting to avoid the throng of carolers in his path. Thankfully the walk back to the halfway house was short.

"I got you some cookies," Marcus said to his roommate as he put the stash on the nightstand between their beds.

"How was your meeting?" the man asked, his voice lighting up at the prospect of the sweet treats.

"I talked about what happened. I don't know why I did. It just, just all came spilling out. Something about this time of the year, I guess."

"You got a Christmas card. Dan already opened it. That's how I know what it was."

Marcus followed where his roommate was pointing to a large envelope with an embossed seal. The administrator had been careful not to break the fancy wax seal that kept it closed. Marcus wasn't accustomed to receiving any mail that didn't have legal documents. The last piece of mail he received was a letter from his sister-in-law's attorney notifying him that his parental rights had been terminated and that his daughter had been adopted by her and her husband.

The front of the envelope had his name and address written in flowing calligraphy. The return address on the back was not one that he recognized. He slid the card out to find the photo of a smiling family in a snow-covered park. He didn't immediately recognize anyone in the picture, but the frozen lake behind him told him the only person it could have been. He taught her how to fish in the summer and how to skate in the winter at that lake. The woman in the center of the photo was the spitting image of his wife, from her thick, curly brown hair to her warm hazel eyes. It was his daughter. It was Mona.

Mona was standing with a man Marcus presumed to be her husband, a little girl at her feet, and a boy in her arms. He held the card close to his chest, tears streaming down his cheeks. He didn't try to stop them or wipe them away.

"Who's it from?"

"My daughter. She says that her children want to meet me. I-I don't think I can go. I don't think I'm ready."

"Maybe not, but you should go anyway. It will make her happy."

Marcus looked at his roommate as if for the first time. Here he is, presented with an opportunity to put someone else's needs above his; he wasn't going to let her down at Christmas. Not again. He dashed to his closet and quickly changed into the only suit he owned. The shirt and jacket were heavily wrinkled, and the shoes were not going to get him to his destination with his kneecaps intact. He changed out of the ill-fitting clothes he got when he came to the halfway house and into the suit.

He went downstairs and asked his program administrator if he would give him a shave and a haircut. It was something the man had done for him in the past before job interviews because the residents were not allowed to have razors in their rooms. He fidgeted as Dan ran clippers and scissors and combs through his unruly hair. For the first time since his trial, Marcus talked about his family, animated and excited.

"Do you have anything for the kids?" Dan asked, brushing stray hairs from Marcus' shoulder.

The color drained from his face. It was Christmas Eve, and he was meeting his grandchildren for the first time empty-handed. He opened his wallet to find a crumpled five-dollar bill and a bunch of receipts. His face fell. Why did he bother hoping something good would happen today? Why would this Christmas be any different from the last fifteen?

As if reading the dejected look on Marcus's face, Dan slid a ten-dollar bill amongst the debris that crowded his wallet. The men shared a knowing smile, and Marcus's faith in humanity was restored. Overcome with emotion in the moment, Marcus wrapped his program director in a tight hug. With a promise to pay Dan back hastily shouted over his shoulder, Marcus dashed out of the halfway house and back onto the icy street.

The people that he avoided as he returned from his AA meeting were the same people he was excitedly smiling at as he walked to the thrift store. How could he make up for all the time lost with his only child with fifteen dollars and a last-minute invitation? Anything remotely appropriate for Mona was out of his price range. He wanted to drape her in the finest silks and give his grandchildren the best toys. All he could find was some alphabet blocks for his grandson, a stuffed teddy bear for his granddaughter, and a knit scarf for Mona.

He took his items to the cashier. She greeted him with a smile he didn't return.

"Did you find everything you were looking for today, sir?" She asked with the cheery, well-rehearsed voice of a veteran retail worker.

Marcus muttered an affirmative as he took out his wallet. He handed the cashier his fifteen dollars, and she handed him back his spare change. She folded the scarf and took the items over to a small table next to the register.

"What- what are you doing?"

"I'm gift wrapping these for you. I assume they are gifts for someone."

"I would love that, but I can't afford to have them wrapped."

"It's something the owner does around the holidays. Because you're my last customer of the day, I'm going to make extra sure that these are wrapped up nicely for you."

Marcus watched as the woman's hands gently wrapped each toy in glittery red and green tissue paper before placing them in their own paper gift bags. She wrapped the scarf in blue and white snowflake wrapping paper. She topped it with a ribbon and handed the packages to Marcus. His hands shook as he took them from her.

"I hope you have a very merry Christmas, sir," the cashier said, this time with a warm and genuine smile that made the corners of her eyes crease slightly.

The adrenaline of seeing Mona again was wearing off, only to be replaced by abject terror. What if he did something to offend her? What if seeing him reminded her of what happened? He started to turn to go back home as the bus pulled up to the stop. He looked at the gifts in his hands and the snow that had gathered on the sidewalk and knew he had to stop running. Whatever she had to say to him, he was going to listen.

Marcus tapped his wallet against the bus's farebox. The satisfying beep was another signal to him that everything was going to be okay. He sat at the back of the bus, holding the gifts gingerly. He didn't want to ruin the wrapping on them before he was able to present them. He watched the street signs as they passed by the windows. He didn't want to get stuck walking in the snow if he missed his stop.

Marcus got off the bus on the outskirts of an affluent neighborhood. Even though he was wearing a suit, he instantly felt underdressed. He stopped a woman walking her dog and asked her for directions to the address on the back of the envelope. She was hesitant at first but softened when she saw the gifts in his hand. She pointed him in the general direction before wishing him a Merry Christmas and continuing her walk.

The house was only a few blocks away, but it might as well have been miles. He rounded the corner to find the house he was looking for at the end of a cul-de-sac with several cars parked out front. Even from where he was standing, he could hear the sounds of merriment from inside. Marcus rang the doorbell and immediately fought the urge to run. He set the gifts by the door and turned to leave when he heard it open.

Standing in the doorway was a man that Marcus recognized from the family photo. The sight of his son-in-law caused his throat to go dry.

"I, um, I'm here to see Mona. I don't want to bother her if she's busy. I got her something, something for Christmas. Something for her and the children."

Marcus knelt down to pick up the gifts and hand them to the man in the doorway. When he looked up again, the man was standing to the side, and Mona stood in front of him. She had been a precocious first grader the last time he saw her. Now she was a mature woman who looked exactly like her mother, except she had his eyes. That was something he had never noticed before.

She stepped out onto the front porch and stood face-to-face with her father for the first time in fifteen years. She covered his shaking hands with hers.

"It's not much, but I got something for you and your kids. I'm sorry I don't know their names. One is a bear for the girl and-"

"Dad, do you want to go for a walk before you meet them?"

Mona took the gifts and handed them to her husband. She slid into her snow boots that were by the door and wrapped her shawl tighter around her. Marcus stood to one side as she led the way down the sidewalk and around the corner.

"I didn't think you would make it. I sent that card two months ago."

"I guess it took some time to get to me at the halfway house."

"John didn't want me to invite you today. He thought, with it being the anniversary of the accident, it might be triggering to see you today."

Marcus stopped dead in his tracks. "I can go. The last thing I want to do is upset you."

Fog puffed from her mouth as Mona laughed. "If I didn't want you here, then I wouldn't have invited you." She slipped her hand into his and pulled him forward. "I've had a lot of time to think about what happened that day. After a lot of therapy and even more meds, I figured some things out. I know now you were scared. I don't blame you for what happened."

"You should. You should blame me for everything bad that has ever happened to you. You were too young to remember, but I was drunk all the time. When I wasn't at work, I was at home running away from my problems instead of facing them. The best thing that could have happened for you was me going to prison. I-I don't deserve your kindness."

"Everyone deserves kindness, Dad." Mona squeezed her father's hand tighter. "Kindness and a push on the swing."

Marcus looked up from his daughter's face to see they were at the playground. A Cheshire grin crept across her face as she took off toward the swings.

She was smiling. She was laughing. She was happy to see him.

He followed behind her as she ran through the snowflakes with her tongue out.

"This was always your favorite time of the year."

Marcus hung his head in shame. She was so young when his choice to drink and drive left her without her mother, and yet she still had love for him. The feeling of her arms hugging tightly calmed his racing heart. Even after all this time, she was still taking care of him. He wrapped his arms around her quaking shoulders.

"Aunt Lisa didn't want me to, but I wrote to you. You never wrote back. I thought you were angry with me. Why didn't you write back?"

Mona looked up at her father, her face shining with tears. Marcus wiped away the tears before they could freeze on her cheeks.

"I couldn't. I wasn't the parent you deserved."

"You were the parent I needed."

Marcus didn't trust his legs to hold him up much longer. He found his way to a bench, clearing off a spot for Mona to sit next to him. "I could live a hundred lifetimes and still not be able to make up for what I did to you."

Mona took her father by the hand and led him to the swings. Her red, puffy eyes sparkled in the winter sunlight. She smiled, taking a seat on the swing.

"I don't need you to make it up to me. I just need you to give me a push."

ABOUT THE AUTHOR

Katrina Rosemond is an up and coming author from Miami Gardens, Fl. She's attending Miami Dade College to become an English teacher while establishing her writing career. Most days, she could be found writing on her laptop with the work of Hans Zimmer playing on her headphones as she works.

When she's not writing, she spends her time dueling her friends in The Saber Legion. It has been her dream since she was ten years old to be a published writer and she is doing her best to make that happen.

ACKNOWLEDGMENTS

Without the dedication of numerous people, this anthology would not be possible.

Thanks to Tom Fowler for completing the formatting; Nydia Pastoriza for designing our beautiful cover; K. McCoy, M. T. Decker and Kaaren Poole for editing and proofreading support; and to Audrey Hughey for guiding each step by reviewing, editing, giving feedback and too many other things to list. Finally, to each member of the Author Transformation Alliance and Sprints and Spirits groups for helping us share this anthology with readers far and wide.

www.ingramcontent.com/pod-product-compliance
Lightning Source LLC
Chambersburg PA
CBHW031702170626
46808CB00005B/1569